ANNA SAYBURN LANE

The Riviera Mystery

A 1920s murder mystery

A sunny place for shady people

Somerset Maugham

Foreword

The Riviera Mystery is the fourth in a series of 1920s murder mystery adventures featuring assistant private investigator Marjorie Swallow.

A word about spelling: I'm a British author, so I use British spelling and grammar.

You can find out more about the books, get free short stories and a prequel novella when you sign up to my Readers Club newsletter on my website: https://annasayburnlane.com/.

Chapter 1

I was far too excited to sleep. The wheels rattled over the tracks, my toothbrush clinked in the glass on my nightstand and Mrs Jameson's gentle snores vibrated rhythmically through the thin walls. Outside, the French countryside rushed past, fields and rivers and lakes and forests, an endlessly changing panorama of the first foreign country I had ever seen.

I reached from my bunk for the cord to pull up the blind. There might not be much to see in the dark, but I wanted to see it anyway. Could it be true that I, Marjorie Swallow, was actually on the famed Blue Train, heading for the French Riviera? Awaiting me was the luxury of a September holiday, a whole month at a villa belonging to a friend of Mrs Jameson, my employer. Travelling as her secretary, I'd been promised turquoise seas, sunshine, white sailing boats and palm trees. I lapsed into a happy reverie.

Then someone screamed.

It was a woman's scream, full of terror. I swung my feet to the floor, heart thumping, and wrenched open the sliding door to my compartment. All my parents' warnings about the perils of Abroad, the danger of being robbed or murdered or worse on a sleeper train, rushed into my head. I'd hoped to get away from murders on this holiday, not be plunged straight into one before we even arrived.

Outside, the door to a compartment three down from mine stood open, light spilling into the corridor.

'I say,' I called, hurrying over. 'Are you all right?'

Sibyl Trent, an Englishwoman we'd met at dinner, stood at the compartment door in a pink cotton night gown, hand at her throat and her eyes wide with fright. She'd removed her smart modern make-up, and looked about ten years younger. She also looked absolutely terrified.

'Oh, thank heavens. Did you see him?' she asked. Her breath was coming quickly as she stared up and down the corridor.

'I didn't see anyone. I just heard you scream. What happened?'

She clutched the door, looking as if she might faint. 'Someone was in my cabin,' she said. 'I woke up and he was just there, moving about. I thought I was going to be murdered.'

'Golly.' I sat her down on the disarranged bunk. 'What a fright for you. Are you hurt?'

I heard running footsteps from the corridor, and swung around.

''Allo?' The carriage attendant put his head around the door. He was out of breath. 'What is wrong?'

'Someone broke into Miss Trent's compartment,' I said. 'Did you see anyone in the corridor?'

He frowned and pulled at his big blond moustache. 'I saw nobody, Mademoiselle. When did this 'appen?'

The fellow wore thick spectacles with heavy wire frames. I wondered how sharp his eyesight was. But I'd seen nobody in the corridor when I opened my door.

'Just now,' said Miss Trent. 'I woke up and he was there.'

I poured her a glass of water from the nightstand. 'Here.

What did you do when you saw him?'

She took a gulp and pulled a shawl around her shoulders. 'I screamed, I suppose. Then I fumbled around for the light switch. By the time I had the lamp lit, he was gone.'

The attendant turned to me. 'Did you also see this person, Mademoiselle?'

'No. But I was awake, and I heard Miss Trent scream. I got up straight away and came into the corridor.'

He stroked his moustache again. 'Perhaps... perhaps, if you will forgive me, Mademoiselle? Maybe it was a bad dream, a nightmare?'

I'd been wondering the same thing.

Miss Trent shook her head vehemently. 'I saw him, all right. He pulled the compartment door open and ran away. Where were you, anyway? I thought you were supposed to stay in our carriage.'

'I ask your pardon, Mademoiselle. I was helping with the baggage when we stopped at Lyon. Can I bring you something to help you recover? A glass of brandy, perhaps?'

I had a sudden thought. 'The painting, Miss Trent? The Renoir?'

She gasped and turned to her suitcase, lifted the lid.

Miss Trent had joined the train at Paris's Gare de Lyon, travelling alone. At dinner, she had been seated with Mrs Jameson and me. After the usual pleasantries, she confided that she was travelling with a rather valuable painting from her place of employment, the auction house Hôtel Drouot, to a gallery in Nice. Miss Trent was an expert on Impressionism, and had been asked to authenticate the painting, by Auguste Renoir, before delivering it back to Nice. I'd been impressed by her professional air. The art world seemed predominantly male, and it was refreshing to meet a woman art expert.

Mrs Jameson had expressed an interest in the painting and Miss Trent had shown it to us after dinner, before we retired. Now I watched, holding my breath, as she opened the suitcase and unwrapped the tissue paper. I exhaled with relief. Glowing in the lamplight was the portrait of a young girl in a white dress, under the dappled shade of an olive tree. The pink of the girl's cheeks, the heavy plait of chestnut hair and the silvery green of the olive leaves made a harmonious, charming picture. I liked it very much.

'Everything is safe?' asked the attendant, his voice anxious. I could imagine the trouble that the theft of a valuable painting on the Train Bleu would cause the Wagon-Lit company, which had only begun running the new train on the Mediterranean Express at the start of the year. The publicity would be appalling.

Sibyl Trent looked dubiously from the painting to the attendant. 'I suppose so. Although I admit, I hardly feel safe myself. I'm quite sure I locked the door before I went to bed.'

I glanced around the compartment. Like mine, it was small and neat, with dark wood panelling, brass fittings and a compact night stand opposite the bed. It was like sleeping in a cigar box.

'If you wanted,' I ventured, 'I could take the second bunk and sleep in here tonight. So you aren't on your own.' It was a bit of a wrench to offer; I had been enjoying the luxury of having a compartment to myself.

'Would you really? That would be so kind. It was such a shock. I don't think I'd get a wink if I was on my own.'

I smiled with what I hoped was good grace. 'Perhaps you could assist with converting the bed, Monsieur?'

'Of course.' The porter rather clumsily pulled out the second bunk and began to make it up.

'I'll do that.' There was barely room for three people in the cabin, even with one bed. He retreated to the corridor.

'I will make sure there is no intruder in the carriage,' he said. 'But really, Mademoiselle Trent, I think it must have been a bad dream.'

Perhaps he was right. But Miss Trent clearly didn't think so, and I knew that even a nightmare could badly shake a person. I glanced at my watch. It was almost three o'clock. I hoped I would be able to get a little sleep before our arrival in Nice.

Chapter 2

To my surprise, I slept soundly until the light coming through the blind woke me. Miss Trent was sitting up, holding back the corner of the blind and looking a little embarrassed.

'I'm so sorry about last night, Miss Swallow,' she said. 'You were very kind to come to help.'

I yawned. 'Not at all.' Now it was morning, I wanted to go back to my cabin to get dressed and freshen up. 'Where are we?'

She squinted out the window, the bright light on her face showing lines around her eyes. 'Just past Marseilles. This is the best bit of the journey, along the coast. You get a wonderful view of the Mediterranean. Is it your first time on the Côte d'Azur?'

I sat up. 'My first time in France.'

'You'll love it. France is so free, compared to England. Everything is better here – the food, the clothes, the weather.' She gave a little laugh, which I found rather annoying. 'And the art, of course.'

'I'm sure I'll have a nice time.' As a proud Englishwoman, I wasn't prepared to admit that France might be better than home. I gathered up my things and opened the compartment door.

'Oh!' I gasped. I shut the door behind me, closed my dazzled eyes and opened them again.

Glorious sunshine flooded the corridor, warming my face and neck. Outside the train, brilliant light danced in diamonds on a sea of such vivid turquoise that it didn't look real. It was almost painful to look at. The rocky outcrops that flashed past were black silhouettes, the sea was flecked with tiny white sails, dark pine trees whipped by. I stood, mesmerised.

'There you are, Marjorie. What are you doing in your pyjamas? I'm going for breakfast.'

I turned guiltily. Mrs Jameson was impeccably dressed in a navy silk day dress with a white polka dot, a matching scarf around her head and neat white kid shoes on her feet.

I considered explaining about the night-time drama, but opted for speed instead.

'I won't be a tick,' I said. 'Isn't it marvellous?'

Mrs Jameson's stern face relaxed into a smile. 'I'm glad you like it.'

Back in my cabin I pulled off my flannel pyjamas, far too hot now, splashed myself with cold water and got the sleep out of my eyes. I'd started the journey in a sturdy tweed skirt and jacket. Gleefully, I selected a cool white linen frock, trimmed with scarlet rick-rack by my mother, and a smart new cardigan jacket I'd saved my wages for.

After a dismal May during which it had barely stopped raining, the British summer had delivered a chilly June, cloudy July and thunderstorms throughout August. Business had detained us in London, while Mrs Jameson scowled at the dark skies and threatened to move back to America. Finally, as September rolled around, she wrote to a friend in Nice and procured an invitation for us to stay at the Villa Beau Rivage.

I'd been glad to get away. Apart from a short break with my friend Evelyn at her Cambridge college, I hadn't left London since our eventful stay at Hawkshill Manor in Kent, back in May. In August Evelyn had departed for a tour of Scotland with her parents. My pianist friend Freddie, who my mother now referred to as 'Marjorie's young man', was on a lengthy tour of English seaside resorts with the All Stars Jazz Orchestra. He sent me brief postcards advising me never to visit Filey, Scunthorpe or Great Yarmouth. London had never seemed drearier.

Now, finally, I was free. I brushed my hair and set out for the dining carriage, which was wafting an enticing smell of bacon along the corridor. I sat opposite Mrs Jameson, so entranced by the scenery I could hardly concentrate on the food.

'I must say, this train is a great improvement on the previous service,' said Mrs Jameson. 'No need to change trains, and the cabins are much more comfortable.'

Sibyl Trent appeared, looking businesslike again in a dark grey two-piece. 'May I join you? I hope you're not too tired from your disturbed night, Miss Swallow.'

Mrs Jameson raised her eyebrows enquiringly. I told her about the midnight drama and my subsequent change of cabin.

'I see,' she murmured. 'And yet Marjorie saw no-one in the corridor. How curious.'

Miss Trent flushed. 'I know everyone thinks I imagined it or had a nightmare. But I'm quite certain. And look. I found this, after you'd gone, Miss Swallow. It was tucked into my shoe.'

She held up a small card. A short message was written across it in curly script: *Be very carfull.*

'How odd,' I said.

Mrs Jameson took it and scrutinised the writing. 'Very odd. Very interesting, Miss Trent.'

'I suppose he must have been after the painting,' I said. Although it seemed surprising that a thief would warn a victim. 'Where is it now?'

Miss Trent indicated the valise at her feet. 'I thought it best to bring it with me.' And yet she'd left it unattended in the cabin when we dined together the night before.

Mrs Jameson was staring out of the window, although her large grey eyes were not focused on the dazzling scene.

'Who knew you were travelling with the painting today, Miss Trent?' she asked.

Miss Trent thought. 'Well, my colleagues in Paris. And the gallery in Nice, of course.' She hesitated. 'I suppose I might have mentioned it to… to my husband.'

I looked up from my bacon and eggs with surprise. She had introduced herself as Miss Trent the night before, with no mention of a husband.

She picked up her coffee and took a sip. 'I go by my maiden name,' she said. 'For professional purposes. It makes life easier.'

Mrs Jameson smiled. 'I understand. People can be so odd about married women working. You live with your husband in Paris?'

'Yes. He's an artist.' Miss Trent set down her coffee cup and I saw disdain in the pinch of her nostrils. 'One of us has to bring in some money.'

The remark hung in the air for an uncomfortable moment. 'Well,' said Mrs Jameson. 'I should very much like to see that painting again. I wonder if my friend Mr Rubin would like it. He is quite a connoisseur. I'm not sure whether he admires the Impressionists, but this is a late painting, I understand?'

Miss Trent's face lit up. 'Mr Solomon Rubin? Oh, that would be wonderful. And yes, this is one of the last paintings that Renoir made, in his final years living at his villa in Cagnes-sur-Mer, just outside Nice.' She leaned forward confidingly. 'In fact, there are a few from those last years which have never been on the open market. A man from Haut de Cagnes, whose wife posed for this painting as a child, owns them. It's very exciting.'

Mrs Jameson nodded briskly. 'I will tell Mr Rubin. Which gallery is handling the sale?'

Miss Trent reached into her bag and brought out a silver card case. 'Here. Galerie Anglaise, on the Promenade des Anglais. It's just along from the Hotel Negresco. The owner is an American I met at art school in Paris, Ashton Montgomery.'

Mrs Jameson handed me the smart pasteboard card and I slipped it into my handbag.

'I'm rather keen on art,' I said. 'I understand there are lots of artists working in the south of France these days.'

'Heavens, yes. You can't move for them in Antibes. It's quite an exciting time,' said Miss Trent. 'In fact, Ashton is holding an exhibition of contemporary art next week. I'll arrange invitations to the opening, if you would like.' She lowered her voice. 'I believe Señor Picasso plans to attend.'

'Goodness.' I was impressed. I'd seen the Spanish artist's work exhibited in London and, although I struggled to under-stand his Cubist paintings, I recognised their jagged power. My friend Hugh, a tutor at the Slade School of Art, explained that you had to imagine you were seeing an object from all angles simultaneously, as if it was in constant movement.

'We shall certainly attend,' said Mrs Jameson. She passed her card to Miss Trent, who took it, then looked up again, surprise in her face.

'Mrs Iris Jameson… I don't suppose you are related to…' her voice broke off. 'I'm so sorry. I recognise you, now. You were married to him, weren't you? Julian Jameson. I've seen one of his paintings of you. '

It was unusual to see Mrs Jameson discomfited, but her pale face flushed, and she pressed her lips together in a way I knew indicated extreme annoyance. She looked out of the window for a moment, and I held my breath.

When she turned back to us, her expression was serene again. 'That's correct, Miss Trent. But it was a very long time ago.' She looked at her wristwatch. 'I think I'll retire to my cabin. Do try the croissants, Marjorie; they're delicious.' She moved away, stately as a dowager.

'Oh dear,' said Miss Trent. 'Have I put my foot in it?'

I wrinkled my nose. 'Don't worry. She never talks about him, that's all.' I'd only recently discovered that Mrs Jameson's late husband was a rather notorious artist, Julian Jameson, who had painted grand canvasses of mythological subjects in a gloomy Symbolist style around the turn of the century.

'I suppose it must be very painful to remember. Such a tragedy.'

'As I said, she never speaks of it.' I had no wish to be pumped for details. Indeed, I would be unable to supply them. Mr Jameson had died many years before I came into Mrs Jameson's employment.

'Well, I do hope you both come to the opening, Miss Swallow. And Mr Rubin, too. I'm sure Ashton would be delighted to have him as a client.' I saw a glint in her eye. From what I knew from Mrs Jameson, any art dealer would be delighted to have Solomon Rubin as a client. He was, Mrs Jameson said, quite possibly the richest man in France.

Chapter 3

It was after eleven o'clock when the blue and gold carriages pulled into Nice central station. The sun was at its height, burning through the glass canopied roof, bouncing off the pale stone platforms.

'Golly,' I said. 'It's so hot!'

Mrs Jameson threw me a glance which suggested I should keep such banal observations to myself in future.

'Now, where is he? Solomon said he'd send a man with a motor car to meet us,' she said.

The porter piled our trunks onto a luggage trolley. A good-looking man of about thirty strode up the platform, wearing a pale blue linen suit and straw boater hat. He was tall and athletic but walked with a slight limp. His face was flushed pink, his blue eyes crinkled with good humour at the corners.

'Are you Mrs Jameson and Miss Swallow?' he asked. 'I'm Andrew Fraser. Mr Rubin sent me. I'm staying at the Villa Beau Rivage.'

Mrs Jameson smiled. 'Thank you, Mr Fraser. If you could tell this gentleman where to take the luggage?'

I gave the porter Mrs Jameson's usual generous tip, while Andrew Fraser loaded our bags onto the luggage rack of a spanking new yellow and black Hispano Suiza, like a very up-to-date bumble bee. Mrs Jameson had opened an elegant Japanese-style parasol and looked perfectly cool. I was perspiring through my precious cardigan jacket, my face pricked with the heat, and I was squinting in the strong light. I would need a wide-brimmed straw hat, not the smart little felt cloche I'd been travelling in.

Mr Fraser held open the car door and I climbed in after Mrs Jameson, glad to be out of the glare. We whizzed through the streets, past tall buildings painted peach, strawberry and lemon, like so many delicious ice-creams. At the end of the road came a flash of breath-taking aquamarine as we rounded the harbour, where gaily painted fishing boats bobbed at the water's edge, yellow and green and pink.

'It's so pretty,' I exclaimed in delight. Then I winced. So hot. So pretty. Maybe I should pipe down until I had something more original to say.

'It is rather jolly, isn't it?' said Mr Fraser, throwing me a boyish grin. 'Not far, now. The villa is around the headland.'

The road rose above the harbour, giving a view of elegant sailing yachts and sleek motor launches, then twisted and turned along a rocky coastline. To our left was a hill dotted with villas. I assumed we were heading up to one of those, but the car suddenly slowed and turned right down a driveway that descended steeply.

'Here we are. You can't see the villa from the road,' said Mr Fraser. He jumped out and opened metal gates into an underground garage, then drove in.

The garage was hewn out of the rock, dark and cool.

'Go through that green door at the end of the garage. There's a passageway straight into the garden. If you wait for me on the terrace, I'll take your things up to your rooms,' said Mr Fraser.

'Maria will bring you some lemonade. Mr Rubin apologises that he has to work this morning. He will be with you as soon as he can get free. There are two other guests staying – Miss Pemberton, and Monsieur Brunot. I expect you'll meet them over lunch.'

Mrs Jameson smiled at me. 'Come, Marjorie. Let's explore.'

We emerged from the passage into the most delightfully unexpected garden. Unlike English gardens with their green lawns and borders of flowers, this consisted of a wide terrace crammed with pots of vivid flowering plants. Above our heads stretched a canopy of vines, bright with apricot, cerise and purple blooms, providing welcome shade. Beneath was a round table and two steamer chairs with cream cushions. However, there was too much to see to sit down.

Steps descended steeply from the terrace into a lower garden, which featured a pretty fountain in a pond where big goldfish swam lazily among the waterlilies. The pond was surrounded by huge terracotta pots from which grew only white flowers – marguerites, white roses and jasmine, smelling exquisite in the sun. A small lawn of emerald grass was damp and had clearly been watered that morning.

I turned and looked up at the villa. It resembled an iced birthday cake. Three storeys of soft pink stucco with curlicues and balconies, sage-green shutters over the windows, and at one end a tall square tower topped with what looked like a Chinese pagoda's green-tiled roof.

A small boy leaned over the railings of the room at the top of the tower and waved.

Mrs Jameson waved back. 'Hello, Benjamin. Are you coming down?'

'Hello, Mrs Jameson! I've got lessons! I'll be down for

luncheon,' he called, before being hustled away.

'Mr Rubin's son,' said my employer. 'A nice child. Doesn't make too much noise.'

I leaned over the wall at the end of the garden and looked down. It dropped sharply to a small beach some ten feet below, hemmed in by jagged rocks.

Mrs Jameson joined me. 'Our own private beach,' she said with satisfaction. 'I haven't swum in the ocean for years.'

'Not quite private,' I pointed out. At the far end of the little cove, a figure in a bathing costume was stretched out on a striped beach towel, her head covered with a wide-brimmed straw hat.

A cast iron spiral staircase twisted down to the beach where turquoise wavelets lapped gently at the flat grey shingle. I had a sudden longing to immerse my hot feet in the water.

'Can we go down and paddle?' I asked.

'I don't see why not.' Mrs Jameson was already descending the stairs, looking more lively than I had seen her since she broke her ankle the previous autumn. The change of climate was working its magic.

I sat on a rock and unrolled my stockings, stuffed them in my pocket and ran into the water. It was clear and cold as gin and almost as intoxicating. I wiggled my toes in delight.

'It's lovely,' I exclaimed. 'Are you coming in?'

Mrs Jameson smiled tolerantly. 'I'll swim later,' she said. 'Did you bring your swimming costume?'

I turned to her, dismayed. 'I don't have one.'

'Never mind, I'm sure you can borrow one. Sea swimming is so good for the soul.'

I gave a lame smile, and wondered whether I'd be able to get out of it. I hated to let Mrs Jameson down.

The woman at the other end of the beach sat up and placed a large pair of tinted glasses on her nose. She pushed up the brim of her sun hat.

'Who are you?' she called, rather rudely.

Mrs Jameson turned towards her. 'I am Mrs Jameson, and this is my companion Miss Swallow,' she said. 'And you are?'

The woman stared at us, as if in disbelief that we did not know. Suddenly I realised. I'd seen that profile before, the sharp cheekbones, precisely cut black bob and small rosebud mouth. I'd seen it four foot wide, spread across the screen of the Obelisk Picture Palace in Lewisham. Oh, my goodness.

'You're Dulcie Pemberton,' I blurted. I seemed to have developed a knack for stating the blooming obvious, as my mother would say.

She gave a faint smile. 'I am.'

'The film star,' I breathed. 'I've seen you lots of times.' I became aware that I was still standing ankle deep in water and retreated from the waves.

'We're guests of Mr Rubin,' I explained, fearing that Mrs Jameson had been unfriendly to the screen goddess. 'I'm Marjorie. We arrived on the train this morning. Isn't it lovely here? It feels like we've arrived in paradise.' I was gabbling, but I didn't seem able to stop. Miss Pemberton's gaze had already passed over me. I followed her eyes.

Mr Fraser was descending the steps. He hurried over. 'Ah, I see you've met already. Dulcie, this is…'

'I know,' she said. 'We've done all that. Is it lunchtime?'

He swallowed. 'Not for an hour. But there's fresh iced lemonade on the terrace, if you would like to join us.'

'Bring me a glass down.' Miss Pemberton reclined, settled the tinted glasses and placed her hat over her face, ending the conversation. Her figure, exposed in a black and white costume that flirted with decency, was flawless. Her manners, however, were not.

Mr Fraser looked flustered, and I felt sorry for him. 'Would you like to come up? Mr Rubin is still working, but I've taken your luggage to your rooms. Shall I show you to them, or would you like some lemonade first?'

'A glass of lemonade would be most welcome,' said Mrs Jameson. 'And then you can show us around. I understand there are hidden passageways, Mr Fraser?'

'There certainly are. Before the villa was built at the end of the last century, this coast was used by smugglers. There were a couple of old shacks standing on what's now the terrace. And there are all manner of old passages and tunnels hewn into the cliff, like the one you came through from the garage. There's another from the beach to the lower garden. The stairs are a bit narrow though, and the entrance is partly blocked. I wouldn't use them.'

I gazed around happily. A private beach complete with famous film star, a luxurious villa, and hidden tunnels to explore if I got bored. This promised to be a holiday I wouldn't forget.

Chapter 4

My room had a tall ceiling, a crisply made bed with white bedspread and an armoire big enough to take double the contents of my trunk. After a struggle I worked out how to unfasten the metal shutters, revealing a perfect view of the garden and the dazzling sea. I washed my face and brushed my hair before luncheon. There was no way I could compete with Dulcie Pemberton, but I could at least look neat.

I was rather nervous about meeting Mr Rubin. Mrs Jameson had told me little about our host, except that she had helped solve an affair of employee theft from his business. Rubin Brothers was London's most successful diamond merchant, and he'd given her a spectacular diamond bracelet in thanks. She'd said he had bought the villa on a whim three years earlier, from an impoverished French count who lost his fortune during the War.

Even though my year with Mrs Jameson had introduced me to people and places far outside of my lowly social circle, this level of wealth was something else.

Mr Rubin stood at the foot of the stairs, beaming. He was short, bald-headed and wiry, although thickening a little in middle age. He wore a perfectly cut dark-blue suit.

'Iris, my dear friend.' He clasped her hand and kissed it. 'And your charming companion?'

I was introduced and managed to talk quite coherently. He seemed rather normal, for a multi-millionaire. I liked the twinkle in his eye, and his evident fondness for Mrs Jameson.

'May I introduce Maxim Brunot, the kinema director? He is making a film at the Nice studios, with our other guest, Miss Dulcie Pemberton.'

A shiny-haired Frenchman bowed formally and kissed our hands. He looked a little careworn.

'Indeed. At least, that is the intention. Miss Pemberton is taking the leading role in *La Femme Honnête*, the honest woman, my fourth motion picture. Monsieur Rubin was kind enough to invite us to stay here for the duration.'

A boy of about twelve years old, bespectacled and formally dressed for a hot day, walked into the room and approached Mrs Jameson shyly. She beamed.

'Benjamin! How good to see you again. How are you enjoying France? I hear you're learning to play chess. We must have a game.'

Mrs Jameson had told me that Mrs Rubin had died in childbirth, and Solomon Rubin had never remarried. Part of his reason for relocating from London to the Riviera was to spend more time with his son, while his younger brothers took a more active role in the business. Benjamin was solemn and old for his years, in the way that only children sometimes were. After submitting to being kissed, he gravitated to Andrew Fraser, and they began to talk about cricket.

Dulcie Pemberton descended the stairs when everyone had been assembled for twenty minutes. She wore a pair of sleeveless beach pyjamas in apricot silk, the flowing fabric shimmering around her long legs with every step. The sun had turned her bare arms golden. She sashayed down, no doubt aware of the sensation her outfit had created. When she reached the bottom, she removed her tinted glasses with a flourish and smiled at Mr Rubin, that languid smile that had set a thousand hearts on fire.

'Hello, darling Sol. You've managed to drag yourself away from work, then?'

He kissed her hand and led her to the table, seating her next to M. Brunot.

'And when do you plan to drag yourself to work, Dulcie?' the film director asked. His English was impeccable, his accent rather delicious, but his tone sharp. Perhaps he was the one man at the table immune to the actress's charms.

She gave him a surly look. 'I worked all day yesterday, you brute. We should be finished by now, you said so yourself.'

He gave a dramatic shrug. 'And we would be, if you had been able to finish a scene without forgetting your lines. I thought we were going to rehearse today, so we can wrap up on Monday and release you for the rest of your holiday.'

I was seated beside Mr Fraser, who would have been a more interesting companion had he not had his eyes mournfully fixed on Miss Pemberton.

'Are you Mr Rubin's secretary?' I asked, hoping to distract him for a moment as I tasted the delicious iced tomato consommé.

'What? No, not exactly.' He looked uncomfortable. 'I'm sort of… well, I help out. Whatever needs doing. Picking people up, helping with the gardens and so on.'

I was puzzled. If he was hired help, why was he eating with the family? And he seemed on familiar terms with the other guests.

'Thing is,' he said, 'I'm a tennis player. At least, I was. I was pretty good, you know, back in the old days.' His voice was wistful. 'Played internationally, for a bit, even got to the semi-finals of the French Open and the quarter-finals at Wimbledon.'

'That's very impressive. What happened?'

He gave a light laugh, with a trace of bitterness. 'The War, of course. I got shrapnel in my left knee at Passchendaele. I came down here in the hope the warmth would help. It has, a bit, but I won't be playing internationally again. I'm the tennis pro at one of the big hotels in Cannes, during the season. But that leaves me at a loose end in the summer. Mr Rubin met me last year; suggested I come and stay here for a bit. While I decide what to do with the rest of my life.'

His eyes rested back on Dulcie.

'She's very lovely,' I said.

He flushed. 'She was rather lovely to me, when she first arrived. But she gets bored quickly. And she needs a rich man. You can't imagine her shacked up in the gardener's cottage, can you?'

I couldn't. 'Perhaps something will come up,' I said, rather lamely.

At the other end of the table, Mrs Jameson was making everyone laugh. I tuned back into the conversation, to discover I was the star of the story.

'So, she offered to sleep the remains of the night in the poor woman's compartment, to guard against further incursions.' She raised her glass towards me. 'And Marjorie is an accomplished martial artist. Any would-be thief would find himself thrown over her shoulder and out of the train window, I shouldn't wonder.'

I joined in the laughter, a little embarrassed.

'Anyway, the point is, we should go to see this Renoir, Sol. It's really quite charming. I thought you might be interested,' my employer added. 'And if you're not, I might be myself.'

M. Brunot looked up with interest. 'A new Renoir? That's very unusual. I thought everything was accounted for. I must ask Jean what else they have hidden away. Although most of the paintings went to Pierre, I believe.'

Mrs Jameson turned a questioning look on the film director.

'Pierre Renoir is the eldest son, a very good actor with whom I have worked several times. His brother Jean is interested in film. His wife would like to be a film star.' He smiled maliciously at Dulcie Pemberton. 'She is most striking; lots of golden hair tumbling around her face like a lion's mane. Perhaps I will cast her in the leading role in my next film.'

'But you said…' Dulcie began, then stopped. She picked up her tinted glasses and put them back on. They gave her the air of an exotic insect, big black eyes beneath her geometric helmet of hair.

'Let us all go tomorrow, when you have had time to recover from your journey, Iris,' said Mr Rubin, diplomatically. 'I know of the Galerie Anglaise, and I am intrigued to see a new Renoir. Andrew, will you drive us down? We can enjoy a morning in Nice.'

'Do you really know martial arts?' Benjamin asked me while the plans were made. His eyes were round with wonder.

I tried to look demure. 'Jiu-jitsu. It can be quite handy,' I said.

'Please, teach me.' He set down his soup spoon and clasped his hands together. 'Before they send me to school. I need to learn how to fight.'

The child was slight and had a bookish air. 'If your father doesn't mind,' I said. 'But you have to be careful. Only use it when you need to. You can hurt someone quite badly.'

'Good,' he muttered grimly, as the plates were cleared away.

Chapter 5

Mr Montgomery and his wife were waiting to welcome our party as the car pulled up on the Promenade des Anglais the next morning, which was Saturday.

Ashton Montgomery wore a cream suit, the lapels and trouser legs wider than was usual in London. His wife was almost as tall as he was. She wore a sporty two-piece in cool green linen, with a smattering of freckles speckling her nose. Her golden hair was neatly shingled, and she looked as if she spent most of her time outdoors.

Mr Montgomery doffed his boater as Andrew handed Mrs Jameson onto the pavement.

'Charmed, Mrs Jameson. So pleased to meet a fellow American,' he said. 'May I introduce my wife Lois?'

He bowed to Mr Rubin, welcomed him to the gallery and then turned a wide, bright smile on me.

'Miss Swallow, I understand I have you to thank for preserving both Miss Trent and the Renoir from thieves on the Blue Train. I am eternally grateful.'

I was rather flattered to be singled out, despite being the least important person in the party, and certainly the one least likely to buy a Renoir painting.

We were ushered into the gallery. Miss Trent waited

inside, her smile a little anxious, even though she had safely discharged her duty in delivering the picture to the gallery. Perhaps she was worried that Mr Rubin would not like it as much as we had.

She need not have worried. 'Ah, very pretty, very charming,' he said, regarding the small canvas with his head to one side. In daylight, placed on a stand, the painting glowed. 'And you say it has never been on the market before?'

'Indeed not,' said Mr Montgomery. 'And I am delighted to say that the owner, Monsieur Leclerc, is here with us today.'

A thin man in middle age with sparse dark hair and a finicky manner stepped forward, as Miss Trent handed Mr Rubin the letter of authentication.

'It's a rather charming story,' said Mrs Montgomery, her American accent soft and lilting. 'The painting is of M. Leclerc's wife, Sophie, made when she was a child of – what was it? Ten, or twelve years? Such a lovely age.'

'My wife was ten years of age when she was first painted by M. Renoir,' said M. Leclerc, stiffly. His accent was strong but his English good, if formal. 'When this portrait was made in 1911, she was twelve years old. M. Renoir presented it to her parents. She was, as you can see, a pretty child.' He folded his hands precisely.

I calculated on my fingers. If Sophie Leclerc was twelve in 1911, she would be only twenty-four now, much younger than her husband. But perhaps that was usual in France.

'And I understand there are other paintings, M. Leclerc,' said Mrs Jameson. 'All of your wife?'

He shook his head. 'Some are portraits of Sophie, and some of her mother. M. Renoir often painted the women from the village.' He permitted himself a small smile. 'The men, not so much.'

'Did you know him?' I asked. I'd seen newspaper photographs of the old man with his straggly beard, struggling to hold a paintbrush in his arthritic fingers.

'I saw him sometimes, being driven through the village. I was the schoolmaster there – in fact, I still am. But it was difficult for him to leave Les Collettes, because of his infirmity. My wife would be able to tell you more about him,' he said.

A schoolmaster. That explained the finicky manner and the formal English.

Mr Rubin smiled expansively. 'I should like that very much. Why don't you both come to lunch with me tomorrow, M. Leclerc? And you too, Mr and Mrs Montgomery, and Miss Trent. I should like to hear more about the great painter. Especially if I am to become a collector of his work.'

I saw the flash of glee in Ashton Montgomery's eyes as he accepted. They started to talk business, and I tactfully removed myself to look at the paintings. Some were still stacked against the walls. They were all contemporary, bright colours reflecting the blue of the sea outside, pink flowers and sparkling light. I bent to read the labels, looking for names I knew. I spotted a painting by Marc Chagall, but others were unfamiliar: Joan Miro, Suzanne Valadon, Albert Gleizes. In some cases, I struggled to work out what they depicted, but I liked the energy and colour.

'Good Lord. What are you doing here, Marjorie?'

I jumped at the sound of the lilting Welsh voice and turned quickly.

'Hugh!'

'Marjorie.' He grinned, teeth white in a face as sun-burned as a pirate. I'd last seen Hugh Williams at his own exhibition of paintings, in the gloom of London in February. The sales had been poor, and he had been despondent. Now he looked – well, rather wonderful. His brown eyes glowed with life, dishevelled chestnut curls framed his merry face and a striped matelot jersey under a blue work jacket outlined his athletic figure. My disloyal heart skipped a beat.

Mrs Jameson joined us, her shrewd grey eyes sliding between us. 'Mr Williams, how unexpected to see you here,' she said. 'Are you also on holiday?'

He removed his blue cloth cap. 'How d'you do, Mrs Jameson. The Slade School shuts down for the long vacation, so I thought I'd come and paint here. I'm staying in Villefranche-sur-Mer, just along the coast. I'm hoping that Ashton will take a look at my latest paintings, but I can see he's occupied.' I noticed the portfolio under his arm.

Mrs Montgomery appeared at his shoulder. 'Can I help with anything, Hugh? Ashton may be awhile,' she said.

He flashed her a smile. 'Hello, Lois. Could I leave these for him to see? I'll call back later. I think he might like what I've been working on this last month. Lots of colour, you know. No more gloomy expressionism.' He laughed, but I sensed a sore spot under his blitheness.

'Of course. I'll be sure he gets to see them.' She took the portfolio with a warm smile.

'Thank you.' Hugh looked consideringly from me to my employer. 'I don't suppose you'd like to join me for a jaunt around the old town? I'll call back to see Ashton later.'

I held my breath.

'Well, that's a tempting offer,' said Mrs Jameson. 'But I have already arranged to take morning coffee at the Negresco with Miss Trent, to discuss the break-in on the train. She is still anxious about it, and I am… curious. Marjorie, would you like to join us?'

She smiled at me, cat-like. She knew full well what I wanted to do.

'Well,' I stammered. 'That would be very interesting…'

'But you are on holiday,' said Mrs Jameson, relenting. 'Go with Hugh, Marjorie. Have a nice morning. I'm sure Mr Rubin will be happy to send Mr Fraser to pick you up later. Shall we say three o'clock, back here at the gallery?'

I could have kissed her.

'Thank you, Mrs Jameson. I won't be late,' I promised. Then Hugh and I headed out into the bright sunshine, gleeful as two children escaping early from school.

Chapter 6

Hugh took my arm, and we stepped across the road to the wide promenade. Men in work clothes bicycled past balancing panniers of bread, women carried baskets of shopping, children bowled hoops and nurses pushed perambulators. A few smartly dressed people strolled like fashion-plates, or sat in the blue-painted metal chairs all along the promenade, taking in the view.

'Most of the posh lot arrive next month,' said Hugh. 'September is too hot for the English. The Americans don't mind, though. Some of them have been here all summer, sun-bathing at St Juan Les Pins. There are rumours that the police are patrolling beaches and measuring women's bathing costumes, to be sure they aren't showing too much flesh.'

At least that was one thing I didn't need to worry about. We descended the steps opposite the strawberry-pink Negresco hotel, with its tower and dome.

'You really are in with the high rollers, staying with Mr Rubin, Marjorie. He's a diamond merchant, isn't he? It's a long way from Bloomsbury.'

'Guess who else is staying?'

'Pablo Picasso.'

I shook my head.

'I know. He's staying with the Americans. I met him, Marjorie. He's terrifying – those black eyes bore into your soul. All right, then. Charlie Chaplin?'

I laughed. 'No. But close. Dulcie Pemberton.'

He whistled. 'La-di-dah! What's she like?'

I walked to the water's edge where the little waves lapped placidly. 'Actually, she's rather rude. She spends all her time lying on the beach when she should be working, and she's horrible to a guest who's in love with her.'

He threw me a sardonic glance. 'I suppose being beautiful is like being rich – you can get away with anything.'

He took off his jacket and slung it over his shoulder. A tuft of dark hair showed at the neck of his jersey. I looked away, then looked back. I unbuttoned my cardigan, slipped it off and felt the sun on my bare arms.

'That's better. Isn't the sun glorious?' he said. He picked up a stone and spun it into the waves. 'I went down to Menton when I first arrived, to see Ralph. He and Winifred are staying there year-round. Death duties broke up the estate at Bessborough, and he can't stand the place anyway.'

'How are they?' I had met Ralph, now Lord Bessborough of Suffolk, and his sister Winifred at a Bloomsbury party, along with Hugh.

'She's just the same. Uptight. Still re-writing her novel. I've never seen an Englishwoman more impervious to the Riviera. He's having a good time, though. Painting again, and making new friends.'

There was an edge to his voice. Hugh had been Ralph's tutor at the Slade School of Art – and their relationship had been a potential source of scandal.

'I expect he was pleased to see you, though?'

He shrugged. 'Not particularly. I don't think he wants any reminders of his old life. Come on, I want to show you the market at the Cours Saleya.'

He led me up the beach and over the road, while I digested this news. If Hugh's involvement with Ralph was at an end, then perhaps he had changed. I remembered something I'd heard from my brother. Boys went through phases. Some took longer than others to grow out of them. Perhaps what Hugh needed was a nice girl.

All such thoughts were banished as we walked through an archway in the ochre-painted buildings into a long market-place.

'Isn't it wonderful?' Hugh led me through the bustling crowds. 'I'm going to paint it sometime.'

I exclaimed over plump tomatoes the colour of oxblood, shiny dark bulbous vegetables that Hugh said were aubergines, courgettes with their yellow flowers still attached, heaps of garlic bulbs and braids of onions. Peaches glowed in their downy softness, baskets displayed brilliant greengages and plums like jewels. I wanted to plunge my fingers into the baskets of fruit and grab handfuls of the glossy produce.

The wares changed as we walked; vegetables gave way to buckets of bright flowers, then stalls heaped with bric-a-brac: discarded furniture, racks of old clothes, second-hand books and stacks of paintings in heavy gilt frames.

'The *marche des puces*,' said Hugh. 'Flea market. You can get anything here.'

'Look!' I saw a stall selling straw hats, which a few young women were trying on, laughing at themselves in the mirror. 'I need one of those. So long as they don't give me fleas.'

Hugh assisted as I picked up, tried on and discarded hats.

Boaters were too severe for my face, and I wasn't tall enough for the style that Dulcie Pemberton wore. The elegant floppy creations made me look like a mushroom, all hat with a short stem.

Finally, we settled on a more modest style with a red silk carnation which matched the trim on my dress. Hugh set it on my hair and adjusted the brim.

'Very pretty,' he said. 'Red suits you, Marjorie. You should wear it more often.'

I laughed. 'I expect it goes with my nose, after being exposed to the sun all morning.' But I was rather thrilled with the compliment. I loved scarlet but didn't often dare to wear it. Feeling extravagant, I bought a useful-looking straw basket, like the ones the French housewives carried over their arms.

We resumed our browsing. 'Let's go to the port,' said Hugh. 'The boats will be back in by now.'

But I was getting hungry. 'Shouldn't we eat first?' I asked. A clock on the side of a baroque-style church said it was gone noon. I noticed some of the stall holders erecting folding tables and bringing out bottles of wine, glasses, cutlery and casserole dishes swathed in tea-towels. They took lunchtime seriously.

'Of course.' Hugh grinned. 'I forgot you need to be fed at regular intervals. I'm used to skipping meals, especially when I'm working.'

'I can pay,' I said, embarrassed. 'If that's difficult.'

He squeezed my hand. 'You're sweet. I admit, money is tight, although if Ashton sells those paintings, I'll be set up for a bit. But how about we get something from the market? We could take it to the beach, have a picnic on the chairs.'

I brightened up. We'd passed several stalls selling delicious-smelling food. I'd prefer a picnic to the awkwardness of ordering and waiting around in a French restaurant, where I wouldn't know what to ask for and would worry about the bill.

Hugh led me to a gaily decorated stall where a round-faced woman in an apron and headscarf was dispensing packets of food to workmen.

'You should have proper Nice street food,' said Hugh. 'Soca – that's sort of between a pancake and an omelette. Delicious. Then pissaladière, which is basically onion and anchovies cooked till they're sweet and baked on bread.'

'I'll try them,' I said, although I was a bit wary of anchovies. My father liked Gentlemen's Relish on toast, but it was too salty for me. 'Can we get some greengages, too?'

As we crossed the market, laden with goodies, Hugh waved to a man bending over one of the bric-a-brac stalls, flicking through the stacks of paintings.

'Hey, Antoine!'

The man jumped guiltily and straightened, shading his eyes with his hand. He saw Hugh and came over, shook his hand.

'*Ça va, mon ami?*' The man appeared rather seedy in his scruffy blue work clothes, his cap pulled down over his eyes. He looked as if he had forgotten to shave that morning and his hollow cheeks were gaunt.

'Marjorie, may I introduce Antoine Rousseau, a fellow-artist. We have lodgings in the same pension in Villefranche. Antoine, this is Miss Marjorie Swallow, a friend from London.'

The man doffed his cap and wiped sweat from his forehead, pushing back straggly dark hair. '*Bonjour, Mademoiselle.*' He kept his eyes on the ground, seeming nervous, as if he had been spotted doing something he shouldn't have.

Hugh looked curiously at the two paintings under his arm. 'What are you up to? Surely you don't like that old rubbish?'

The scuffed frames contained indifferent nineteenth-century paintings of landscapes and seascapes, in murky colours that were completely out of style. They were a million miles away from the vibrant new work I'd seen in the gallery.

'I was going to paint over them. Cheaper than buying new canvasses.' Antoine shifted them awkwardly so we couldn't see the pictures. 'Have you seen Montgomery today? I want to talk to him about the exhibition.'

'He was in the gallery this morning,' said Hugh. 'I wanted to ask him the same thing. I left my portfolio there. Why don't we go back together? We're about to have lunch on the beach. Will you eat with us?'

Antoine looked hungrily at the packets of food in my basket. But he shook his head. 'I am sorry. I have no time. I must get back to work.'

'Go on. You don't mind, do you, Marjorie?'

I'd rather enjoyed having Hugh to myself, but I smiled as warmly as I could. 'Of course not. Do join us, Monsieur.'

Antoine wiped his forehead again and replaced his cap. 'You are kind. I must go now, however. *A bientôt.*'

He headed off with determination. I frowned. He'd seemed almost scared of us. What had worried the man about our encounter?

Chapter 7

'Poor chap,' said Hugh. 'He hasn't sold anything for months. It's cheap to live in Villefranche, but not free. I hope Ashton accepts something for the show. Antoine's not a bad painter, but he's too old fashioned. Technique isn't enough, these days. You have to cater to what the people want.'

We sat in the sun and ate. The flavours were quite different from English fare, but I was getting to like them: sweet onions took away the saltiness of the anchovies and the bitterness of the little black olives.

Hugh didn't used to think like that about art, I reflected. I remembered the big, dramatic canvasses he'd displayed in London, full of the horrors that he'd seen in the War. Frightening pictures, ugly and jagged. As he'd predicted, they were not the sort of paintings people wanted to hang on their walls. Everyone wanted to forget, even those of us who had lost loved ones in the conflict. Perhaps he was right. It was time to move on from the past.

By the time we got back to the Galerie Anglaise, my feet hurt. We'd toured the pretty harbour, admired the yachts and watched the fishermen's wives selling mackerel while their husbands tended to their boats. My head ached from the heat and the glass of pink wine I'd drunk in a cafe after lunch. I began to realise why people in hot countries retired for a siesta in the afternoon.

My spirits rose again when Andrew Fraser roared up to the kerb in a racy three-wheeled scarlet Morgan sports car.

'I say! That's a beauty,' I exclaimed.

He jumped out and shook hands with Hugh. 'Isn't it? A special edition Aero, one of Solomon's favourites. It's pretty nippy, I can tell you.'

I inspected the driver's seat. 'Right-hand drive. How do you find that on French roads?'

'You adjust pretty quickly. You just have to remember which side of the road to keep to when you come out at a junction. It has two speeds; no reverse gear but it's so light you don't need one. Turns on a sixpence.'

I looked covetously at the walnut steering wheel and dashboard. 'I'd love to try it.'

'Can you drive?' asked Andrew.

Hugh laughed. 'I've seen Miss Swallow commandeer a London taxi and chase a murderer halfway across London, Mr Fraser. She drives like a demon. Now, I must go and talk to Ashton. I don't want to miss him.' He made his excuses and disappeared into the gallery.

'I learned on ambulances during the War,' I explained, seeing the surprise on Andrew's face. 'If you can drive those, you can drive anything. And sometimes I drive Mrs Jameson's Lagonda.' I imagined how much Frankie, Mrs Jameson's chauffeur, would love the Morgan. I'd have to tell her all about it.

Andrew looked dubious. 'I suppose you could take it for a run the length of the promenade, then I could drive back to the villa. Those twisty roads take a bit of getting used to, especially if you're not familiar with driving on the right. Rear brake only, so don't go too fast. It takes a while to stop.'

I climbed in, determined to show him. I stretched out my legs until I was sitting a couple of inches above the road, and put it into gear. To my relief, I managed to pull smoothly away from the kerb and soon I was breezing down the sea front, grinning like a fool as the palm trees whizzed by. Being so close to the road made it feel much faster than a normal car.

Andrew handily fielded my new hat as it flew off, and I laughed. This was glorious.

At the far end of the bay, I drove into a side street wide enough to make a U-turn. Mindful of Andrew's advice, I was careful to keep to the right as we returned along the promenade. There was little motorised traffic, but a few horses pulled carriages or carts. I smiled to see the horses too wore straw hats, with holes cut out for their ears.

'Can I keep going?' I asked.

Andrew threw up his hands in surrender. 'You drive as well as I do. Go on, then. Watch out for the steep climb on the far side of the harbour.'

I've rarely enjoyed a drive as much since. The car handled like a dream, the engine growled with excitement and the steering responded to every touch on the wheel. I allowed myself to accelerate out of the bends, as Frankie had shown me, scattering grit on the cliff-top road. I had to restrain myself from singing.

'We're almost there,' shouted Andrew. 'Don't miss the turning – just past that white-painted rock.'

I pulled on the brake, slowed just in time, and we dropped smoothly into the motor garage. The sudden shift from bright sunshine to gloom left me blinking to adjust.

The green door from the tunnel to the garden opened, and Mr Rubin stood in the doorway. I couldn't see his expression, and I hoped he wasn't angry to see me in the driving seat of his beautiful car.

I scrambled out, feeling guilty.

'You are a keen motorist, Miss Swallow?'

'I am rather,' I said. 'I hope you don't mind, Mr Rubin. I persuaded Andrew to let me drive. I was very careful.'

'She's a very good driver,' said Andrew heartily. I wondered if he too was worried about Mr Rubin's disapproval.

Solomon Rubin walked over and caressed the shiny dome of the chrome bonnet. 'And how did you find it?'

'Oh, it's marvellous,' I said, relieved to see he was smiling. 'The nicest car I've ever driven.'

He laughed. 'Then you must drive it again. I find it a bit too exciting, now I am so old. It needs to be used. Please, Miss Swallow. Borrow it whenever you like.'

'Really?' I gasped. 'Thank you so much. I'd love to.'

Mrs Jameson and Miss Trent followed through the green door.

'There you are, Marjorie. I thought you had run off with your artist friend,' said Mrs Jameson, tartly.

'I'm sorry.' I wasn't late, but it was always easiest to apologise when Mrs Jameson was annoyed about something.

'I have had a most interesting discussion with Miss Trent. Marjorie, when you came out of your compartment on the train, did you look down the corridor both ways? To the rear and the fore of the train?'

I thought back. 'Yes, I think so. There wasn't anyone in the corridor towards the front of the train. And when I looked back, I saw Miss Trent's door was open and the light on.'

'And from which direction did the carriage attendant arrive?'

'From the rear. He'd been helping with the baggage.'

Mrs Jameson smiled, as if satisfied. 'As I thought. Well, Miss Trent, I wish you a safe journey back to Nice. I believe Mr Fraser is to take you.' She cast another caustic glance in my direction. 'Unless you would prefer to be chauffeured by my assistant, of course.'

Miss Trent, cool and businesslike in her grey suit, took in my dishevelled hair and crumpled white frock. 'I expect Marjorie wants to freshen up, after her drive,' she said. 'Mr Fraser, would it be too much trouble to run me into Nice? I'm staying at a pension in Cimiez.'

As Andrew opened the car door for Miss Trent, Mr Rubin ushered us into the garden.

'I must go back to my study to look over some letters, Iris. But I believe it is the perfect time of day to bathe. Benjamin and Nanny Braithwaite are probably already on the beach. Why don't you and Marjorie go down, and I will join you when I can?'

I smiled my acquiescence, but I was privately dismayed. To my embarrassment, I'd never learned to swim, and I was too scared to try.

Chapter 8

Mrs Jameson went to her room to change. I paused at the top of the spiral staircase to the beach. Benjamin was knee-deep in the sea, watched over by a sturdy middle-aged woman in an ankle-length beige dress and white apron – Nanny Braithwaite, I assumed. Benjamin was a bit old for a nanny, at twelve. I wondered why she had stayed so long.

'Blast.' I turned to see Dulcie Pemberton had materialised beside me, wearing a ravishing turquoise silk wrap over her bathing costume. She had a beach towel in one hand and a book in the other. Her rosebud mouth was pursed.

'Is something the matter, Miss Pemberton?'

'I wanted to sunbathe in peace.'

One small boy splashing in the water didn't look too disturbing. I wondered how she would fare at Margate on August Bank Holiday.

'I'm sure they will leave you alone,' I said. I took a peek at her book. It was by Dorothy L Sayers, a new author I very much wanted to read. 'Ooh, is that good?' I loved a decent detective story.

She glanced at it. 'Not bad. I've almost finished it.' She looked at me again, dark eyes narrowed. 'Where did you get that hat?'

I reached up to touch it. 'This? I found it in the market at the Cours Saleya this morning. Cheap, but it does the job.'

She raised her pencil-thin eyebrows. 'It looks just like one from Jean Patou's latest collection. You must have a good eye. Marjorie, isn't it?'

I beamed. 'Thank you. I did try on the big ones like yours, but I think I'm too short for them. They look lovely on you.'

'I know. Call me Dulcie, why don't you?'

We descended in surprising harmony. Perhaps I had misjudged Dulcie Pemberton.

'Come and paddle,' pleaded Benjamin. Dulcie marched to the far end of the beach and settled herself on a deckchair. I slipped off my shoes and ventured into the water.

'Don't bother the guests, Benjamin,' said Nanny Braithwaite, her Yorkshire accent disapproving.

'I'm happy to paddle with Benjamin,' I said. 'The water is lovely and cool.' It seemed a rather lonely life here for a child.

'Will you really teach me jiu-jitsu?' he asked. 'Can we start now?'

The stony beach wasn't ideal. Sand would have been better, and for the first time I wished we really were at Margate rather than Nice. However, I spread out our beach towels and we stood opposite each other, knees bent and arms loosely at the sides, like gorillas at the zoo.

'It's all about balance and weight,' I told him. 'Especially for you and me, because we're small. We're never going to beat someone in a fight by muscle power. We have to use their weight against them.'

His face was deadly serious. 'Show me.'

I ran through some exercises. 'First you have to learn to fall without hurting yourself, and roll over so you can get quickly to your feet.'

We did this a couple of times. 'This is boring,' complained Benjamin. 'I thought you said you could hurt someone.'

I shot a look at Nanny Braithwaite. She was sitting heavily in a deckchair and had her knitting out.

'I'll show you how to trip someone who's coming towards you, so they fall backwards,' I said.

He grinned with enthusiasm.

'Walk towards me and grab me by the shoulders,' I instructed.

He complied. I placed my ankle on the outside of his and tipped him over, throwing him onto his back. He yelled, lying on the ground looking up at me in shock. Oh, goodness. That was a bit more effective than I'd expected.

Nanny Braithwaite shot out of her deckchair. 'What on earth are you doing to the poor bairn?' she demanded.

'I'm sorry.' Flustered, I extended a hand to Benjamin to pull him to his feet. 'I was just teaching him some jiu-jitsu techniques. Are you all right? I didn't mean to hurt you.'

'That was brilliant,' he said, eyes shining as he sprang up. 'My turn next.'

'Certainly not,' said the nanny. 'I'm surprised at you, Miss Swallow. I shall inform Mr Rubin.'

'I did ask Mr Rubin yesterday,' I said apologetically. 'He said it would be fine, so long as Benjamin didn't get hurt.'

'That looks awfully handy,' said Dulcie, who had roused herself from her book. 'Perhaps you could teach me too, Marjorie?'

'Over my dead body,' said Nanny Braithwaite.

'That can be arranged,' muttered Dulcie. 'Come on, Marjorie. Show us how you did it.'

Nanny Braithwaite folded her mouth primly and stalked

back to her chair. I demonstrated again, more cautiously this time. Then I let Benjamin have a go, but he couldn't get the co-ordination right.

'I'm rubbish.' He flopped down on the beach.

'You just need practice,' I assured him. 'We've got plenty of time. When are you going to school?'

'I don't know,' he said, gloomily. 'I don't want to go. Nanny Braithwaite says boarding schools are horrible. She says the older boys all make fun of the younger boys and the masters cane you for nothing.'

I shot a sharp look at Miss Braithwaite. 'I'm sure that's not true,' I said, although actually I had heard pretty awful things about English boarding schools. 'I bet you'll make lots of friends and have fun. Wouldn't you like that?'

He picked up a stone and rubbed it dry. 'Maybe. I don't know if I like other boys. They make such a dreadful noise.'

It sounded to me as if he should be sent to school as soon as possible, before his too-old manner became priggish and odd.

Mrs Jameson descended the spiral staircase in a floor-length yellow wrap, holding a towel over one arm.

'Are you going to bathe?' Benjamin asked her. 'I've been in twice today. It's topping.'

She smiled. 'I certainly am. Marjorie, ask the housekeeper if you can borrow a bathing suit. Mr Rubin keeps a selection for guests who forget to bring them.'

I hesitated. Much as I loved paddling, I was actually rather afraid of the sea. 'I'm quite happy like this,' I said.

'Nonsense. Run along, now. Right, young Benjamin. Shall we race out to that rock? I bet you can beat me.'

She disrobed and strode confidently into the waves, her modest navy blue bathing costume disappearing quickly as she struck out with a firm breast-stroke, hair wrapped in a towelling turban. Benjamin threw himself after her and doggy-paddled in her wake.

Dulcie sat down and picked up her book. 'I'd go in myself, but I don't want to mess up my hair before dinner. Why don't you borrow a suit?'

Minutes later, I was back on the beach, feeling self-conscious in the rather old-fashioned red and white costume the house-keeper had found, with flounces around the elbows and knees. Mrs Jameson and Benjamin stood on a rock in the bay, impossibly far out it seemed to me. Maybe I should just give it a try.

I tried to walk in casually, but I was hollow with nerves. The cool water gave me goosebumps as it moved up my legs, then made a cold ring around my waist like a belt. Pebbles pinched my bare toes and I stumbled, a clutch of fear at the thought of falling and being unable to get up again.

When the water reached my chest I stopped, trailing my fingers through the waves. What should I do now?

Experimentally, I leaned forward in the water as Mrs Jameson had done, arms out in front of me, then stretched wide. My feet lifted gently, and I toppled over, gasping as my face went under and swallowing a great gulp of sea water. I panicked, kicking my legs and trying to find the bottom, my hands scrabbling for the surface. My flouncy costume felt heavy, pulling me down. I kicked hard, my foot connecting with something solid.

Then someone had hold of my arm and was pulling me upright. With relief I emerged, spluttering and gasping for air, and found my feet.

'Whatever are you doing, Marjorie?' Mrs Jameson held me

firmly by the shoulders while I coughed up brine. 'Stop kicking me.'

'I'm sorry,' I gasped. 'I was trying to swim. I don't really know how.'

'Dear girl, you should have waited for me to teach you,' she said. I saw concern and amusement mingled in her face. 'You gave me quite a fright. I haven't swum that fast for years.'

Benjamin was paddling around us in circles like a terrier. 'You need lessons. I learned when I was five.'

'I want to get out,' I said, feeling like I was five years old myself. I didn't feel safe out here at all.

'Nonsense,' said Mrs Jameson. 'If you get out now, you'll never get back in again. You can float perfectly well, if you don't panic. I'll show you.' She let go of my shoulders, leaned back into the water and drifted backwards, her toes appearing at the surface a second later. I seriously doubted the same would happen if I tried it.

'Your turn,' she said. 'I'm right here. Try to relax and let the water hold you up. Then let your feet drift up to the surface.'

I took a deep breath, expecting to sink like a stone. I started to lean, then fear claimed me, and I struggled back upright with a cry.

'I can't do it.'

Mrs Jameson was unperturbed. 'You can. Close your eyes and lean gently. Relax your muscles. You're not an ironing board.'

I tried again. This time, my feet lifted gently from the stones and the water cradled me. I opened my eyes, saw the perfect azure sky stretching above me and spread my arms wide. I stretched my legs out and my toes broke the surface.

'It's working!'

Mrs Jameson laughed. 'Well done, Marjorie. Now, any time you feel you are sinking, just flip onto your back and float.'

'I'll remember that,' I said. As it turned out, it was rather lucky I did.

Chapter 9

The Montgomeries were the last to arrive for Sunday lunch. They walked through the terrace arm in arm, like a *Vogue* advertisement for modern America. Lois looked pristine, from her white sunray-pleat skirt and sailor-collar blouse, to her black and white Oxford pumps and sheer stockings. They both glowed with good health and bonhomie.

Mr Rubin stepped forward, hands outstretched in welcome.

'We are so pleased to visit the Villa Beau Rivage,' said Ashton. 'I knew the place under the previous owner. The Comte d'Aubigny was a keen host. It's wonderful to be back.'

Lois Montgomery smiled warmly as Mr Rubin raised her hand to his lips. Across the room, I saw Dulcie frown with annoyance. The American's wholesome style made the film star's glamour look rather tawdry. Dulcie wore a vampish scarlet and black silk tunic with flowing scarlet pyjama trousers. It was a bit much for Sunday lunch.

Sibyl Trent was again deep in conversation with Mrs Jameson, and M. Leclerc stood looking nervous with his wife, who apparently spoke little English. She was very pretty, easily identifiable as the child in the Renoir painting, despite her old-fashioned ankle-length dress.

Nanny Braithwaite bustled across the terrace, bearing down

on Benjamin and the Leclerc's daughter Claudette, a doll-like child of six who took after her mother.

'Come along. The children are having their lunch in the garden,' she said.

'But I want to talk about sensible things,' said Benjamin, with a look of outrage.

Claudette took one look at Nanny Braithwaite and began to wail. Her mother looked exasperated and chided her in French.

'What a sweet child,' said Lois Montgomery. 'Come along, dear. Let's go and look at the pretty flowers in the garden, shall we?' She held out her hand and the girl stopped crying. 'Won't you show us around, Benjamin? I'd so like to see the garden and the beach.' The scowl left Benjamin's face and he stood taller, his face flushing with pleasure.

Nanny Braithwaite nodded her approval and they disappeared down the steps.

'Your wife has a way with children,' Mrs Jameson said to Ashton Montgomery, who was watching with a fond smile.

I felt a little sorry for the Leclercs and decided to try out my French. I quickly discovered that Sophie Leclerc had been a pupil of her schoolmaster husband. She seemed to find this very funny, although it made me uncomfortable. What sort of man married a schoolgirl?

'I was seventeen when we married,' she said, her eyes round. 'Can you imagine? I was... what is the word? Impatient. I wanted to get on with my life. And Marcel, *le pauvre*...'

He raised his hands, palms up, and gave me a rather greasy smile. 'What chance did I have?' he asked.

I swallowed down my cocktail. I needed something to shift the bad taste in my mouth.

'I thought life would be more exciting once I was married,' said Sophie, rather wistfully. She looked around the terrace. 'Like this, with lots of people and parties and a pretty house with a garden.'

Her husband tutted. 'We have a perfectly good house,' he said. 'You just need to learn to make it look pretty.' He looked irritated. I wondered how having a much younger, more vivacious wife was working out for him.

To my relief, we were called to take our places at the table. Unfortunately, M. Leclerc was on my left. I turned quickly to Andrew Fraser, seated to my right, but he was making the most of being seated next to Dulcie Pemberton. I tuned into their conversation for a moment.

'What am I supposed to do, Andrew? He's been talking to that American woman ever since she arrived, and now that blasted Englishwoman from the gallery. She's got her eye on him. I'm not stupid. And as for Miss American Pie over there, she makes me sick. Pour me another glass, will you?'

Poor Andrew. I realised what I should have spotted before. Dulcie Pemberton was hoping to become the next Mrs Rubin. No more learning lines, no more posing for the cameras. An extremely wealthy husband and a lovely lazy life. Andrew's words came back to me. She needs a rich man. Well, she'd certainly found one. Whether or not she would hook him was another question. I suspected that Mr Rubin had plenty of experience of women after his wallet rather than his heart.

Mrs Jameson and the Montgomeries were discussing acquaintances in common from New York, where Ashton had grown up, and California, where Lois's family owned fruit farms.

'My people have farmed there for generations,' she said, her soft sing-song accent rising effortlessly above the babble of voices in French and English. 'Apricots and peaches. They're moving into vineyards, now. They plan to make their own wine, as soon as this prohibition nonsense is over.'

'How brave of them,' said Maxim Brunot, his tone acid. 'Do you think Americans will drink wine made in California? I can't imagine the rest of the world will want it, when French wine is so superior.'

She laughed. 'Perhaps we should wait until we can make the comparison, M. Brunot. Although I don't drink wine myself. Alcohol is very ageing for women, you know. It coarsens the complexion.'

Dulcie, who was on her third glass, almost spat it out. 'Teetotallers bore me,' she said, too loud. 'Don't you think, Sol? I should hate to be at a dinner party where everyone drank water. Too tedious for words.'

M. Brunot rolled his eyes. 'Perhaps you should try it. You might be able to concentrate on set the next day.'

Mr Rubin smiled uneasily. 'I believe in everything in moderation,' he said. 'Now, perhaps we could hear a little more about this painting. Madame Leclerc, I understand you had the honour of posing for M. Renoir. We would all love to hear a little about that experience.'

Sophie Leclerc seemed to enjoy an audience. Despite her limited English, between her and her husband, she managed to tell us a lot about posing for the great master. Her mother had taken her to his farm, Les Collettes, along with other women and children from Haut de Cagnes, the medieval village perched on a hill above the sea.

'There was a pretty garden, with lots of flowers, and many olive trees. Oranges, too. They smelled so sweet in springtime.

We played under the trees and M. Renoir picked out the girls he wanted to paint.' She smiled at us gleefully, her small white teeth glinting. 'He picked me, because I was so pretty. He said he liked my hair.'

Her hair was indeed rather stunning, a great pile of chestnut curls twisted up into a bun on the top of her head.

'It was nice, to be looked at and admired. I enjoyed it very much. And he painted Maman, too.' She dimpled at us. 'Without her clothes. *Nue*, you understand? She didn't mind, because he was so old. His son had to wheel him into the studio in his chair, then set up the easel and put the paintbrush into his hand. The old man was in pain, but when he started to paint, he seemed to go…' she waved her hand. '*Un rêve*. Like there was nobody there.'

'A dream,' said M. Brunot, his expression soft. 'That's what Jean told me. He was in so much pain. Then when he started to paint, it all fell away.'

'You know his son?' asked M. Leclerc.

'Jean Renoir asked me to show him my cameras and lighting equipment, when we met in Paris. He plans to make films of his own.'

Ashton Montgomery broke in. 'How wonderful to hear about those memories of the great man,' he said. 'Thank you, Madame Leclerc. As you can tell, Mr Rubin, this painting of Sophie is very special. I sold a similar one for the Leclercs last year, to a collector whose name I am sure you would recognise. He asked me to offer him first refusal on any others. It is only because Miss Trent recommended you that I have shown it to you first.'

Mr Rubin nodded. 'And you say there are more paintings?' he asked. 'How many, Mr Leclerc?'

The schoolteacher swallowed a mouthful of the beef stew, which was tasty but rather heavy for such a hot day. 'Quite a few,' he said, hesitantly. 'We did not even know of their existence until my wife's mother died last year. We discovered them in the attic of the farmhouse, which she left to Sophie. Of course, we don't really want to sell such beautiful things, but…' He gave an expressive shrug. 'A schoolteacher's salary is not high, and there are taxes and bills to pay. Since the War, everything is more expensive.'

Everyone murmured in sympathy.

'Do not hesitate too long, Mr Rubin,' said Ashton. 'I have many clients who would be interested in a newly discovered Renoir. And buying now would put you in a very good position if others are released for sale.'

'They all need to be authenticated, of course,' said Sibyl Trent, hastily. Perhaps she was worried that Ashton was pressing too hard. 'Which is where I come in. Checking the composition of the paint, the labels, the canvas. I have been working on the *catalogue raisonné*, so I am very well placed.'

Mr Rubin turned to her with courtesy. 'Of course. And I'm sure your skills and experience are most valuable. I will be glad to have you as an advisor, Miss Trent.'

She smiled. 'And I would love to see your collection. I hear you have been quite the connoisseur. Perhaps we could take a look?'

'Well, maybe.' Mr Rubin looked cautious, but a clamour of voices urged him on.

After luncheon, which concluded with absolutely delicious raspberry ice-cream, the party ascended to the first floor of the villa, where Mr Rubin had his study. He led us through the room with its desk, telephone and bookshelves, then pressed a switch beside the books. A section of the wall of shelves glided back, revealing a long gallery running across the rear of the villa, lit by electric lamps illuminating dozens of paintings.

'I made a study of Symbolist paintings at the turn of the century,' said Mr Rubin, glancing uneasily at Mrs Jameson. 'I have several by Gustave Moreau, for example. And others.'

My employer had stayed by the door, her face frozen and a hand to her throat. I was about to ask if she was feeling unwell, when I saw the picture.

The canvas stretched floor to ceiling, a swirling seascape with a new moon emerging from heavy storm clouds. A sea monster reared up in the foreground, its scales silver and green. Shrinking back against a rocky outcrop was a chained figure draped in flimsy gauze, auburn hair flaming against the pewter-coloured backdrop.

My jaw dropped. There was no mistaking the large grey eyes, the firm jaw and patrician nose.

Miss Trent stepped forward. 'I have wanted to see this for many years,' she said. '*Andromeda and the Sea Monster*, by Julian Jameson. It's magnificent.'

I turned back to Mrs Jameson in astonishment, but she was gone.

Chapter 10

'I am truly sorry, Iris.' Mr Rubin wrung his hands, pacing the length of his study. 'I didn't realise how much it would pain you to see that painting again.'

Mrs Jameson sat in an armchair, her face pale. 'Please, say no more about it,' she said. 'I had almost forgotten you owned it. It's all such a long time ago.'

The luncheon guests had departed, and even Dulcie Pemberton had been tactful enough to withdraw from the scene. I had tried to disappear too, but Mrs Jameson had asked me to stay.

She drew a deep breath, then raised her head and looked steadily at Mr Rubin.

'My husband painted me as Andromeda during the first year of our marriage,' she said. 'I had already begun to realise that the wedding had been the most serious mistake of my life. This painting confirmed my worst fears.'

She clutched her wrists, steadying herself. 'Julian was obsessed with Greek mythology, with the concept of sacrifice. Iphigenia, sacrificed by her father for a favourable wind to Troy. Polyxena, sacrificed to assuage the spirit of Achilles. And Andromeda, chained on the rocks to be devoured by a sea monster to appease Poseidon, god of the sea.'

She smiled, a little tartly. 'Andromeda, of course, didn't die. Perseus rescued her. Perhaps that's what Julian thought he was doing. Rescuing me. But he had to sacrifice me first. I'm not sure what for. His genius, I suppose.' She chafed her left wrist in her hand, as if she could still feel the fetters.

'He chained me up in his studio in Rome. It was January. Even in Rome, January is cold. I wore… well, you could see what I was wearing. I stood there for days. He would go out and leave me there, in chains. My wrists bled and blistered. The scars have never completely disappeared. I developed pneumonia, almost died.

'But he said he could not paint Andromeda unless I despaired. When he could see despair, then he would let me go. He was relentless.'

Her face was rigid. 'As you may have realised, I don't despair easily. It took some weeks. But he got what he wanted in the end.'

'That's so awful,' I said, tears starting in my eyes. 'How cruel. I can't imagine. How dreadful for you.'

She turned her proud face to me. 'I don't need pity.' She took a sip of the whisky from the glass by her elbow. 'He is… he is history.' She gave a grim smile. 'Art history, it is true. But I'm alive and living on my own terms. Living well, as they say, is the best revenge.'

Mr Rubin took out a big white handkerchief and blew his nose. 'Iris, I cannot begin to apologise enough. I am appalled. Had I known its history, I would never have bought it. I will destroy that odious painting. I never want to look at it again. It should be burnt.'

'No!' She turned back to him, chin held high. 'It is an important work of art. He was a great artist. You must not destroy it, Sol. Keep it here, for my sake. But perhaps… do not show it to people who know me. I do not enjoy my friends seeing what I look like when I despair.'

I put a tentative hand on her arm. 'Mrs Jameson, I know you don't want me to feel sorry for you. I'm sorry I saw the painting, really. But I want you to know I didn't see despair when I looked at that picture. You looked exhausted, and scared. But you also looked really, really angry.'

She paused for a moment, and I worried that I'd said the wrong thing. Then she threw back her head and laughed. 'Bless you, Marjorie. Bless you for seeing that. You're right. I was furious. Mostly with myself, for being fooled when I agreed to marry him. But also with him, for his cruelty.'

Her face became solemn again. 'Cruelty is so difficult to fight. Most motives for violence are at least comprehensible. Avarice, or fear, or rage can make us do terrible things.

'But the cruel person, who takes delight in causing pain – it is almost impossible to believe. So, we don't expect it. It takes us by surprise, to find savage cruelty behind a civilised mask. At first, I thought I must have been imagining it, that I was misunderstanding, or that this was merely artistic temperament. And to experience this from someone I had thought myself in love with…' She shivered. 'It is not easy to explain how that feels.'

It was true; I didn't think I'd met anyone motivated solely by the desire to cause pain to others. We had met murderers, swindlers, blackmailers and gangsters. While many of them had been thoroughly nasty pieces of work, they had all been motivated by something else. For them, the ends had justified the means. Here, the means were the end.

'Well, then.' Mrs Jameson rose to her feet. 'Enough of the

past. Let's talk about something else. Marjorie, have you worked out yet who was the midnight intruder to Miss Trent's train compartment? She tells me the Nice police have declined to investigate, as the attempted crime did not happen within their jurisdiction.'

I struggled to keep up with the shift in the conversation. 'So, you don't think she just had a bad dream, then?' Insofar as I'd thought about our late-night adventure at all since our arrival, that had been my conclusion.

'Goodness me, no. A woman travelling alone with a valuable painting, asleep on a night train from Paris? It's hardly surprising she was a target. And, of course, you yourself met the intruder.'

'I did?' Bewildered, I reviewed the events of the night. The scream, the open door, Miss Trent, the arrival of... light dawned.

'You mean the carriage attendant?'

She smiled briskly. 'Finally. You described him as having a big blonde moustache and thick spectacles. That alone was enough to rouse my suspicions. A fake moustache and spectacles is the most rudimentary disguise. And when the attendant came to make up the compartments the next morning while you were at breakfast, he was a small, dark-haired man, clean-shaven and sharp-eyed enough to notice a hat-pin I'd dropped on the floor. The question is, where did your fake attendant come from, and where did he alight?'

I was embarrassed that I had not thought of it before.

'We had passed Lyon about an hour before it happened. I looked out of the window and saw them loading and unloading luggage. He could have got on there,' I said. 'The next stop was Avignon. Perhaps he left there. Before everyone got up and went through for breakfast.'

Mr Rubin shook his head. 'Perhaps it does not matter so much, now. The painting has been safely delivered to Mr Montgomery's gallery and resides in his safe. The thief failed in his attempt.'

Privately I rather agreed, but Mrs Jameson did not look convinced. She never liked to give up on a mystery.

'You are forgetting the card,' she said. 'A warning. Miss Trent says she doesn't understand it, but I wonder how true that is.' She gazed out of the window and lapsed into silence.

'I have something to tell you,' said Mr Rubin, after a moment's awkwardness. 'I hope it will be welcome news. I have offered to host a party here for Mr Montgomery and his artist friends, after the opening of the exhibition on Wednesday. You don't mind, Iris?'

She turned to him with a smile, her face serene again. 'I shall enjoy it very much,' she said. 'What a splendid idea. And Marjorie loves to dance.'

I'd already been looking forward to seeing Hugh at the opening of the exhibition. Now, perhaps, he would be able to attend the party. I remembered dancing with him in Bloomsbury, fox-trotting to the Tiger Rag. He danced beautifully, graceful and light of foot. My heart began to beat a little faster.

'I certainly do,' I said. 'What fun, Mr Rubin! I can't wait.'

Chapter 11

The next few days were blissful. I sun-bathed with Dulcie Pemberton, letting my face and arms get brown; had daily swimming lessons with Benjamin and Mrs Jameson; played tennis with Andrew Fraser. Jiu-jitsu lessons took place every evening on the beach, and Benjamin could now throw me handily over his ankle.

Then came Wednesday. When we arrived in the evening, the Galerie Anglaise was packed with people. Mrs Jameson, Mr Rubin, Dulcie and I descended from the Hispano Suiza into the late sunshine.

Ashton and Lois Montgomery stood by the door, shaking hands and welcoming guests.

'Do come through, Mr Rubin, Mrs Jameson. I'm so glad you could attend.' Mr Montgomery clearly revelled in his role as host. 'Ah, Miss Pemberton, Miss Swallow. You both look very elegant. And Mr Fraser, isn't it?' Andrew joined us, having parked the car across the road.

Dulcie sailed into the room in a dramatic black chiffon dress, cut low at the back with fringing on the skirt that swished between her shapely legs as she walked. I'd put on my favourite of the two evening dresses I possessed, a cream crepe de Chine frock with black beading around the square neckline and a black sash. I'd brushed my dark hair until it shone, despite the amount of salt water it had seen in the last couple of days. It was hard not to compare myself to Dulcie's exotic beauty, but I knew that I looked well enough.

No-one seemed to be looking at the art. Everyone was gabbling away nineteen to the dozen, laughing loudly and knocking back champagne. I took a glass from a circulating waiter. Mrs Jameson was talking to a pleasant-looking American couple who planned to buy a house in St Juan les Pins.

'We're going to call it Villa America,' said the woman, laughing. 'A cultural embassy, open to artists, writers and all manner of reprobates. It's going to be such fun.'

With a thump of my heart, I noticed Hugh behind them, wearing an unusually smart suit and talking to a short, dark-haired man. I squeezed through the crush.

'Hugh!'

He looked up and smiled. 'Hello, Marjorie.' His hair was neatly combed, his hands mostly clean of paint. Scrubs up well, as my mother would say. He looked thrilled. 'I was showing Señor Picasso my work,' he said proudly. 'Señor, may I present Miss Marjorie Swallow?'

The dark-haired man turned and I almost gasped. The face, familiar from newspaper photographs. The casual matelot jersey. But above all the eyes, obsidian black, hypnotic in their intensity.

I held out my hand and stammered a greeting. 'I am so pleased to meet you. I admire your work very much, Mr Picasso.'

He smiled, an even row of white teeth in his walnut-dark face, then brushed my hand with his lips and spoke a few words in French. I got the gist of them: he had been admiring Hugh's painting and wanted to know if I liked it.

I turned to look. Hugh had abandoned the monochrome expressionist style of his war paintings for intense colour and light. The lines were fluid, elegant. Against a backdrop of cerulean blue was the head of a young man, but doubled, so one face looked to the left and another to the right. The expression of both faces was yearning, the lips parted and the eyes wide. Splashes of yellow and white denoted stars and moon to one side, sun the other. Curtains framed the scene, as if before a window, and high in the sky a white-sailed yacht traversed the canvas.

I puzzled at it, then realised the great artist was waiting for an answer.

'*Je l'aime beaucoup*. But I need to look at it some more. I'm not sure I understand it, Hugh. You'll have to explain it to me.'

Picasso chuckled, long and low, his gaze penetrating first me and then Hugh.

'*Vous regardez, Mademoiselle Swallow. Beaucoup de gens regardent. La question est: verrez-vous?*' You look, Miss Swallow. Many people look. The question is, do you see?

With which enigmatic words, he passed through the crowd to where a slim woman with the poise of a ballerina was standing by the door.

'I'm so sorry, I shouldn't have interrupted,' I said, hoping Hugh wasn't cross. 'I didn't realise who you were with.'

He turned a dazzling smile on me. 'Did you hear? He said he admired it. Picasso admired my painting. God, Marjorie.' He clenched his fist. 'I'm getting somewhere. Finally. I was right to come out here, get away from dreary old London. Can't you feel the way life is here? It fizzes. It's all about colour and energy. To hell with the Slade. I'm going to stay.'

His eyes glittered. I'd never seen him so excited before.

'I'm so pleased for you,' I said. Did he mean it? Would he really not come back to London? A rebellious thought took root. What about me? Was there a place for me in this warm and colourful playground, too?

Out of the corner of my eye, I saw Dulcie bear down on Picasso, Andrew Fraser trailing behind her. Perhaps she had given up on Mr Rubin, who was again in conversation with Sibyl Trent. Miss Trent looked smart as usual, a long string of pearls over a black crepe dress, her dark hair held back from her face with a cream silk scarf.

Raised voices in French caught my attention. 'What's happening?' I was too short to see through the crowd.

Hugh stood on tiptoes to look across the room.

'Oh my word. It's Antoine. Poor chap. Ashton hasn't included any of his stuff. He was so angry about it. He said he was going to come and have it out with him here. It sounds like he's been drinking.'

He took my hand, and we squeezed through the people. I saw Mrs Jameson talking to Maxim Brunot, the film director. There were lots more people I didn't know, many of whom affected the same work clothes that Hugh usually wore: the artists' uniform of matelot jersey and *bleu de travail*. I supposed they were all trying to look like Picasso.

'Come along, old chap. This really isn't on, you know,' Ashton was saying, grasping the painter's elbow and manoeuvring him towards the door. 'I didn't sell a single piece of yours in the Spring show. You have to show me something new.' Lois hovered nearby with a look of distress, clutching a glass of orange juice.

'*Tu est un faux-cul!*' shouted Antoine, who was red in the face and stumbling. '*Je leur parlerai de toi, Ashton. Entendez-vous? Vous le regretterez.*'

Hugh grabbed his other arm. 'Don't be a fool, Antoine. Don't make threats. Come outside for a smoke.'

People were edging away from the disturbance, the women with looks of distaste on their well-fed faces. I remembered how hungry Antoine had looked when we met him in the Cours Saleya.

'Get him something to eat,' I implored Hugh. 'Can you? I'll pay you back later.'

'Thanks. I will.'

I could see the fight going out of Antoine. He slumped against Hugh. Ashton held the door open as Hugh half-carried the drunken man out.

He called over his shoulder to me. 'I'll put him into a taxi back to our lodgings. But then I'll come back for the party, I promise. Save all the dances for me.'

Grinning like an idiot, I rejoined the party.

'Getting a bit lively,' said Andrew Fraser, handing me another glass of champagne. 'Are you all right?'

'Absolutely,' I said, taking a gulp. It fizzed up my nose. Golly. What an evening. I'd talked to a world-famous artist, and Hugh had asked me to save him all my dances. I tried again to look at the paintings on the walls, but it was far too crowded to get a good view of them.

'Do you like art?' I asked Andrew.

He scrunched up his face. 'I shouldn't say, in this company. But I don't really see the point of it. I mean, I like pretty stuff. But I think pictures should look like what they are. You know, flowers or horses or sailing yachts. Or portraits of people you can recognise. Half of this lot, you can't even tell what they're supposed to be.'

He sounded like my father. I hid a smile. 'What's your cup of tea, then? Tennis?'

He gave a sad laugh. 'It used to be. Now I find it rather depressing. But I like to swim, and play a bit of cricket.' He rubbed his nose. 'The casino, although I shouldn't. I lost a packet, last April. That's why I'm still here. Couldn't afford the ticket home. I'd be in a real hole if Mr Rubin hadn't taken me in.'

Dulcie Pemberton flounced over, took Andrew's half-full champagne glass and downed it.

'Well, that really takes the biscuit,' she said.

'What's happened?' I asked.

'I just heard that Trent woman telling Sol that she needs to talk to him privately when they get back to the villa. I suppose she's going to whisk him off to that gallery he has hidden away with all those creepy pictures. Ugh.'

I looked at her in astonishment. 'It's probably about the painting he's going to buy,' I said.

'She's making a play for him, Marjorie, you mark my words. I know the signs,' she said.

Ashton Montgomery appeared at Andrew's shoulder. 'Everything all set for the party, Mr Fraser? It really is good of Mr Rubin to have us.'

Dulcie instantly switched on her dazzling smile. 'I'm so looking forward to it. You must promise to dance with me, Mr Montgomery, won't you?'

He looked wary but smiled. 'Of course. Now, I should just see where Lois has got to.'

Andrew looked at his watch. 'I'm going to head back to the

villa and make sure the band has arrived. I'm taking Mr Rubin. Who else wants to come with me? I'm sure there will be plenty of people heading that way if you want to wait.'

I set down my glass. 'I'll come. I'd like to freshen up before everyone arrives.'

'Me too,' said Dulcie. 'I'm not letting that Trent woman get in ahead of me this time.'

Chapter 12

The villa had never looked lovelier. Candles twinkled in lanterns hanging from the pergola over the terrace, softly illuminating the trailing bougainvillea. The staff had set out a tempting buffet of delicious foods – cold chicken, salmon mousse, and salads of sliced tomato and peppery basil. Flowers spilled over the huge terracotta pots that punctuated the terrace and torches illuminated the lower garden, where the fountain played.

The band was tuning up. The singer crooned gently into the microphone, her silky voice suggestive. She wore an exquisite silver-beaded frock which glowed against her dark skin. All of the musicians were Black, and American by the sound of their voices. I thought of my friend T-bone Tommy, the trombonist with Freddie's All Stars Jazz Orchestra, and wondered how they were getting on with their tour of the English seaside. Tommy always complained about the rotten English weather: perhaps the All Stars should try for a Riviera tour.

Andrew came back from talking to the band leader, looking pleased. 'How do you like them? Florrie Briscoe and the Beau Belles, from New York. We were lucky to get them,' he said. 'They were booked for the Monte Carlo casino, but there was a muddle over the dates.'

'They sound marvellous. How long are they going to play?' I hoped Hugh wouldn't miss them.

'They're doing a couple of sets. Nine until ten thirty, then a second set after the speeches. Do you enjoy dancing, Marjorie?'

'I certainly do. In fact,' I told him, 'I once worked as a dance hostess in a Soho nightclub.' His look of shock was very satisfying. 'Undercover, of course. In pursuit of the Limehouse criminal drugs gangs that were infiltrating West End venues.'

'Really? Did you use jiu-jitsu on them?' asked Benjamin, who had arrived unnoticed at my side, his face and hands scrubbed clean, wearing a smart evening suit that looked rather comical on such a young boy.

I laughed. 'I don't think you should have heard that. But yes, I did have to use my skills to get out of a tight spot.' My fingers found the slight raised line of the scar across my cheek. It was barely noticeable, but a reminder that investigations could turn nasty very fast.

'My goodness, Marjorie. Your job seems to involve some rather terrifying escapades,' said Andrew, whose eyes had gone as wide as Benjamin's.

'Which is why it's so nice to have a holiday,' I said. 'Get away from all that for a while.'

Guests started to filter through the tunnel, the band began to play, and Andrew Fraser disappeared to help take coats. I accepted a glass from a waiter and took a sip. It caught in my throat, and I realised they were not serving wine, but Mrs Jameson's favourite cocktail of gin, lemon and champagne, the redoubtable French 75. I knew how lethal they could be, and resolved to take it slowly.

I leaned back against the terrace wall and looked up at the

pink-washed villa, a fingernail sliver of silver moon hanging in the dark sky above. Lamps were lit in the tower room, which gave the most magnificent view over the Bay of Nice. It was a romantic spot, open to the sea breeze on all sides, looking down onto the rocks that enclosed the beach. I'd enjoyed sitting up there in the shade during the afternoon, reading a book until it was cool enough to bathe.

Someone was up there now, I saw, leaning over the railings. Tall and slim, in a dark frock, dark hair falling over her face. Dulcie, I supposed. Her room gave onto the base of the tower, just below Benjamin's nursery. I waved to her, but she didn't seem to see me.

'Ah, there you are, Marjorie.' Mrs Jameson was already part-way down her glass. 'I've been having a most interesting conversation with Mr Montgomery about the art market. I have some paintings by my late husband which I do not wish to display. He says they might be worth selling now, given that there will be no more.' She smiled in satisfaction. 'I shall send him an inventory.'

'Good idea.' I could quite understand Mrs Jameson wishing to be rid of Julian Jameson's artwork, especially if it could be done at a profit.

Mr Rubin was greeting guests at the door, Benjamin by his side. I wondered if Mr Picasso would come. I had felt a little afraid of him: he didn't make for comfortable company. I wondered what he'd meant about looking and seeing. What had I not seen? A waiter passed by and I swapped my empty glass for a fresh one.

My head jerked up as the band swung into one of my favourite numbers. The Harlequin Shimmy, composed by T-bone Tommy and the All Stars Jazz Orchestra, had been the hit of the summer. I'd have to tell them it had been picked up by American bands playing in France.

I thought of the way Freddie charged through the number, grinning from ear to ear, then put him firmly from my mind. He'd be in Blackpool or Bournemouth or the Isle of Wight, performing for staid English holidaymakers.

'Care to dance, Marjorie? If you promise not to use martial arts on me.' Andrew Fraser held out a hand.

'Go.' Mrs Jameson flapped her free hand at me. 'Dance, for heaven's sake. That's what we're here for.'

Andrew was a competent, but not brilliant dancer. He didn't step on my feet or get out of breath, and his embrace was firm. But he had no imagination, and it was a rather stolid dance for such a lively number. Never mind, I told myself. Hugh would be back soon. I tried not to make it obvious that I was scanning the room over his shoulder. How long would it take Hugh to get Antoine fed and into a taxi back to Villefranche?

'No, you don't, you conniving…'

There were gasps and shrieks from the far side of the dancefloor. Andrew let go of me abruptly.

'Oh, good Lord,' he said, and shot across the room. 'Dulcie.' I followed with trepidation.

Dulcie Pemberton was pulling at Sibyl Trent's long pearl necklace, which snapped and sent beads rolling all over the floor.

'Fake,' Dulcie shrieked. 'Like the rest of you. I've watched you inveigle your way in here, you manipulative little madam, cosying up to Mr Rubin. Well, I was here first!'

Sibyl, scarlet with mortification, was on her hands and knees trying to collect the escaped pearls. I crouched down to help her. They were indeed costume jewellery, but they would have been worth a fortune if they had not been.

Andrew had seized Dulcie by the arm and was trying to disengage her. I saw Maxim Brunot, looking horrified at the antics of his leading lady.

He stepped forward and called her sharply. 'Dulcie. Behave yourself, and come with me.'

'Please stop it,' Andrew hissed. 'You're making such a fool of yourself. Honestly, if you think Mr Rubin will like this sort of behaviour…'

Mr Rubin appeared through the crowd, his face creased with concern. 'Is something the matter?' he asked mildly.

Dulcie, her face streaked with eye-black and her dark hair mussed, stared at him, then burst into tears. She let go of Miss Trent and turned to Andrew, beginning to wail. He put an awkward arm around her shoulders.

'Nothing to worry about,' said M. Brunot smoothly. 'Actresses can be temperamental, I'm afraid. Here, Mr Fraser. Let me help you take Miss Pemberton for a rest.'

Between them they manipulated Dulcie off the dancefloor. I wondered if I should go with them, but they seemed to have her well in hand.

Mr Rubin crouched beside Miss Trent and me. 'I am sorry. Are you all right, my dear? I will pay for any damage, of course.'

She nodded, her colour subsiding. 'It was just a silly misunderstanding, Mr Rubin. No harm done. Please, do go back to your other guests. We can talk later,' she said.

I handed her a pile of beads.

'What a nuisance,' she said. 'I'll have to re-thread them.' Her little handbag was full of pearls, and she put the rest in the pocket of her black frock. Up close, I saw that the dress was a few seasons old, the hem taken up and a new sash fastened around the hips to give it a fresh look. The knee of her white stocking was neatly darned. I remembered what she said about needing to earn money, and realised how hard she worked to keep herself looking up-to-date.

'Are you all right?' Lois Montgomery stopped by, her soft voice full of concern. 'How upsetting for you, Sibyl.'

'I'm fine.' Miss Trent's long silk scarf had slipped off her shiny brown bob. 'I'd better go and find the cloak room to get myself straight.' She shook out the scarf and folded it over her arm.

I offered to help. 'No need,' she said. 'I can manage.'

Lois put her hand on my arm, her voice confidential. 'Look, isn't that the painter you were chatting to earlier at the gallery? Ashton's rather impressed with his work.'

I swung around. Hugh was making his way through the crowd, his curls wind-blown out of their former neatness and a wide smile on his face. The band was playing *The Sheik of Araby*, a favourite from two years ago.

'Marjorie.' He took my hand. 'How about that dance?'

Chapter 13

Dancing with Hugh Williams, after trotting around the floor with Andrew Fraser, was like eating chocolate mousse after tapioca pudding: light, delicious and pure, decadent pleasure.

He held me just a little closer than he should, so I could feel the warmth of his chest through his shirt. His arm circled firmly around my waist. He had impeccable rhythm, knew all the latest steps and had none of the self-consciousness that most British men display on the dance floor.

'I like this band,' he murmured. 'Who's the singer?'

'They're wonderful,' I agreed. 'She's called Florrie Briscoe. Is Antoine all right?'

'Mmm. I expect so. I say, Marjorie, you danced well before, but you've improved no end. Have you been taking lessons?'

I explained about my time at the Harlequin nightclub, and he chuckled. 'Is there nothing you can't do?' The band finished their number and moved smoothly into the next, a slower tempo with a romantic lilt. 'Don't even think of going anywhere, Miss Swallow. I'm enjoying myself too much to share you.'

I twirled around the floor in a cloud of bliss. As we turned, I saw Mr Rubin dancing with vivacious Sophie Leclerc, Maxim Brunot taking a turn around the floor with Sara Murphy, the lively American woman from the gallery, and Mrs Jameson dancing with Sara's husband Gerald. They were all lovely, I thought. Lovely people, in a lovely place, with lovely music. It was possible I'd had a bit too much lovely champagne. I started to feel rather dizzy.

'Are you all right, Marjorie? You almost trod on my foot.'

'Sorry. Maybe I need a drink.'

Hugh brought us gently to a pause at the side of the dancefloor and we headed for the refreshment table. I drank a glass of lemonade.

'That's better.'

'Come along, Benjamin,' said a bossy Yorkshire voice. 'It's well past bedtime, and that rich food will upset your tummy.'

I turned and saw Nanny Braithwaite dragging a reluctant Benjamin away from the buffet.

'I want to hear the speeches,' he protested.

'Speeches are always very dull,' said Lois Montgomery, laughing as she topped up her orange juice. 'Even when my husband gives them. Your nanny's very sensible. Everyone else here will feel lousy in the morning.'

Hugh squeezed my hand. 'Don't listen to her,' he whispered. 'Have another cocktail.' He procured one for each of us. 'Let's have a breather. Why don't you show me around?'

The refreshment table was at the top of the stairs that led down to the fountain garden. 'Come on, then,' I said. The exotic smell of jasmine mingled with the sweetness of the white roses. I stumbled on the small lawn and kicked off my shoes, enjoying the cool damp grass under my stockinged feet.

'There are fish in the pond,' I said. 'Big orange fish. Swimming around.'

Hugh nodded gravely. 'I'm glad to hear it,' he said. 'Marjorie, how many of these cocktails have you had?'

I ignored him. 'And down there is the beach. I'm learning to swim. Mrs Jameson says you have to float on your back and then you'll be all right.'

'Unless you're a goldfish, I suppose.' He brushed an escaped curl back from my face and tucked it behind my ear. 'I'd rather like to see you floating on your back. How about a midnight dip?'

I laughed. 'Don't be silly. I haven't got my bathing costume on.'

'Indeed. Good point. But shall we go down to the beach, anyway?'

We abandoned our glasses and descended the spiral staircase. Hugh went first, in case I tripped. At the bottom he lifted me down, hands firm around my waist. The music and laughter sounded distant, far above our heads, and I heard the ripple of black silk waves as they broke on the shingle.

The darkness was opulent, soft and warm as velvet. The rocks enclosing the beach sheltered us from the lights of Nice harbour. The night breeze was gentle, and I could smell the salt of the sea. Hugh stood very close. I wondered if he could hear my heart, skittering like a snare drum. I tried to think about Freddie playing the piano.

'Marjorie.'

'Hugh?'

He cupped my face in his hands and kissed me, his lips brushing sweetly over mine. Oh, goodness.

'I thought…' I thought he preferred boys. But right now, that didn't seem to be the case.

'Don't think,' he murmured. And then he kissed me again, wrapping his arms around me, pulling me close to his chest.

This time his lips lingered longer, and I didn't think of anything at all for quite some time.

Until somebody screamed.

We both jumped. Oh, not again, I thought, despairingly. Hugh pulled away from me, stepped back and looked up towards the sound.

'What the devil's going on? What's happened to that woman?'

Someone was shrieking up in the tower room, waving something and pointing down towards the beach. Had we been spotted? I gasped in horror. How shaming.

'Oh, no,' I mumbled. 'They're looking at us.'

'No, she's not.' Hugh stepped away from the shadow of the rocks. 'She's pointing down that way, the other end of the beach.'

I stumbled after him as he raced down the beach. Shielding my eyes against the light from the tower room, I saw it was Miss Braithwaite, the nanny. She had something white in her hands and was pointing to the rocks at the foot of the tower.

'Fallen over… an accident…' I heard, snatches of sound from the tower. Other people were crowding into the tower room now, leaning over the railings and giving little shrieks. The music had stopped.

'Marjorie,' called Hugh. His voice had a break in it, his tone urgent. 'Can you come here?'

I clambered onto the rocks, feeling sick. What had he found? My thoughts flashed back to the start of the party, Dulcie leaning over the tower room railings and looking out to sea. Dulcie drinking too much, making a fool of herself. Being taken back to her room, at the foot of the tower.

I clambered onto the ledge of rock, the sea gleaming beyond

it. Hugh stood over a crumpled heap in a pool of dark liquid reflecting the lights from the tower above.

Carefully I picked my way over the treacherous surface, slick with weeds. The woman lay prone, her black dress risen up above her knees. Dark hair splayed out across the rock.

I knelt by the body, felt around on her neck and wrist. No pulse. The head was twisted sideways, too far around. I looked for a long moment into the open staring eyes. There was nothing I could do. Sibyl Trent was dead.

Chapter 14

'I'll see if there's a doctor,' said Hugh. He looked as sick as I felt. 'Marjorie… are you all right? I don't like to leave you. But we need to get help.'

I shivered. 'Go,' I said. 'But she's dead, you know.'

'Yes. I know.' He stripped off his jacket and put it around my shoulders. 'I'll be as quick as I can.'

Sibyl Trent. I knelt on the rock beside her body, trying to make sense of it. My head was muzzy. How could this be happening? One second I was in Hugh's arms… and now I was alone with a corpse. The shock of it sobered me a little, but I was having trouble thinking straight.

The nanny was still up in the tower room, squawking away. She'd said something about a fall. But you couldn't fall from there easily. The railings came to waist-height. I could believe that Dulcie might have done something silly – perhaps threatened to throw herself off, or climbed onto the railings in a fit of drunken despair. But sensible, businesslike Miss Trent?

I thought of the scene on the dance floor and shuddered. It had been shocking to see a woman attacking another, pulling at her pearls and shouting at her. Could Dulcie have taken it a step further? Perhaps enticed Sibyl up to the tower and pushed her off? Absurd, surely. Dulcie was selfish and manipulative, but I persisted in believing she had a good heart. Yet how else had this horrible thing happened?

There were voices on the beach. I took a deep breath. I must be calm, measured. Think about the scene, remember what I saw. I'd been trained for this. It was important. I just wished I'd not had quite so much to drink. If I looked properly, the crumpled body on the rocks would tell me its story. I forced myself to use Mrs Jameson's training.

Sibyl Trent lay on her front, her head sideways and a little blood showing at her nostrils. The angle of her neck suggested it was broken. I supposed that was the probable cause of death, although a doctor would have to confirm it. There was no sign of the long cream chiffon scarf that she'd worn around her hair. I glanced up, but Miss Braithwaite was gone. Was that what she had been waving from the tower?

I couldn't see Miss Trent's bag, but perhaps it was still in the tower room. I looked at her hands: no sign of broken nails or scratches, but perhaps any push had been too sudden for her to fight back. She wore black suede heeled shoes, one of which had slipped half-off. What else? From what I could see, her maquillage was intact, lips painted in a perfect cupid bow. If she'd been eating or drinking, she'd repaired the damage recently.

'Miss Swallow, are you all right?' Mr Rubin climbed onto the rocks, the tall figure of Ashton Montgomery close behind him. Mr Rubin stopped short, pressed his hand to his mouth and turned quickly away, leaning against the rocks.

'Good grief,' said Mr Montgomery. 'Is that Sibyl?' He knelt next to me, passed his hand over his face. 'How frightful. Poor, poor woman.'

'*Excusez-moi, m'sieur, mademoiselle? Je suis médecin.*' A middle-aged man I did not know, with a professional air and a calm demeanour, eased us aside. I rose and stepped away with relief. The doctor laid his finger on Sibyl's neck, took a little electric torch from his evening jacket pocket and shone it into her eyes, then held the back of his hand above her open mouth.

He sat back, shook his head. '*Rien,*' he said, regretful. '*Elle est morte.*'

'Sol, you must call the police.' A firm, familiar voice broke through. Thank goodness, I thought. Mrs Jameson. She always knew what to do.

I scrambled down the rocks towards her. She observed me for a moment: my dress wet and torn at the knee, Hugh's jacket around my shoulders, my lack of shoes.

'Were you down here when she fell? Did you see it happen?' she asked.

'Yes… but no. I was on the beach, but I didn't see anything. I just heard Miss Braithwaite screaming from the tower. And then we… Hugh found the body.'

I forced myself to meet her eyes. There was absolutely no point in trying to hide from Mrs Jameson what I'd been up to on the beach. I knew she would read me as clearly as any crime scene.

'Go back up with Mr Rubin, Marjorie,' she said firmly. 'Make sure the police have been called. Nobody should leave before they arrive. Wait for me on the terrace. You'd better drink some water and have something to eat. It may be a long night.'

When I reached the terrace, collecting my shoes on the way, Miss Braithwaite was sitting in an armchair sipping a cup of tea, surrounded by an avid audience. The band had stopped playing and looked unsure what to do.

Mr Rubin, pale as death, went to his study to telephone the police. I hunted around for my abandoned handbag, which contained my pocketbook and pencil, then joined the circle around the nanny and began to take notes.

'I heard something, sort of like a cry. I'd just finished putting Benjamin to bed, and I ran up the stairs to the tower. I was puffed out,' she said. She seemed to be enjoying her audience, her little eyes gleaming.

'That was when I saw the scarf, caught up on the railings.' She brandished the long streamer of cream silk, and I winced. It should have been left where she found it, for the police to see. 'It must have got caught up, when the poor woman went over,' Miss Braithwaite continued. 'So, I looked down, and that's when I saw her. Splattered on the rocks.'

I frowned in distaste. Sibyl Trent had not been splattered. The dramatic phrase had its effect, however. Women gave little shrieks, men turned their heads away. Cries of 'how awful' and *'quelle horreur'* rippled through the crowd. Sophie Leclerc buried her face in her husband's chest; Lois Montgomery pressed her hand over her mouth.

'What time was it?' I asked. I remembered seeing Nanny Braithwaite check the watch pinned to her apron as she hauled Benjamin Rubin off to bed.

She looked me up and down. 'You have a rip in your skirt, Miss Swallow. What have you been doing?' Her gaze was censorious, as if my dress had been torn from me in the throes of passion. I hoped no-one else would think such a thing. Mrs Jameson, for example.

I flushed. 'I tore my frock climbing up onto the rocks where poor Miss Trent was found. I was trying to help her.'

Mr Rubin rejoined his guests, a glass of whisky in his hand.

'The police are on their way,' he said. 'They have asked if you would kindly stay here for the moment. Please, do help yourselves to the refreshments.' He looked around. 'Where is Andrew Fraser?'

The ubiquitous Andrew did not seem to be present. I frowned. Who else was missing? Sibyl Trent, of course. Dulcie Pemberton, who I supposed was still in her room. Ashton Montgomery and Mrs Jameson were down on the beach with the French doctor. Maxim Brunot was smoking on the terrace, a few paces away.

And Hugh… I couldn't see Hugh anywhere. Had he already left? I felt a distinct pang, despite the seriousness of the situation.

Mr Rubin went to speak to the band, who began playing a quiet instrumental number. The singer, Florrie Briscoe, sat by the side of the little platform that had been set up for them, her shoulders slumped wearily. On impulse, I went and sat with her.

'You were wonderful, Miss Briscoe,' I said. 'I'm so sorry we didn't get to hear your second set. Can I get you anything?'

She smiled. 'That's kind of you, Miss. A lemonade would be very welcome. But don't wait on me; I can get it myself.'

We went to the buffet together. My stomach was empty, apart from rather a lot of liquor sloshing around. I loaded up a plate and urged her to do the same.

'No sense it going to waste,' I said. 'We might have to wait a while for the police.'

We sat together at one of the little tables dotted around the terrace. I tucked in, hoping it would settle my queasiness.

'Do you like jazz music?' she asked.

'I certainly do.' I told her about my friendship with the

members of the All Stars Jazz Orchestra, feeling more than a twinge of guilt about Freddie. There had never been any formal engagement between us. But I knew full well how hurt he would be about Hugh. I pushed the thought away.

'You know T-bone Tommy? That's amazing. I used to sing in a band with him at the Cotton Club in Harlem,' said Miss Briscoe, her smile warm. 'He's a diamond.'

'He is. I like him very much.' I took another mouthful of chicken salad. 'This is delicious.'

'Sure is.'

'What happened up here, when Miss Braithwaite screamed?' I asked. 'I was down on the beach.'

Miss Briscoe chewed and swallowed. 'We had just paused for the speeches. Mr Rubin welcomed everyone and introduced a tall American man, and his wife. The man thanked Mr Rubin and started talking about an art exhibition, then we heard the scream.'

She took a breath. 'Well. Then half the guests rushed up to the tower, and the other half rushed to the edge of the terrace. It was a muddle. No-one knew what had happened until a young man came down from the tower and said the nanny had seen someone throw herself over the railings. Then another man came up from the beach and called for a doctor.'

'That was my friend Hugh. So, you didn't see Miss Trent fall?'

The singer shook her head. 'I was going through my music, getting ready for the next set. I don't know if anyone else saw her. I guess they were watching the speeches.' She looked at her wristwatch. 'Eleven, already. I hope we aren't too late tonight. We've been on the road for months, and I'm tuckered out.'

I looked up as the butler bustled through the green door to the terrace, leading a middle-aged man in a dark suit and crumpled white shirt, with the disgruntled air of someone pulled away too soon from a good dinner. At the same time, Andrew Fraser appeared at the bottom of the stairs from the tower.

'Inspecteur Grignot, M'sieur Rubin,' said the butler. 'From the *département de police.*'

Mr Rubin shook the inspector's hand. He was still very pale and looked like he might faint at any moment.

'*Bonsoir, Inspecteur.*' He paused. 'I say, *parlez-vous Anglais?* It would be so helpful if you did.'

The policeman gave a weary smile. 'Good evening, Sir. I am accustomed to communicating with our visitors in Nice, in whichever language is most commodious to them. Please, be so good as to explain to me what has happened here.'

Chapter 15

It was long after midnight by the time the inspector and his colleagues left, and all the guests departed. I fell into a dream-laden sleep and woke, with a feeling of doom, at seven.

I drank a pint of water from the carafe by my bed, then opened the shutters, wincing as the bright light poured into the room. My head hurt. Fragments of the night crowded in: dancing on the terrace, drinking cocktails, talking to Picasso in the gallery. Pushing all other memories aside, Hugh's kiss. And, inextricably linked to it, Sibyl Trent's body, broken on the rocks. I groaned, fought off the temptation to hide under the covers and go back to sleep.

It was too hot to sleep, anyway. I was sticky with sweat. My hair smelled of cigarette smoke, making my stomach churn unhappily. What I needed, I told myself firmly, was a bathe. I pulled on my borrowed bathing costume, picked up a towel and walked through the quiet house to the terrace.

The housekeeping staff must have been awake even longer than the rest of us. The tiles were swept clean, the empty glasses and trestle tables had vanished, the lawn was raked and the fountain twinkling. Even the goldfish looked like they'd been scrubbed.

I made my way down to the beach, wishing I had a pair of

Dulcie Pemberton's tinted glasses to shield my bleary eyes from the sun. I walked into the gentle surf, splashed my face with cool water, then carefully pushed off into a rather wobbly breast-stroke. The waves were cleansing. I turned onto my back and floated, eyes closed against the glare. If only I could stay out here, and not have to think about Hugh, or Freddie, or poor Miss Trent.

When I opened my eyes, I found I had drifted almost onto the rocks. I twisted around and started to paddle away. Although the police had removed Miss Trent's body the night before, I had no wish to swim where she had been found.

I spotted something gleaming in the sunshine. Cautiously, I swam back towards it.

Pearls glimmered in a tiny pool in a cleft between the rocks. I pulled myself out of the water. A pile of pearls. Or rather, fake pearls. Sibyl Trent's broken necklace, spilled out of her pocket or handbag.

I hunted around, scooping up a few more pearls. Then I found a small black beaded reticule lodged in the cleft, its mouth open. Sibyl Trent's handbag. I picked it up, rescuing it from a puddle of seawater. Triumphantly I returned to the beach, wading through the water holding the bag above the waves.

By the time I went down for breakfast, I felt almost myself again. My white linen frock, returned to pristine condition by the maid, was cool and businesslike. I was ravenous and piled my plate high. While the lack of eggs and bacon provided for French breakfasts was disappointing, the buttery flakes of croissants certainly made a delicious alternative.

'Someone's got an appetite,' said Mrs Jameson with asperity, as she joined me at the breakfast table. 'How are you feeling this morning, Marjorie? Not too wretched, I hope. We have a busy day ahead. Mr Rubin is already in town. He's wiring Sibyl's family in England, to ask about funeral arrangements. He feels very responsible.'

'I'm quite well, Mrs Jameson. I've had a swim. And I found Sibyl Trent's handbag. It was caught between the rocks.' I held up the bundle, wrapped in my towel to dry, with my sunniest smile.

'Oh, splendid. Well done. Have you looked inside yet?'

I had, but the contents were soaked with water, so I had left them to dry.

'There's a coin purse, the remains of her pearl necklace, a comb, and a pocket book,' I said. 'With a letter tucked in the flap. But it's too wet to read at the moment.'

She smiled her approval. 'Well, that gives us a head start over that rather lackadaisical policeman. Do you know, he says he doesn't plan to be in the *département* until ten o'clock this morning, to make up for his late night?'

I'd rather liked the urbane Inspector Grignot, who had taken a death at a party very much in his stride, as if such things were not unexpected on the Riviera.

After breakfast, we repaired to Mrs Jameson's sitting room on the first floor, which had a balcony looking over the terrace and voile curtains blowing gently in the breeze. She had moved a card table into the centre of the room and placed upon it a pile of paper on which she had begun to draw up timelines, lists of suspects, and motives.

'Do you have a theory yet?' I asked. I didn't need to ask if she considered the death suspicious. In Mrs Jameson's mind, every death was suspicious until proven otherwise.

She shook her head. 'Too soon. But I went up to the tower

room last night. The railings are intact. There are no loose tiles to trip over. There's nothing to suggest a person could accidentally fall off, unless I suppose you were leaning very far out with your feet off the floor. So, I think we can assume she did not die by accident. Now, describe to me how the body looked when you found her.'

I summoned up the image of that horrible discovery. 'She was lying on her front, fully clothed. From the angle of her head, I think her neck was broken.'

'Was there much bleeding?'

I considered. 'A bit, from her nose. There was seawater on the rocks, so it looked as if she was lying in a pool. But it wasn't blood, or it would have stained my skirt.'

'And you found her handbag, which means she must have had it in her hand. Unlikely if she flung herself off the tower deliberately,' said Mrs Jameson. 'Now, what do we know of her circumstances? Did she seem to have any reason to take her own life?'

'There's the husband in Paris,' I ventured. 'She didn't seem very happy about him. And I think she was short of money.'

Mrs Jameson looked up. 'Why do you say that?'

'Her clothes were quite good, but several seasons old. She darned her stockings, re-trimmed her hats and turned up her skirts to keep in with the fashion,' I explained. I was more than familiar with the tactics, having used them all my life to keep my good clothes current.

Mrs Jameson once again smiled her approval. 'She told me a little about her marriage. Her husband is a penniless dipsomaniac. Without money she was unable to leave him. Her family in England disapproved of her liaison, and she felt unable to apply to them for assistance,' she said. 'She had hoped that her work in the art world would finance her escape, but her husband was capable of drinking all the money she brought in. We should look into her financial affairs.'

I made a note.

'However, I do not believe she was suicidal. Miss Trent was in a difficult position, but she had a plan to extract herself, and seemed purposeful and self-reliant.'

That had been my impression too – except for that first night, when she had been so disturbed by the intruder in her train compartment.

'What about the break-in on the Blue Train?' I asked. 'Do you think it has something to do with that?'

Mrs Jameson tapped her chin. 'That was a curious affair,' she said. 'I wish I had made more progress with it. Who knows – it might have made a difference.'

I frowned. 'But the thief was after the Renoir,' I said. 'And that's in the Galerie Anglaise. So why would someone want to kill Miss Trent now?'

We heard a commotion from the terrace and rose to look down from the balcony. Dulcie Pemberton flounced down the steps in her beach robe, with Andrew Fraser behind her carrying a towel and a jug of iced lemonade. Maxim Brunot tried to block her path.

'I can't possibly work today,' Dulcie declared. 'You're an unfeeling brute, Max. A woman has died, and all you can think of is your wretched film.'

Mrs Jameson's eyes glinted. 'Where was Miss Pemberton at the time that Miss Trent died? I think we might have to interrupt her sunbathing, Marjorie. Are you feeling brave?'

Chapter 16

'Hello, Dulcie.'

I dropped down onto the shingle beside her. She raised herself on one elbow, tipped up her tinted glasses to look at me, then settled them back in place.

'What do you want? I'm not feeling well.'

'Miss Pemberton, are you aware that Miss Sibyl Trent died last night?' asked Mrs Jameson, standing above me like a sentinel.

Dulcie yawned. 'Of course. It's dreadful. I've found it very upsetting. Suicide, I suppose. So selfish, to do it so publicly. I would prefer not to discuss it.' She picked up an illustrated fashion magazine.

'I do understand,' I said. 'But I thought it would be best if we asked you about it before the police interview you. The inspector will be here this morning. You might want to think about what you're going to tell him.'

She sat bolt upright. 'What on earth do you mean, Marjorie? Tell him about what?'

Mrs Jameson lowered herself into a deckchair. 'Your whereabouts at the time of the fall, for a start. Most of the party was assembled on the terrace to hear Mr Rubin and Mr Montgomery speak. A few people,' she glanced at me, 'were absent. You were one of them.'

Dulcie regarded her coldly.

'I retired to my room early. I'm not fond of large parties. They bore me; so many people wanting to talk to me. I wasn't enjoying myself, so I left.'

Mrs Jameson smiled, cat-like. 'Come, Miss Pemberton. You were escorted away after an altercation with Miss Trent.'

Dulcie's small mouth trembled, as if she was acting the part of a misunderstood heroine from one of her films. 'I do not need to be reminded of that painful incident,' she said. 'That's why I decided to stay in my room. I know one shouldn't speak ill of the dead, so I will say no more about Miss Trent's behaviour.'

'And what was the cause of this altercation?'

Dulcie looked away. 'I believe Miss Trent was jealous of my friendship with dear Solomon,' she said. 'She seemed to want to come between us. I suppose she thought he might marry her. Perhaps it was seeing her plans foiled that led her to jump from the tower.'

Dulcie clearly did not know that Miss Trent was already married.

'Did anyone see you to your room?' asked Mrs Jameson.

Dulcie paused, as if trying to remember. Yet we had all clearly seen Andrew Fraser and Maxim Brunot manhandling her away from Miss Trent.

'Andrew escorted me to the door. He was concerned about me,' she said. She pouted. 'I think that ghastly nanny saw us. She came down the stairs from the boy's room on the floor above.'

'And what happened then?'

She shrugged her elegant shoulders. 'I had a headache. I

took an aspirin and went to sleep. I didn't wake up until this morning. I've been working very hard. I need rest.'

I'd been taking discreet notes in my pocket book. Dulcie noticed.

'What are you doing?' Her voice was accusatory.

'Just making sure we get it straight,' I said. 'For the investigation.'

'What investigation?' Dulcie looked from one to the other of us. 'What are you accusing me of?'

'Nothing, as yet,' said Mrs Jameson, coolly. 'I am a private investigator, Miss Pemberton. I had already been working on one matter on behalf of Miss Trent. Now that she is dead, I will investigate the circumstances of her death. As, I sincerely hope, will the French police.'

'Well, that takes the absolute biscuit.' Dulcie flung down her magazine. 'I won't sit here and be interrogated.' She took off her glasses, the better to shoot me a look of contempt. 'I had assumed I was consorting with friends of Mr Rubin, fellow house guests. I will remove myself to a hotel at once. I cannot have my privacy invaded in such an outrageous manner.' She rose. 'Now, I am required on set at the studios. M. Brunot is waiting.'

She swept away, leaving her beach towel and other possessions for someone else to clear up. I felt as if I should applaud. When I turned to Mrs Jameson, her face was creased with mirth.

'At least M. Brunot will get some work out of her,' she murmured. 'I suppose we should talk to Andrew Fraser, and to the nanny. But even if they did see her go to her room, there's no guarantee she stayed there.'

I was thinking. 'Was Andrew on the terrace when it

happened, Mrs Jameson? Only he wasn't there when I went back up from the beach. Mr Rubin was asking for him. He didn't turn up until the police arrived.'

Mrs Jameson's eyes narrowed. 'I don't believe he was. Indeed, I don't remember seeing him after the scene between Miss Pemberton and Miss Trent. It's hard to be sure, of course, with so many people around.'

We retreated to our investigation room and began filling in the timeline.

'Miss Pemberton and Miss Trent argued when?' asked Mrs Jameson.

I frowned. It was before I danced with Hugh, but after Andrew Fraser.

'The band started playing at nine o'clock. I was dancing with Andrew when we heard the disturbance, maybe half an hour or so after they began their set?' I wrote it down. 'And that's when Dulcie Pemberton went to her room. I don't remember seeing her afterwards, Mrs Jameson. Do you?'

'No. But more importantly, when did we last see Miss Trent?'

I thought back. 'I helped her pick up the pearls that had been spilled on the floor. She said she was going to the cloak room.' Then Hugh arrived, and I'd had eyes for little else.

'Hmm. She danced with Ashton Montgomery, while you were dancing with Hugh Williams. And later I saw her in the lower garden, on her own.' She paused. 'Now. Let's get this out of the way, Marjorie. What happened after you and Hugh left the dancefloor?'

I tried to remain matter-of-fact. 'We got some drinks from the refreshment table, then went down the steps to the beach. We were on the beach, close to the steps, when we heard Miss

Braithwaite scream.'

Mrs Jameson, much to my relief, did not ask what we were doing there. 'And what happened then?'

'Hugh saw she was pointing to the rocks. He went over, then called me. I climbed up and saw the body. I checked for a pulse, and Hugh went up to the house to ask for a doctor. I stayed there, until you arrived.' I swallowed. 'I haven't seen him since. I think perhaps he left the party after sending the doctor down.'

Mrs Jameson held me in her sharp gaze for a moment, her grey eyes as penetrating as Picasso's, but with more understanding than his basilisk stare. Then she gave me a brisk nod.

'Write it all down,' she said. We would add to the timeline as we spoke to each of the guests, trying to piece together who had been where at which point in the evening. And, perhaps more importantly, who had been missing when Miss Trent had her fatal fall.

'Now, can we establish at what time the nanny screamed?' asked Mrs Jameson.

'It was just after the speeches began, wasn't it? I talked to the singer later, Miss Briscoe. She said they'd just finished the first set, so it must have been half past ten, if they stuck to the schedule.'

Mrs Jameson picked up another piece of paper, which I saw included just four names: mine, Hugh's, Dulcie's and Miss Trent's. 'People not on the terrace when Miss Braithwaite screamed from the tower,' said Mrs Jameson. 'You had better add Andrew Fraser.'

'And Benjamin,' I said. 'Nanny Braithwaite took him off to bed just before we went down to the beach.'

'Indeed. I think it's time to talk to Miss Braithwaite, don't you?'

Chapter 17

I tapped on the nursery door. Benjamin often did his lessons in the tower room during the mornings, but for obvious reasons that was out of bounds today. The police had asked that no-one go up the stairs beyond the nursery until they had been back to examine it during daylight hours.

Miss Braithwaite opened the door a crack.

'Please be quiet,' she began. 'Benjamin is working on his algebra.'

'It was you we wanted, Miss Braithwaite. Would you mind talking to me and Mrs Jameson for a moment?' I asked. 'Mr Rubin has asked Mrs Jameson to look into the events of last night. To assist the police, of course.'

She stepped into the corridor and looked at me with disapproval. 'I'm surprised you can remember anything of last night, Miss Swallow. You seemed a little the worse for wear.'

I flushed, but would not let her get the better of me. 'My memory is perfectly clear. Now, will you be kind enough to join Mrs Jameson in her sitting room?'

She trailed after me, complaining that this was not part of her duties. Then she sat heavily in one of the upright chairs, her back to the window.

'Please,' said Mrs Jameson, rising from her armchair. 'This one is more comfortable.' Miss Braithwaite sat again, the light falling obliquely on her square face. She screwed up her small eyes against the sun. I had seen Mrs Jameson do this before, to be sure that we had a clear view of the person we were interrogating, while they were slightly off-balance with the sun in their eyes.

'Thank you for helping us,' said Mrs Jameson. 'I am sure you were quite tired of questions by the time the police had finished last night. But Mr Rubin has asked me to help with the inquiry. I may ask some questions the police did not ask.'

The woman sniffed. 'I can't see how. That Inspector Grignot kept me up till midnight. I've told him everything already.'

'Indulge me, if you would. How long have you been Benjamin Rubin's nanny?'

'Nine years, since he was a bairn of three. You know the poor child was left motherless when he was born?'

Mrs Jameson smiled blandly. 'Indeed, I do. You were an experienced nanny at that stage?'

She puffed out her chest. 'I certainly was. I've been working with children since I was one myself, almost. I have more than thirty years' experience. I've seen that many children come and go.'

Mrs Jameson nodded thoughtfully. 'And do you plan to retire when Mr Rubin no longer requires your services?'

'He'll be needing me for a while yet,' she said. 'My work is my life, Mrs Jameson.' She crossed her arms defensively.

I wondered how she had come to pick such a profession. She didn't strike me as the maternal sort. But of course, options were limited for women needing to earn a living.

'And you moved out to France with the family three years

ago?' asked Mrs Jameson.

'For my sins.' She sniffed again. 'I can't say I like it. This heat isn't healthy. But I couldn't leave the bairn to be neglected by some French slattern. It's been hard, insisting on proper food for the nursery. Especially when his father lets them cook all that sloppy French stuff. Garlic and snails and I don't know what else. I suppose it's because he's foreign himself.'

I wasn't sure this was getting us very far. 'But isn't Benjamin rather old for a nanny, Miss Braithwaite? Surely he should be at school by now, or at least working with a tutor?'

She looked at me as if I'd suggested sending him out to sweep chimneys. 'The poor wee bairn! Isn't it enough that he has no mother?' She clutched her hands to her bolster-like bosom. 'I've looked after him for almost a decade. He's like my own. Mr Rubin only has to mention the word school, and Benjamin begs him to let me stay.'

A good, well-paid position with an indulgent employer and a motherless child who no longer needed much looking after would be hard to relinquish. No wonder Miss Braithwaite was in no rush to leave. Finding another such position at her age would be difficult, and her reaction to Mrs Jameson's question about retirement suggested she had few financial resources to fall back on.

'How affecting,' said Mrs Jameson, her grey eyes unreadable. 'Now, let us move to more recent events. Miss Pemberton says you saw her going to her room last night, at about half past nine. Is that correct?'

The woman's eyes gleamed. 'Oh, I saw her, all right.'

Mrs Jameson waited, wearing a polite look of inquiry. I poised my pen. Few people could resist Mrs Jameson's judicious pauses.

'All over that poor man like a rash.' Miss Braithwaite shook her head, lips pursed. 'If I was Mr Rubin, I'd send her packing. Carrying on like that under his roof, and thinking no-one would notice? Well, I notice. I can tell you that for nothing.'

'Who was Miss Pemberton with, Miss Braithwaite?'

She looked surprised. 'That Mr Fraser, of course.' She sniffed again.

'And,' Mrs Jameson said, 'I appreciate this is delicate, Miss Braithwaite. But did Mr Fraser leave her at the door, or did he go into her room?'

Miss Braithwaite folded her lips closed like an envelope, then opened them to spit out one venomous syllable. 'In.' She re-crossed her arms. 'And I didn't see him come out again, either.' She glanced around, as if she might be overheard. 'It wasn't the first time, either. I'm thinking of saying something. It isn't right, with the nursery just above her room.'

'That is most helpful,' said Mrs Jameson. 'Now, let us talk about the main event of the evening. Where were you when you heard Miss Trent call out, and can you tell me as nearly as possible what time that was?'

Miss Braithwaite settled herself in her chair, perhaps satisfied that she'd destroyed a woman's reputation. 'I'd been knitting in the nursery. I don't like all that modern jazz music, so I kept away from the terrace. I went down to find young Benjamin at half past nine. That's when I saw... well, I'll say no more about that. I finally managed to find the wee lamb and took him up at ten. I checked my watch on the way up. He'd been allowed to stay up late to talk to guests at the party.' Another sniff. 'Which wouldn't have been my choice, but Mr Rubin was insistent. By the time I'd seen him washed and dressed in his pyjamas and into his bed, it was almost half past ten. Much too late for a growing boy. And I was more than ready for my own bed, I can tell you. I'd just shut the door to the nursery and was about to go to my room, when I heard something. A sort of cry.'

'A scream?' asked Mrs Jameson. 'Loud? Would anyone else have heard?'

She hesitated. 'Not very loud. More of a gasp, I suppose. But it came from the tower room. I never liked that room. Not safe, with that horrible drop down to the rocks. So I ran up the stairs and saw the scarf, caught on the railing. I wondered what had happened and picked it up.'

She pressed her hands to her chest again. 'Then I looked over the edge and saw the body. Horrible, it was. Like something out of a film.'

Mrs Jameson was watching her closely. 'You were sure you were seeing a body? There was no doubt in your mind as to what you were looking at?'

Miss Braithwaite looked puzzled. 'Well, it was obvious. She wasn't sunbathing, was she?'

Mrs Jameson smiled grimly. 'Indeed not. And, of course, you were right. So, you saw the body, screamed for help, and then people rushed up into the tower room. Is that right?'

'Correct,' said Miss Braithwaite, briskly.

'And do you often scream? I would have thought a woman of your experience would take most things in her stride,' said Mrs Jameson.

Miss Braithwaite looked offended. 'I have never been present at the scene of a violent death before,' she said. 'I'm not sure what your experience is, Mrs Jameson, but I work in respectable households.' She checked the time on the watch pinned to her apron. 'I must be going. Benjamin should have finished his algebra. He'll need to move on to French verbs.'

Chapter 18

By eleven o'clock we had established a tentative timeline, interviewed our first suspect and our key witness. We went down to the terrace in search of coffee.

The housekeeper made it Italian-style, serving up what she called a 'cappuccino' with a lid of frothy milk on top. I much preferred this to Mrs Jameson's usual tiny thimbleful of thick black coffee. I also tucked into the little sugared biscuits that were served alongside. I was on my third when the door from the garage opened and Mr Rubin returned, Andrew Fraser a step or two behind him.

Mr Rubin looked downcast. 'Good morning, ladies. I'm glad to see you are being looked after. Iris, I am so sorry that your longed-for holiday has turned out like this.'

'Nonsense, Sol. I admit, I was getting a little restless without a case to investigate,' said my employer. 'And I am determined to find out what happened to poor Miss Trent.'

For myself, I could quite happily have spent a month relaxing on the beach. But each to their own, I supposed.

'I'm glad to see you back, Mr Fraser. Mr Rubin has asked me to investigate Miss Trent's death,' said Mrs Jameson. 'After we've had coffee, would you kindly join me and Marjorie in my sitting room upstairs? I should like to ask some questions regarding your whereabouts at the time of Miss Trent's fall.'

He pulled at his collar, looking troubled. 'Anything I can do to help, of course. But I'm sure Mr Rubin will need me to see to arrangements here. There's bound to be a lot to do.' He looked at Mr Rubin, pleadingly.

'Don't worry, Andrew. Everything is under control,' said Mr Rubin. 'Please, go and talk to Iris.' He smiled at her fondly. 'I've seen the way she works. I have no doubt that she'll get to the bottom of this dreadful affair.'

When we'd finished our elevenses, we returned upstairs, a reluctant Andrew with us. He stood on the little balcony, looking out over the glorious Bay of Nice.

'If you wouldn't mind sitting down, Andrew.'

He turned and dropped into a chair. Mrs Jameson got straight to the point. Where had he been, between walking Dulcie Pemberton to her room at about half past nine, and eleven o'clock, when he reappeared on the terrace?

He tugged at his collar again. A sheen of sweat coated his forehead and top lip. He stared out of the window, as if longing to escape.

'I... I took Dulcie to her room.' He licked his lips. 'She'd had a bit of a skinful, as you probably realised.' He paused. Mrs Jameson waited. 'That's it, really. I left her at the door and went up the tower.'

'You went to the tower room?' Mrs Jameson jumped on his words. 'What time? Who was there?'

He shook his head. 'Just for a minute. There was nobody up there. I just... looked at the view, I suppose.' He swallowed. 'Then I suppose I was helping out in the kitchens, making sure the staff had everything they needed. That sort of thing.'

Mrs Jameson watched him narrowly. 'So, the housekeeper

and the kitchen staff would have seen you?'

He licked his lips again. He really was a very poor liar. Surely he knew we would check on his movements?

'I don't know. Lots of people there, you know. Everyone was rushed off their feet.'

'And when Miss Trent's body was discovered? What were you doing when you heard?'

He swallowed, looked wretched. 'I don't think I heard anything at the time. Then, when I came through later, I realised something terrible must have happened, because the police were there.'

I interjected. 'You arrived at the same time as the police. And when you came onto the terrace, you came from the stairs to the tower,' I said. 'Not the kitchen. I saw you. Mr Rubin had been asking where you were, and nobody knew.'

He looked at me in desperation. 'Perhaps I'd been to check on Dulcie?'

Mrs Jameson sighed. 'Andrew, please don't treat me like a fool. If you went up the tower, before or after Miss Trent's death, what you saw there is of great importance. If you did not, then I need to know where you were. I have absolutely no interest in what you were doing, unless it pertains to Miss Trent's death.'

He covered his face in his hands and heaved a great sigh.

'I can't tell you,' he said.

'Then let me assist you. Miss Braithwaite saw you taking Miss Pemberton into her room. She did not see you come out again. The next time you appeared at the party was after eleven o'clock, when Marjorie saw you come from the direction of Miss Pemberton's room.'

He did not contradict her.

'Miss Pemberton, on the other hand, says you left her at the door at half past nine, and she then went to sleep until this morning. Only one of those accounts is true. Which is it?'

He rose from the chair and walked to the doors onto the balcony. 'I took her into her room. I was worried about her. She seemed quite upset.'

'And when did you emerge from Miss Pemberton's room?'

The back of his neck was brick red. He did not turn around to look at us. 'About eleven o'clock.'

Mrs Jameson gestured towards me, and I wrote on our timeline.

'Thank you, Andrew. May I ask if Miss Pemberton remained in her room during the whole of that time?'

He stared down at the terrace. 'Yes.'

'That is most helpful to know. Now, did you hear anything during the period before Miss Braithwaite screamed? A cry, a gasp, anything like that?'

He turned, his face puzzled. 'No. Nothing at all. I've been trying to remember. I heard Miss Braithwaite scream, and then lots of people charging up the tower steps. I stayed where I was until they'd all gone back down again. I didn't know what had happened, of course, until later.'

'Well,' said Mrs Jameson, smiling brightly. 'That has been most illuminating. You may go.'

He tugged at his collar. 'I say, you won't tell Dulcie what I said, will you? She'll be furious. And it's rather a damnable thing to do. A chap shouldn't talk about such things. Or Mr Rubin. He's been very good to me. I wouldn't like him to think I was abusing his hospitality.'

Mrs Jameson rose and opened the door. 'Thank you, Andrew.' He slunk out.

I felt rather sorry for him. As I'd discovered, the Mediterranean night could play havoc with one's sense of moral propriety. And if what Miss Braithwaite said was true, his liaison with Dulcie was not a new one.

'Dear me, you young people do get yourselves into scrapes,' said Mrs Jameson, moving to the balcony. 'However, we have only his word that they remained in the room. Miss Pemberton claims she was alone. The first resort of both of them was to lie. And the room is at the base of the tower. If either of them had been responsible for Miss Trent's fall, they could have been in and out of the tower room in minutes.'

She checked her wristwatch. 'Now, perhaps it is time for us to raise Inspector Grignot from his slumbers. It's half past eleven. I should like to hear what the police doctor has to say about Miss Trent's death. Let me see if I can fold myself into that tin can on wheels you've been driving, and we shall pay a visit to the inspector.'

Chapter 19

The police station was a big, plain building of white stone, the tricolour flag flying over the door, situated in a leafy avenue of ornate villas some way back from the sea. I parked the Morgan and Mrs Jameson entered the building like Wellington reviewing his troops.

'Madame, it is midday,' said the desk clerk, pointing to the clock above the grand waiting room.

'And so I suppose Inspector Grignot has finally arrived at work,' said Mrs Jameson. 'Despite his late night.'

'But it is *l'heure du déjeuner!*' the man expostulated. Despite this heinous breach of etiquette, Mrs Jameson insisted he ring through to the inspector's office. A moment later Inspector Grignot descended the marble staircase, adjusting the cuffs of his dark jacket.

'Madame Jameson, Mademoiselle Swallow.' He bowed formally. 'To what do I owe this pleasure?'

Mrs Jameson expressed her desire to know the progress of his investigation. He looked surprised. 'But we have barely had time to begin, Madame!'

She smiled. 'Then I have the advantage of you, Inspector. I have constructed a timeline and established the whereabouts of some of the key players in this affair. Perhaps I will share these findings with you, and you can tell me what the medical report says.'

The policeman shook his head sorrowfully. 'Perhaps that is the way investigations are conducted in America, Madame Jameson. In France, the amateurs leave such matters to the professionals. Now, if you will excuse me, I am late for my luncheon.'

He walked across the hall and down the steps into the sunshine. We accompanied him.

'Allow me to treat you, Inspector.' Mrs Jameson wasn't going to let him get away so easily. 'We can talk as we eat.'

It was his turn to look shocked. 'I do not mix *l'affaires et le déjeuner*, Madame. It is very bad for the digestion.'

She laughed. 'All right, then. Let us eat, at any rate. *Le plaisir avant le devoir*, Inspector. Pleasure before business. *N'est ce pas?*'

The inspector, defeated, ushered us into a shady restaurant at the corner of the avenue. It was panelled in dark wood, with frosted glass partitions between the tables and brass lamps on the walls. Mrs Jameson smiled in approval as a black-clad patron, a big white apron wrapped around his waist, showed us to a table covered in a starched cloth and laid with heavy silver cutlery.

'I do like your French brasseries,' she said. 'I enjoyed many excellent meals in these establishments in Paris, even during the War years.'

His face lit up. 'You were in France during the War, Madame?'

'Indeed. Perhaps you will be familiar with some of the people I worked with.' Mrs Jameson dropped a few names that meant little to me but were clearly meaningful for the inspector. He looked at her with respect.

'On behalf of my country, Madame, I thank you for your service.'

Meanwhile, I was struggling with the French phrasing of the menu, trying to find something familiar. The inspector noticed.

'Miss Swallow, will you allow me to take charge? It is my habit to be guided by Albert, the patron. He will tell us what is best today.'

After a brief but intense discussion, Albert left wreathed in smiles, returning with a chilled bottle of pale pink wine. I shuddered slightly and put my hand over my glass.

'It is very gentle, Mademoiselle. Almost like water,' said the inspector. 'It helps me to concentrate on my work.'

He poured half a glass, and I sipped cautiously. It was rather pleasant, but I made sure I had plenty of water from the carafe, all the same.

We ate a very good lunch of consommé soup, followed by grilled fish and fried potatoes. Inspector Grignot was excellent company, making us laugh with indiscreet stories about the English and American tourists who visited Nice.

'And the clothes, *mon Dieu!*' He laughed. 'I ask your pardon, Madame and Mademoiselle, who both dress charmingly. But some of your compatriots believe that the only purpose of clothing is warmth. When the sun shines, the need for clothes is all but removed.' He shuddered. 'It is not a matter of decency, so much as a question of aesthetics. Not every form is designed to please the eye without drapery, *ne c'est pas?*'

'You are unkind,' said Mrs Jameson, although she too was laughing. 'Why should those of us past our youthful peak not feel the sun on our skin? American women like to enjoy ourselves.'

'*Alors*, that is good, and good for the economy of Nice. That, too, is my philosophy of life,' said the inspector, as the plates were cleared and replaced with little pots of chocolate mousse. '*Le bon Dieu* puts us on this earth to enjoy the good things of life. We would be remiss not to make the most of them.'

I dived into the chocolate mousse, which was rich, slightly bitter, and definitely one of the good things of life.

'I agree, up to a point,' said Mrs Jameson. 'But then there are times when one has to work. Are there not?'

He twinkled at her. 'Very good, Madame Jameson. As it is you, I will explain what has happened so far. And my philosophy of investigation, which is not so far from my philosophy of life.'

The doctor had concluded that Miss Trent had died of a broken neck, he said. Her body bore no other major injuries, although there were scratches and bruises consistent with a fall. Two detectives would visit the Villa Beau Rivage that afternoon, to conduct a thorough investigation of the scene of the accident. He had telephoned to a colleague in Paris, who had called on Miss Trent's husband to break the unhappy news.

'Perhaps you can help me with one puzzle,' he said. 'Is it usual for an Englishwoman to continue to use her *nom de jeune fille*, her maiden name, after she has married?'

'It is unusual, Inspector. But I understand the marriage was not happy. Miss Trent wished to be independent and needed to earn her own living. Perhaps that is why she chose not to use her married name. What is her husband called? She never told me.'

'Henri Lejaby. They live in Montparnasse, which is infested

with many artists of minimal talent,' he said. 'I understand why Miss Trent may have felt she had made a mistake. My colleague said he had to roust the man out of a bar, where he was already half-drunk at eleven in the morning. He has a reputation as a drunkard and a womaniser.' He twinkled at us. 'I refer to M. Lejaby, you understand. Not my esteemed Parisian colleague.'

Poor Miss Trent. I remembered her dignity as she explained to us that she needed to bring in money.

'Do you know about the break-in on the train?' I asked. 'Miss Trent said she reported it, but nothing happened.'

The inspector raised an eyebrow. 'Tell me more, Mademoiselle.'

I explained about the attempted theft. 'Mrs Jameson thinks it was someone pretending to be the carriage attendant,' I added. 'Because they had disappeared by breakfast time.'

The inspector frowned. 'I had not heard about this. I will ask some questions of the railway authorities.' He sat back, picked up his tiny coffee cup and beamed at Mrs Jameson. 'You see, Madame? There is no need to charge about and waste energy. If I wait, the information comes to me. And when I have the information,' he leaned forward, 'I spring into action. I imitate the action of a tiger!' He looked proud. 'Is that not what Shakespeare says?'

Mrs Jameson laughed. 'Very good. But someone has to bring you the information, Inspector Grignot. Perhaps you will allow that?'

He inclined his head with courtesy. 'Of course. And I am most grateful. Tell me, do you have any further information?'

Mrs Jameson brought him up to date with our conversations with Dulcie Pemberton, Miss Braithwaite and Andrew Fraser.

'Mr Fraser and Miss Pemberton both lied, at least initially,' said Mrs Jameson. 'Which is always suspicious. However, I'm inclined to suspect a clandestine affair of the heart, rather than a plot to throw Miss Trent off the tower.'

Inspector Grignot heaved a sentimental sigh. 'Ah, the romantic intrigues of the young. And Miss Pemberton is very beautiful. However, I will remember their lack of candour. And you say Miss Pemberton had developed an enmity with Miss Trent? *L'amour* can lead young men to do very foolish things for those they love.'

Chapter 20

Mrs Jameson insisted on paying the bill for lunch. After the inspector had returned to the police department, she lingered over a second cup of coffee, thinking.

'Did you bring Miss Trent's bag?' she asked. It had dried during the course of the morning, and we had yet to examine it. I withdrew it from a straw basket I had bought in the Cours Saleya, which I'd been using in place of my rather battered leather handbag.

It was a simple drawstring pochette of black silk with beaded embroidery, which looked home-made. I loosened the ribbon and removed the contents: the imitation pearls, a comb and powder compact, Miss Trent's pocket book. This I opened with care. The pages, which had been stuck together with salt water, eased apart. Tucked into the cover was an envelope.

'Aha!' Mrs Jameson pounced. The envelope had no name or address, the flap tucked inside without being sealed. Mrs Jameson removed the letter and smoothed it carefully on the table. The ink was blurred with water, but the clear hand was legible.

'Dear Ashton,' we read. 'Thank you for settling my invoice for the valuation so promptly. I do not like to ask this, but you are aware of the difficulty of my situation.

'I need more. Considering the work I have done for you, and how far we go back, I ask you to reconsider your previous offer. Five per cent is very little, especially as I have delivered at least one potential client.

'I propose fifteen per cent, on this and related sales. I know you would not want me to share our secret more widely. I do not wish to make threats, but my financial situation is desperate. And desperation leads people to use whatever they have, I'm afraid.

'I hope it will not come to that. I look forward to talking further on this matter.

Your friend,

Sibyl.'

We looked at each other in surprise. 'She was trying to blackmail him!' I said. Our previous experience had demonstrated that blackmail was a rather dangerous activity.

'It sounds like it.' Mrs Jameson folded the letter back into its envelope and put it into her handbag. 'How interesting. It seems this letter has not been delivered. Perhaps we should remedy that.' She looked at her wristwatch. 'Two o'clock. I wonder if Mr Montgomery is in the Galerie Anglaise. Let's find out.'

Ashton was indeed in the gallery, talking to a prospective client. We waited while a dapper man in a striped linen suit dithered over a sunny scene of the Bay of Nice. Eventually he said he would have to ask his wife and took his leave.

Ashton advanced towards us, his head on one side and his expression sombre. 'Mrs Jameson, Miss Swallow. How are you both today? What a tragic turn of events. I hope Mr Rubin does not feel too badly.'

Mrs Jameson did not waste time. 'Mr Rubin is well, thank

you. He has asked me to investigate Miss Trent's death. As you were an old friend of hers, I hope you will be able to assist.'

He ushered us to a low table and armchairs at the back of the gallery. 'Of course. I'm happy to help, if I can. Poor Sibyl's life was not happy, I'm afraid, since her marriage.'

We sat. 'Tell me about M. Lejaby. Did you know him?' asked Mrs Jameson.

'I haven't seen him for years. Sibyl and I were both students at the Académie de la Grande Chaumière in Montparnasse, taking drawing classes and hanging around on the fringes of the Parisian art world. She had run away from her stuffy family in England, and I was enjoying a rather extended European tour, courtesy of my father.

'Lejaby was one of the stars of the Académie, when he was sober. He always had a crowd of women around him, partly because of his talent but also because he had that artistic look they all liked. Dark soulful eyes, long hair – you know the sort of thing.' He chuckled. 'About the opposite of me. Anyway, I thought Sibyl was immune, until she announced she had moved into his studio.'

'And was this type of liaison usual?'

'Not unusual, among that crowd. But it was the final straw for Sibyl's family. Her brother came over and tried to force her back to England. She refused, and they cut her off completely. To our surprise, Lejaby then married her. I think he hoped they would change their minds and give her a decent allowance, but it made no difference.'

'How long ago was that? Did you stay in touch with Sibyl?' asked Mrs Jameson.

He calculated. 'It must be eight or nine years since the Académie. I didn't see much of Sibyl after I married Lois.

She persuaded me to come south, to Hyères. Then my father died, and we went back to the States for a while. It's been almost a year since we moved to Nice and set up the Galerie Anglaise.

'That's when I heard that Sibyl was working at Hôtel Drouot. And so, when I needed someone to authenticate paintings, she seemed like the obvious choice. I soon found out that she and Lejaby were struggling financially, so it was good to be able to help her out.'

Mrs Jameson reached into her handbag and retrieved the letter, which she unfolded on the table. 'And can you tell me why Sibyl Trent was asking you for more money, and about the secret she was threatening to reveal?'

He looked startled, as well he might, but remained courteous. 'May I see?' He looked over the letter. 'Where did you find this?'

'It was in her handbag when she died,' said Mrs Jameson.

'I see.' He passed a hand over his face. 'Poor old Sibyl. That's a bit desperate. I would have helped her without threats. I was reluctant to give her money that I knew Lejaby would spend on wine. But I could certainly have arranged a loan if she was in particular difficulties, or paid off a few bills.'

'And the secret?'

He gave an impatient shrug and glanced around the empty gallery. 'I assume she is referring to the romantic liaison we had in Paris,' he said. 'I'm afraid it meant more to her than it did to me.' He sighed. 'In fact, I feel rather guilty about it. You see, she took up with Lejaby after I'd called the thing off. I wondered if it was a desire to make me jealous that first pushed her into his bed.'

Mrs Jameson was watching his face closely. 'And you think

this was the secret she was referring to in the letter?'

'I know it. She referred to it when we began working together again. It made me uncomfortable. She made a few passing comments – you know, asking if I'd told Lois about us. Suggesting we had shared some great secret love that could be rekindled at any moment. Which, I can assure you, was not going to happen. I felt sorry for her, but I'm very happily married.'

He picked up the telephone on the desk. We heard it ring on the floor above. 'Darling? Can you come down here for a moment?' He replaced the receiver. 'We're camping out in the flat above the gallery, until we can find a proper place to live. Lois is just on her way.'

'What about the Renoir?' I said. My mind had been running on the attempted theft on the train.

Ashton looked puzzled. 'What do you mean?'

I flushed, realising that Mrs Jameson was looking impatient. 'Well, I can't help thinking Miss Trent's death has got something to do with the painting,' I said. 'Because of the break-in on the Blue Train. Could the theft have been organised by her husband, for example? Have you checked that it's safe? Maybe we should look at it again.'

He gave a hearty full-throated laugh. 'Don't you worry about that, Miss Swallow. It's safe in the vault. I checked it this morning. I'm sure it doesn't have anything to do with this awful business with poor Sibyl. Lejaby can barely organise a trip to the bar.'

A door opened at the back of the gallery and Mrs Montgomery came through with a warm smile, her golden curls held back with a sporty blue headband that matched her fresh cotton frock.

'Mrs Jameson, Miss Swallow. Such a horrible thing to happen. Are you both all right? How is poor Mr Rubin faring?'

'Lois, I hate to ask. But could you tell Mrs Jameson here what I told you about Sibyl Trent?'

'I don't know what you mean,' she said, a faint hint of a frown creasing her smooth forehead.

'About my… relationship with her. Before we met.'

'Oh.' Her brow cleared. 'If you wish. You told me she was an old girlfriend from your time at art school, and that you felt sorry for her because of her unfortunate marriage. You wanted me to know, because she kept dropping hints about it.' She turned her gaze on us. 'Why ever would you wish to know such a thing?'

For once, Mrs Jameson looked abashed. 'It relates to the investigation into Miss Trent's death. I'm sorry to trouble you, Mrs Montgomery.'

'No trouble,' she said. 'Anything we can do to help.' She switched her gaze to her husband. 'I'm planning to go for a swim at the beach club, darling. Do you want to come?'

He rose. 'Are we done here, Mrs Jameson? As you can see, I have no secrets from my wife. But do ask if there's anything else I can help you with.'

We rose too and were about to take our leave, when the gallery door opened, and my heart gave a great crash. Hugh stood in the doorway, a portfolio under his arm.

Chapter 21

It was all rather awkward.

'I'm sorry if I'm interrupting,' said Hugh, glancing nervously from me to Mrs Jameson and the Montgomeries. 'I was in Nice, and I thought I'd check to see if anything of mine sold last night.'

I'd already noticed a red dot on the label next to the Janus painting that Picasso had admired at the opening. I wondered who had bought it. I tried a smile, but Hugh seemed to be avoiding looking at me. I supposed he was embarrassed.

'Not a bit of it. Mrs Jameson was telling me about her investigation into poor Sibyl Trent's death,' said Ashton smoothly. 'And yes, I'm pleased to say we sold both of your oils. Congratulations.'

Hugh grinned like a schoolboy at that. 'That's great. Thank you, Ashton. I brought some more over for you to look at.' He laid the portfolio on the table. 'I hope you don't mind. I brought a couple by Antoine Rousseau, too, and a letter for you from him. He's been working hard, but he's a bit downhearted. He's worried that you haven't bought anything of his for a while.'

Ashton shook his head. 'I'll take a look, but I've told him. His style is too old-fashioned. He needs to move with the times.

Like you have done, Hugh.'

He opened the portfolio and started to flip through, then paused to read the letter.

'Did M. Rousseau get home all right yesterday?' I asked, remembering Antoine's ejection from the gallery opening.

Hugh glanced at me again. He seemed unable to hold my gaze. I began to feel rather put out. Given his ardour the night before, I'd expected him to at least be pleased to see me.

'I expect so,' he said.

'Poor man,' I said. 'I hope you managed to get him something to eat.'

Ashton gave me a curious look. 'I wasn't aware that you knew Mr Rousseau, Miss Swallow.'

I flushed. 'I don't, really. But we met him in the market the other day, buying old paintings to work over. You need to pay him more, Mr Montgomery, if he can't afford to buy new canvasses.' I tried to make a joke of it, but he frowned in disapproval.

'To be honest, after the scene he made at the opening, I'm not sure I want to do business with the man again,' he said, folding the letter and putting it into his jacket pocket. 'I can't have him getting drunk and throwing tantrums in front of potential clients.'

'What was Mr Rousseau upset about?' asked Mrs Jameson.

'I didn't include his work in the exhibition,' said Ashton. 'I can't include everything. And I didn't sell a single picture of his in our Spring show.'

'He was talking a whole load of nonsense when we went for something to eat,' said Hugh. 'He was drunk, of course. I don't suppose he knew what he was saying, poor chap. But I'm worried about him. Maybe I should go back to Villefranche and see if I can find him. He's probably in a bar somewhere, spouting rubbish.'

Ashton mused for a moment. 'All right. I'll give him another chance. Let me give you something for him, Hugh. And an advance on your own sales, too. A bonus. You deserve it.' He clapped Hugh on the back and led him to the desk at the rear of the gallery, where he scribbled a note and abstracted some bills from a strong box under the counter.

'Well then,' said Mrs Jameson. 'Are you ready to go, Marjorie?'

I dragged my eyes away from Hugh. I felt rather hurt by his lack of notice. My own feelings about our kiss were complicated enough, without trying to work out what it had meant to him.

'Of course.' I picked up my straw bag. 'Where to now?'

Mrs Jameson watched me silently for a moment, then switched her gaze to the men.

'Actually, I've had a better idea,' she called to them. 'How about Marjorie drives you back to Villefranche-sur-Mer, Hugh, and you can both look for Mr Rousseau? I need to go into the American Express offices, and I can take a taxi back to the Villa.'

Hugh swung around and I was mortified to see a flash of panic in his eyes.

'There's really no need,' he began.

'Nonsense,' said Mrs Jameson firmly. 'Marjorie likes driving, and the car is just outside. And you're good at finding things, aren't you, dear? I'm sure you'll help Hugh find his friend.'

Chapter 22

I slipped the car into gear, and we moved off in silence. I was determined not to act as if anything was bothering me. If Hugh was going to pretend nothing had happened between us, then so would I.

I drove smoothly along the seafront, taking pleasure from my growing familiarity with the car. I'd tied my sun hat on with a scarf, which streamed out behind me, and felt rather chic. I was aware that heads turned as I drove past the pavement cafes along the Promenade des Anglais, although whether they were looking at me, the car, or my companion was questionable.

'I wanted a chance to talk to you alone,' he said eventually, with the enthusiasm of a swimmer braving icy water. That sounded ominous.

'Well, off you go, then,' I said, turning the wheel a touch sharply as we rounded the harbour. I kept my eyes on the road, hoping they would not betray me by filling with tears.

'I'm sorry I left without saying goodbye. I should have made sure you were all right.'

Rather than leaving me with a dead body and a whole lot of explaining to do about why I'd been on the beach.

'So why didn't you?' I tried to keep the sulk out of my voice.

'It was all… It was all too much. And the doctor fellow said he would go down, and Mr Rubin, and your Mrs Jameson. So, I knew you'd be all right.'

'Did you?' I relented. 'Too much what?'

'Oh, you know.' I thought I probably did, but he owed me an explanation. 'Just… it's like it's always there. Just below the surface. Everything's going well, everyone's having fun, the sun's out and the sky's blue. And then, suddenly, it comes crashing in.'

I didn't need to ask what he meant by 'it'. Hugh, like so many men his age, had seen their fill of death in the trenches. For a whole generation, death had been their ghastly daily companion, the only constant as their friends and brothers died. Working in the hospital, I'd seen more than my fair share of it, too. But although I'd endured losses, I had never been in constant fear of my own life. I supposed that made a difference.

'Where did you go?' I asked.

'I walked home to Villefranche. It took me a couple of hours.' He put a hand on my knee. 'I had a lot to think about.'

I pushed his hand off. 'No doubt.'

'Ah, don't be like that. I think you're fabulous, really I do.'

'Fabulous,' I said, grumpily.

'Wonderful, then. Marvellous. The cat's pyjamas, the bee's knees. You're the cherry on the top of the Bakewell tart. The kipper's knickers.'

I started to giggle, despite myself.

'And I've been wanting to kiss you for I don't know how long. Since that party in Bloomsbury last year. But you were rather serious and disapproving.'

I gasped. 'Me? That's not fair.'

He laughed. 'You were, though. You told me off about Ralph. Quite rightly too. I didn't behave well at all.'

I said nothing. It was true; he had behaved badly. But no woman minds being told that a handsome man has wanted to kiss her for a year.

'Anyway. Then I was rather occupied with one thing and another, and you took up with that pianist fellow. How's that going, by the way?'

If there was one thing I wasn't going to discuss with Hugh, it was Freddie Gillespie. 'None of your business,' I said, sternly.

'No. No, I suppose not. Unless, of course, you wanted to take up with me instead.'

I took a quick look at him, expecting to see him mocking me. But he looked quite serious, his brown eyes soft and appealing. Did I want to take up with him? What exactly would that involve? I thought again of his kiss, the willingness with which I'd returned it, and a shiver of excitement ran through me.

'I… I don't know what I want,' I said. Or perhaps I was too scared to admit it.

'Ah. Well, then. That's a bit tricky.'

We lapsed into silence once more. After a few hair-raising bends, we began the long descent into Villefranche-sur-Mer.

He sighed. 'The thing is, I'm struggling to work out what I want, too. I like it here. It feels free, liberating. I think I have a chance of making a success, with Ashton's help. I like you, too. But I can't make commitments. I'd like us to be friends. Maybe more, if you'd be willing. But definitely friends. Don't you think?'

Friends, maybe more. No commitments. I pulled up beside the yachts moored in the harbour, grinding gears, scraping one tyre along the kerb and making a complete hash of my usually competent parking.

'Friends, then.' I climbed out and looked at the yachts, willing the tears welling up in my eyes to go away. I wasn't sure what I'd been expecting after last night – vows of eternal devotion? That would have been most out of character. I couldn't imagine him dropping to one knee and producing a ring. Neither could I imagine him calling around to my parents' house on a Sunday afternoon to drink tea and make polite conversation, like Freddie did. Hugh wanted the cherry, but not the cake.

'Come on.' He took my arm, a hint of impatience in his voice. 'Let's walk into town. Don't look so sad.'

I thought of Ashton's comments about the artistic crowd he'd been part of in Paris, with irregular liaisons and people living together without bothering to get married first. Was that what I wanted? A frivolous and impermanent life, throwing away my affections? I suspected my parents would react much in the same way as Sibyl Trent's family.

But an impatient voice in my head told me to stop being – what were Hugh's words? – so serious and disapproving. I was walking along a beautiful seafront with a handsome man who thought I was marvellous. The breeze caressed me, the sun soaked into my skin. Was it so wrong to stop thinking at all for a while?

In the old town, a small fish market was in full swing, boats bobbed by the quayside and women lined up with straw baskets to pick out the catch of the day. On the other side of the cobbled street, old men sat under awnings, drinking pastis and watching the world go by.

'I'll go up and see if Antoine is at home,' said Hugh, stopping in front of a jolly-looking apricot-hued hotel, appropriately called the Hotel Welcome. 'The entrance is up those stairs, in the Rue Obscure. Why don't you wait for me in the hotel?'

'Can't I come?' I was rather intrigued by the Rue Obscure.

He hesitated. 'Best not. I don't know what sort of state he'll be in. And my landlady is a bit of a gorgon.' He grinned. 'I don't want to risk your reputation.'

I took a seat at one of the small green-painted tables outside the hotel. The waiter arrived and I ordered tea, which came without milk or sugar, and was too weak for my taste.

I sipped my tea and waited. The harbour was busy with fishing boats. Sailors strolled by, and women stepped into the pretty little chapel opposite the hotel. There was plenty to see, but I was getting restless.

I pulled the Baedeker guidebook from my basket. The Rue Obscure, or dark road, had been built in the fourteenth century by soldiers defending the town from invaders, I read. A 'curious and romantic remnant of medieval Villefranche', it was now covered over by houses and shops.

I put a few coins on the table to pay the bill and walked up the steps. The Rue Obscure was off to the right, a long tunnel underneath the ramparts, dim gas light gleaming off the wet stone floor. The atmosphere was rather spooky, the medieval timbering of the roof giving it a gothic feeling.

I heard footsteps behind me and jumped. I turned quickly.

'Oh! M. Rousseau, we were just looking for you,' I said. 'Hugh's gone to your lodgings. He has something for you from Mr Montgomery.'

The man stared at me, as if he wasn't sure who I was. I supposed it was the contrast between the light outside and the dark tunnel. He wore a workman's cap, its peak shading his eyes. But I was certain it was him.

'Sorry,' I said, advancing towards him. 'It's Miss Swallow. We met before, remember? In the Cours Saleya.'

He shook his head, although I could see recognition in his eyes. Recognition, and fear.

'*Non. Non, c'est un erreur. Pardon.*' He turned on his heel and scurried away, then ran up the steps and turned off into a side street. I watched him go, puzzled. What was wrong with the man?

More footsteps in the Rue Obscure. I turned again. With relief, I saw it was Hugh, coming down a set of steps from an old timber door.

'Exploring, I see! I can't leave you alone for a minute.' His voice was hearty, a little false. 'Well, that's all fine. Antoine's at home, sleeping it off. He woke up when I came in and insisted on making coffee. That's what took so long.'

He paused, seeing the confusion on my face. 'What?'

'But… Nothing. You saw him, then?'

'Yes. He was pleased to have the money,' he said. 'So that was good. Now, what shall we do? Would you like to go down to the beach at the far end of town? It's very pretty, and sandy. Better than the beach at Nice.'

Hugh had lied to me. Deliberately. And now he was trying to distract me, get me away from the place. My chest felt hollow. Why would he do such a thing? And what was he lying for?

I took a deep breath and pasted a smile on my face. I would sort out my hurt feelings later. The important thing was to find out what Hugh was hiding. I wasn't a private detective's secretary for nothing.

'Come on, then,' I said. 'I'll drive us to the beach.' At the far end of the sandy crescent surrounding the shimmering turquoise sea, I parked and walked with him as far as the sand.

'Bother,' I said. 'I quite forgot. Mr Rubin asked me to help Benjamin with his lessons this afternoon. Never mind; you enjoy the beach. I'd better go.'

I was back in the car and driving into town before he had time to protest. I parked by the harbour, dashed up the steps and into the Rue Obscure. I turned at the entrance that Hugh had emerged from and tapped on the door.

'*Allo?*' A woman in a faded floral overall, looking suspicious, opened it a crack.

'*Bonjour, Madame. Je cherche M. Rousseau, s'il vous plait? J'ai un message de M. Montgomery, de la Galerie Anglaise,*' I said, carefully reciting my schoolgirl French.

The woman shook her head. '*Il n'est pas là.*'

So, I hadn't been mistaken. Hugh had definitely lied. I passed over a couple of francs. '*Est-ce que vous savez où il est maintenant?*' Do you know where he is now?

She took the coins. '*J'espère qu'il est a Cagnes, comme toujours,*' she said. I expect he's at Cagnes, like always.

That was unexpected. 'Cagnes-sur-Mer?'

She nodded. '*Oui, bien sûr.*'

I thanked her and jumped back into the car. I had a momentary qualm at the thought of Hugh, abandoned on the beach. Well, serve him right for lying to me. I pulled out into the traffic and accelerated onto the road back to Nice.

Chapter 23

I was full of confusion. Antoine Rousseau wasn't in his lodgings, so why had Hugh pretended to have seen him? And I'd seen him myself on the streets of Villefranche, so he wasn't at Cagnes either, although his landlady presumably thought he was.

Why had he pretended not to know me and run away? We'd only met the once, in the Cours Saleya, but I was sure it was him. I'd recognised him straight away. A worm of doubt wriggled into my brain. Was I absolutely certain? Perhaps I'd made a mistake.

I swung the wheel as the corniche turned sharply right at the furthest point of the headland, the sea glittering like a mirage to my left. Immediately ahead, a big tree branch had fallen into the road. I pulled on the brake lever. The car slowed, but not enough. Rear brake only, I remembered. I wrenched the wheel to the left to swerve around the obstruction, gasping at the close call. I'd have to stop and clear it before someone had an accident.

But now there was a car coming straight at me, a low red sports car revving madly, tooting its horn. It didn't seem to be slowing at all. I knew I was on the wrong side of the road, but I'd had little choice. I gestured at it to stop, but it kept coming.

To my left was a pavement, then a low wall and a sheer drop towards the ocean. The car ahead pulled its nose to my right, forcing me towards the wall and the edge of the precipice.

Heart in my mouth, I pulled hard on the inadequate brake, changed down to the lower gear, felt the front left wheel of the Morgan mount the pavement, and tried to keep a steady course. With a horrible shriek, metal scraped along the wall. I feared the car would tip over, but thankfully I was still upright when it came to a juddering halt. I looked back in fury towards the car that had forced me from the road. It didn't stop.

I sat for a moment, heart thumping, sweat springing out on my forehead. What had just happened? I replayed the crash. The branch on my right, the car coming straight for me. I had no memory of the driver's face; just a blur of a leather motoring helmet. The fellow had been driving far too fast, but he might at least have tried to get out of the way. And why didn't he stop to make sure I was all right? If the car had flipped over the wall, I could have been killed.

I scrambled out and surveyed the damage. The paint had scraped off all along the left wing and the headlight was smashed. Poor Mr Rubin's lovely car. I wondered how much trouble I'd be in. Then I looked over the edge at the steep, rock-strewn slope and felt rather green. I sat on the wall and took deep breaths.

Two people rounded the bend on bicycles: a sporty-looking young man and woman.

'I say,' called the man. 'Are you all right?'

I tried to stand, then realised my legs were shaking rather hard. I sat down again.

'Of course she isn't all right, Dick,' said his companion. 'What happened? Can we help? *Parlez-vous Anglais?*'

'I had a bit of a near miss,' I muttered, mouth dry. 'As you can see. Sorry.' I burst into tears.

They were perfect angels. Dick cleared the branch from the road and the girl, Eleanor, poured me a cup of tea from their thermos flask. They picked up the broken glass, then Dick examined the side of the car and looked underneath.

'I think it'll drive all right,' he said. 'Shall I start her up? Where are you going? I could drive for you. Or would you prefer us to cycle to a garage for help?'

Not for the first time, I wished our chauffeur Frankie was here. She'd know what to do. I could drive and change a flat tyre, but I'd never learned about the mechanical aspects of a car.

'I don't know,' I said. 'I was going to the Villa Beau Rivage. I'm staying there.'

'Oh,' exclaimed Eleanor. 'We know that place. We went to a party there a few years ago. Don't you remember, Dick? We can take you, can't we?'

Dick drove the car slowly and carefully back to the villa, while Eleanor and I rode behind. I rang the bell at the gates in the rock and – somewhat to my relief – Andrew Fraser opened them. After his initial exclamation of horror, he ushered me and my rescuers through to the terrace, where Mrs Jameson and Mr Rubin were sipping pre-dinner cocktails.

'Mr Rubin, I'm so sorry,' I said. 'You were so kind to lend me your lovely car. I can't apologise enough for what's happened.'

I explained, with added interjections from Dick and Eleanor. Thankfully, Mr Rubin seemed more concerned about the danger I'd been in, than the damage to the Morgan.

Mrs Jameson's face darkened as I described what had happened.

'You say the other car came straight at you?'

I swallowed. 'I know it sounds like an excuse. But I had to swerve around the branch, and it had plenty of time to stop, or at least slow down and let me pass.'

She frowned. 'I think we should tell Inspector Grignot. That doesn't sound to me like an accident. At the very least, the other person was driving irresponsibly. At worst, it was deliberate.'

I was embarrassed. 'There's no need, Mrs Jameson. I expect they were just taken by surprise when they saw me on the wrong side of the road.'

My two rescuers, having refused refreshments, were looking confused by the altercation.

'We'd better be off,' said Dick. 'I'm just glad we could help.'

I thanked them effusively.

'Don't mention it.' Eleanor looked around the terrace. 'It's even lovelier than I remember here. The garden looks much prettier now. Have you explored the tunnels? When we were here before, the previous owner took us all over them.'

I shook my head. 'Not yet,' I told her. 'I've had enough excitement for one day.'

They departed, and I flopped down into a chair. Mr Rubin had gone to examine the car with Andrew Fraser. I felt wretched for betraying his trust and making such a mess of it. But Mrs Jameson was pacing, throwing out questions.

'Who knew you were driving back from Villefranche?' she asked.

I frowned. 'What do you mean?'

'Hugh?' she asked. 'I don't like to ask, but...'

Cold seeped into my stomach. 'Well, yes. I left him on the beach. I told him I had to help Benjamin with his lessons. But surely you don't think...'

She turned her piercing grey eyes on me.

'He lied,' I admitted. 'And I was trying to find out why.'

Chapter 24

After dinner, Mrs Jameson and I retreated to her sitting room to review the progress of our investigations. I had resolved to put my heartache on hold until I knew exactly what Hugh was playing at. I explained how I had seen the painter in the street, going towards his lodgings, moments before Hugh emerged from the apartment and claimed to have talked to him.

'That's why I went back. But I don't understand why he lied,' I said. 'It doesn't make sense.'

Mrs Jameson was especially interested in the landlady's assertion that Antoine Rousseau was probably at Cagnes.

'The home of the late M. Renoir – and, of course, of the Leclerc family. Marjorie, I'm finally getting a handle on this case. I think we should take a trip to Cagnes tomorrow.'

'All right.' I still felt despondent about Hugh's behaviour. Was I such a terrible judge of character? And was it really possible that he had somehow arranged for the car that ran me off the road?

Mrs Jameson gave me a sharp look. 'Don't grouch, Marjorie. I'm sorry that Hugh disappointed you. But Miss Trent is dead, and I am beginning to understand why. When I sent you off with Hugh, I had hoped that you would learn more from M. Rousseau. It sounds to me as if we will need to look for him ourselves.'

'I'm sorry.' I was contrite. 'I didn't mean to be gloomy. But I feel very badly about the car. I don't suppose Mr Rubin will let me drive it again, even if it is repairable.'

Mrs Jameson looked a little more kindly. 'It was only thanks to your driving skills that either you or the car survived at all. Mr Rubin can always buy another car, but you are one of a kind. I can't afford to lose you, Marjorie.'

'Thank you.' I felt a little better. At least someone appreciated me.

'Meanwhile,' said Mrs Jameson, 'my inquiries into Miss Trent's background are proving fruitful. I have a friend working at the Banque du Nord in Paris. She and I worked together during the War, and I telephoned her this afternoon from their branch in Nice. She was kind enough to take a look at some of the recent transactions on the account of M. Lejaby, of Rue Huysmans in Paris. Not strictly legal, but she was very understanding.'

She pulled out her pocket book and flipped the pages. I never ceased to be amazed by the useful connexions that Mrs Jameson was able to call on, even in a foreign country.

'Here we are. A regular deposit of four hundred francs every month, drawn from the account of Hôtel Drouot. Not a great deal for two people to live on in Paris, but possible. During the past year, three additional deposits of cash, each of three hundred francs. Despite this extra money, the account is usually running close to empty. Large sums of cash are withdrawn shortly after deposits are made.'

She sat back and looked at me triumphantly. 'What can we deduce from that, Marjorie?'

I forced myself to concentrate on the facts. 'I suppose the

regular amounts are Miss Trent's salary.' It seemed most unfair that her money would go into her husband's account, but I supposed the system was the same in France as in Britain. A married woman would find it difficult to open a bank account in her own name. 'And from the sound of it, her husband takes the money out and spends it.'

'And the additional cash deposits?'

I remembered the letter to Ashton Montgomery. 'Payments from the Galerie Anglaise, for validating paintings. Which she said were insufficient, given her expertise.'

'Exactly.' Mrs Jameson beamed. 'And do you know how much Mr Montgomery proposed to sell that Renoir for?'

I didn't.

'Thirty-five thousand francs.'

I gasped, although I had yet to get a proper handle on French prices.

'That must be a fortune!'

Mrs Jameson took a pen and scribbled calculations on a sheet of paper. 'Around seven hundred British pounds, or two thousand dollars. A small fortune. But a bigger piece by Renoir sold this year for ninety-three thousand francs, or so Mr Montgomery told Solomon. You can see why Miss Trent was requesting a commission on the sale, can't you? Fifteen per cent would be more than five thousand francs. An order of magnitude above the three hundred she was paid for validating authenticity.'

I looked up from the calculations. 'So, what does that mean? Miss Trent was asking for a pay rise – but she couldn't force Ashton to give her more money, could she?'

Mrs Jameson smiled. 'Her letter suggests that she hoped to do so.'

'But he'd already told his wife about their relationship. And anyway, would Ashton kill Miss Trent just because he didn't want to pay her a better commission? He said he'd help her. And he gave money to Hugh, and to Antoine Rousseau.'

Mrs Jameson waved away my questions. 'Even if we accepted money as a motive, we have yet to establish the means. Mr Montgomery was on the terrace giving his speech, in front of everyone at the party, when Miss Braithwaite heard Miss Trent fall.' She shuffled the papers together. 'No, we are still lacking some of the pieces of this puzzle, Marjorie. Let us see what we can gather in the morning.'

There was a tap on the door. One of the maids hovered on the threshold, looking nervous. Mrs Jameson had asked not to be disturbed when we were working.

'A visitor for Mademoiselle Swallow,' she said. 'A gentleman. Monsieur Williams.'

I'd half-risen, but dropped down into my seat again.

'Do you want me to see him?' asked Mrs Jameson. 'Or we could send him away.'

I rose again. 'No. No, I think I should talk to him. I want to see what he has to say.'

\#

Hugh had been shown into the library, its long windows overlooking the terrace. He stood with his cap twisted in his hands, staring out to sea. I entered the room silently, closed the door, and waited.

'You saw Antoine,' he said, without turning. 'While I was in the apartment. He told me this evening.'

I said nothing. Whatever the explanation, he would have to offer it himself.

He turned then, and I saw his eyes were shaded with weariness.

'I'm sorry I lied to you. It's all a bit complicated.'

'You didn't want me to talk to him,' I said.

'It seemed best.'

I swallowed. 'Are you… is he?' I took a breath and just said it. 'Is he your lover, Hugh?'

Light sparkled suddenly in his eyes, and he laughed. 'Is that what you thought? No, he's not. Honestly.' He grinned. 'Was that what you were worried about? Poor Marjorie. No wonder you were cross. You should have more faith in your own charms.' He reached out his hands.

I didn't take them. It had seemed one possibility. The man's shiftiness, his evasiveness, combined with Hugh's lie. But there were other possibilities, and they were worse.

I took a step away from him. 'I was almost killed on my drive back to Nice,' I said. 'Someone tried to run me off the road.'

'What?' He stopped halfway across the room, his grin frozen in place.

'Hugh, what's going on? Why didn't you want me to talk to Antoine? Did you tell someone I was driving back from Nice?'

He'd gone white beneath his suntan, colour draining from his lips. 'I… that's awful, Marjorie. Are you all right?'

I wasn't going to be deterred. 'Well, did you? Did you know something like that would happen?' All my hurt and anger bubbled to the surface. 'I really thought you liked me, Hugh. What a fool you must think me. Whatever's going on, you're quite happy to put me in danger, aren't you? So long as you're all right, so long as whatever scheme you've got going with Antoine isn't interrupted.'

'It's not like that,' he shouted, running his hands through his curls until his hair stood up all over his head. 'I'm trying to keep you safe.'

'Then perhaps you should tell me what's going on, so I can keep myself safe. Because it doesn't seem to be working very well so far,' I spat.

He shook his head, shot me a look of despair and slammed his way out of the room.

Chapter 25

I slept badly. Every time I was about to drop off to sleep, I seemed to see the red car coming towards me, forcing me from the road. The memory of that steep, rock-strewn descent to the sea, and what would have happened if the car had rolled over the wall, made me shudder. Eventually I sat up and put my light on, hoping to read for a while. Dulcie had passed her book to me once she'd finished it. But even the adventures of Lord Peter Wimsey could not keep my mind off Hugh.

Now that I knew he had lied to me, I questioned every aspect of his behaviour. Had he really wanted to dance with me at the party, or had he been distracting me from something that he knew was to happen to Sibyl? And why did he suggest we went down to the beach just then? Did he know what would happen? I even asked myself if he could have been responsible for her death – yet of course he had been with me when it happened. Rather disgusted with myself, I got out of bed and unlatched the shutter, breathing in the salty night air.

Hugh, from what I knew of him, was not a bad person. He was yet another damaged man, trying to put the horrors of the Great War behind him and make a new life. I thought of his excitement at selling his art, his fierce enjoyment of the pleasures of the Riviera. If Hugh was caught up in something that required him to lie, he was shielding himself. Hugh Williams believed nobody would look out for him. He'd told me that a year ago. But I couldn't truly believe that he would be involved in murder.

I listened to the gentle shushing of the waves down on the beach, distant sounds of music. The night was dark, but up in the tower room a light flickered. A lantern, or a candle. I caught the murmur of a man's low voice. Then came a soft laugh, which broke and turned into a sob. I watched a figure rise and walk quickly across the room before disappearing down the stairs.

I slipped my cardigan over my cotton pyjamas and tiptoed down to the ground floor. At the bottom of the tower staircase outside Dulcie Pemberton's room, I paused but could hear no footsteps. Whoever had come down the stairs from the tower room had already gone.

I padded up the stairs in my bare feet, past the nursery on the first floor. At the top I heard sobbing. I pushed through the door into the tower room.

Dulcie sat on the floor next to a candle, a whisky glass by her side. She was crying like a child, her nose running and her eyes red. She looked up anxiously as I came through the door, then dropped her head.

'It's you.'

I sat down next to her. At least she hadn't shouted at me to go away. 'Who did you think it was going to be?'

'I thought Andrew might have come back.' She looked up, rubbed the tears from her lovely face. 'But I shouldn't let him see me like this. I must look awful.'

I sighed. 'Dulcie, he's madly in love with you.' Compared with my own situation, her romantic entanglements seemed simple to resolve.

She turned her face and I saw from her sideways smile that she knew.

'And you like him, don't you? Even though you're so mean to him.'

She sighed and ran her hand through her sleek bob. 'I'm mad about him, Marjorie. I have been since I arrived.'

'So what's the problem? You should tell him so,' I said. But even as the words left my lips, I doubted them. Was it really that simple? Should I just tell Hugh what I felt when he walked into the room?

Dulcie heaved another heartfelt sigh. 'Marjorie, I'm twenty-five. I have maybe five years left before I'm too old for this job. You heard Max the other day at lunch. He's looking for new faces already. I won't be able to support us. Andrew can't support us. It's not going to happen.'

'But if you love each other…'

'We can live on what – fresh air and kisses? Come on, Marjorie. It's all right for you. You've got brains, and a profession that means you use them. I've just got this face.' She grasped her chin. 'And it won't look like this by the time I'm thirty.'

I was silent for a moment. 'That's why you want to marry Mr Rubin?' I asked.

She sighed again. 'I know I've blown that one. But when life deals you a hand of cards, you have to know when to play it. And my hand happens to have a time limit. I don't even have a role lined up when this film wraps. I'm scared I've left it too late.'

'Do you have savings?' I asked, hopefully.

'D'you think beauticians, hairdressers and French couture

come cheap? I invest in my assets, Marjorie. I always have.'

I opened my mouth, but she cut me off. 'And if you're about to suggest I go back home to live with my family, I will throw you off this tower.' I winced at her choice of words in the light of Miss Trent's death, but Dulcie ploughed on unperturbed. 'My mother and father live in Forest Hill, in a house backing onto my father's builders' yard. I have five sisters and two brothers still at home. I didn't so much leave home as get squeezed out when the last baby arrived.'

I smiled. 'Forest Hill's nice,' I said. 'Lovely view over London.'

She burst out laughing. We gazed out over the ocean, the lights from the yachts in Nice harbour twinkling. 'We're doing all right, for a pair of south London girls, aren't we? And I don't know about you, but I don't fancy going back.'

'Maybe something will come up,' I suggested, remembering I'd said the same to Andrew. It sounded even lamer now.

'Maybe.' She yawned. 'Andrew told you he stayed in my room last night, didn't he?'

I didn't know what to say.

'It's all right. I got it out of him. That blasted nanny woman probably knew, anyway. Fortunately people expect that sort of thing here. It's not like London, everyone gossiping and pretending to be scandalised while they're all carrying on behind each other's backs.'

'I suppose not.'

She was overtaken by an enormous yawn. 'Time for my beauty sleep.' She rose, picked up the candle and knocked over the glass. 'Bother. Can you get that, Marjorie?'

I took the glass and followed her down the stairs, thinking.

Chapter 26

I was bleary-eyed by the time I met Mrs Jameson on the terrace for breakfast.

'Good news,' she said, her brisk manner warning me that no sleepiness on my part would be tolerated. 'Andrew called out a mechanic, and he says the car is fine. He's had the wing mirror replaced and the garage will repaint it tomorrow. But there's no reason why we can't take it to Cagnes today.'

'You want me to drive?' I asked. I couldn't imagine getting back in that car again, let alone driving along the coast.

She took a sip of tea and reached for a second croissant. 'We could ask Andrew to take us in the other car, I suppose, but he's busy here. This would be more convenient.'

I buttered a croissant. 'But… doesn't Mr Rubin mind?'

'Not a bit of it.' She gave me a severe look. 'Marjorie, you have to learn to recover from shocks quickly. You had a near miss, but you managed the situation. If you sit around moping about it, you'll never drive again. Drive today, and you'll have forgotten all about it by the time we get back. It's much the best way, believe me.'

My mouth was dry as the dusty road as I inched the Morgan out of the garage. I waited until I was completely sure there was nothing coming in either direction for some distance, then cautiously moved onto the carriageway towards Nice.

'Cagnes-sur-Mer is to the west of the city,' said Mrs Jameson, who had a touring map unfolded on her lap. 'Keep on this road along the Promenade des Anglais and over the river Var. I'll direct you inland from there.' She glanced at the speedometer. 'It's only about five miles. It would be nice to arrive sometime this morning.'

She'd been right, of course. I gained confidence as I went, taking corners smoothly but slowly, alert for obstructions. There were none; we drew up at the gates of Les Collettes, the Renoir property, promptly at ten o'clock.

The big green iron gates were closed and chained together, a padlock holding them shut. We got out of the car and peered through. There was a meadow of wildflowers: big white daisies sprinkling the long grass. The twisted branches of olive trees held up a canopy of silvery leaves, their colours shifting as the wind ruffled through them. It was the background to the Renoir painting, brought to life. I felt almost as excited as if I had seen the great painter himself.

An elderly man was sweeping up leaves in the shade of a pine tree on the drive. Mrs Jameson called a greeting, and he came towards us.

'*Bonjour, Monsieur. Est-ce que Monsieur Claude Renoir est à la maison?*' she asked.

The man leaned on his broom and shook his head regretfully. '*Non, Madame. La famille est à Paris,*' he said. '*M. Claude et son femme rendent visite à M. Jean et M. Pierre.*' Claude Renoir and his wife were visiting his brothers in Paris.

Mrs Jameson thanked him and we returned to the car. 'That's a pity. If anyone could tell us about the painting, it would be the painter's sons. However, we have one other visit to make, Marjorie. The address of the Leclerc family was on the documentation that Mr Montgomery gave to Mr Rubin.'

We retraced our path along the Chemin des Collettes to the Avenue des Tuileries and continued to drive west.

'I believe that must be Haut de Cagnes,' said Mrs Jameson, pointing. My heart sank into my white Mary-Jane shoes. The village perched on what looked like a small mountain, narrow streets winding almost vertically up the slope to a turreted castle on the top. I glanced at Mrs Jameson. Would she accept a suggestion that we park at the bottom and walk up? I knew her better than to try.

I inched up the hill, expecting the car to stall at any moment. It laboured away in first gear, and I worried it might overheat with the combination of the effort and the sun, which was also climbing high in the sky. Mrs Jameson craned out of the window, checking off the house numbers. Finally, as I sweated my way around another sharp bend, she called out.

'Here we are. Well done, Marjorie. Now, why don't I get out here, while you find somewhere to leave the car?'

Easier said than done. However, I followed the road around and came to a wider section overlooking the edge of the village, with a view to proper mountains beyond. I parked and retraced my steps to the house where I had left my employer. Now that I could take my eyes off the road, I appreciated what a pretty old village this was, its cobbled streets and tall, narrow houses decorated with flowers.

The houses looked ancient, the doors barely wide enough for a person to squeeze through. Cats lazed in the sun, blinking slowly as I passed. One wound itself around my ankles and I bent to stroke it, thinking with a sudden pang of homesickness of my little black cat, Sooty, who Freddie had rescued.

Freddie. I remembered him emerging from a burned-out building, Sooty in his arms. Freddie wouldn't have abandoned me with a dead body on a beach. He'd never lied to me. He was kind, and brave, and he made me laugh. He was polite to my parents, fiercely loyal to his friends, and he played the piano like a man possessed. What on earth had I been thinking to prefer Hugh over him?

I turned the last corner.

'There you are, Marjorie. Now, let's see if the Leclercs are at home.' Mrs Jameson rapped smartly on the door.

Chapter 27

Sophie Leclerc answered the door, pushing back the scarf that held her heavy chestnut hair off her forehead. She had a grubby white apron tied around her striped skirt and blouse, and rough wooden clogs on her feet.

'*Oui?*' She didn't seem to recognise us at first, her greeting the harassed reaction of any housewife interrupted in the course of her duties. Then she saw Mrs Jameson's erect figure, upright in a tailored grey travelling coat and hat. I saw a flash of dismay, quickly covered up with a welcoming smile.

Mrs Jameson was all politeness, begging forgiveness for disturbing her without notice and asking after her health, that of her husband, and her daughter. No, she said, there was no need to fetch M. Leclerc.

'I will not keep you for more than a moment,' she said, the French phrases rolling smoothly off her tongue. 'Is it possible that I could come in and have a glass of water? It is hot work, walking up the hill in this weather.'

She left Madame Leclerc with little choice but to invite us into the bare parlour at the front of the narrow house. It was rather cheerless: three worn armchairs, their chintz roses fading; dying daisies in a chipped crystal vase on the dusty mantelpiece; a rag rug that needed shaking out, and a pencil sketch of a woman in a cheap frame on the table. Madame Leclerc did not seem to be an enthusiastic housewife.

As we waited for her to fetch refreshments, a small head of chestnut curls peered around the door, the blue eyes mischievous.

'Hello,' I said. 'Claudette, isn't it?'

The girl giggled and disappeared, then reappeared again. '*Bonjour, Madame, bonjour, Mademoiselle*,' she said. She stepped boldly into the room and performed a curtsey, clearly much-rehearsed. I gave her a little round of applause.

'Claudette!' Her mother tried to shoo her away as she carried a tray into the parlour.

'She's not bothering us,' I said. The little thing made me laugh, so clearly was she imitating her mother's mannerisms as she walked across the room behind her, pretending to balance a tray and sway her hips.

Sophie Leclerc had whipped off her apron, tidied her magnificent hair and was again all dimpling smiles. She served cool water in heavy glasses and asked how she could help us.

'I wondered if you knew an artist who has been working in Haut de Cagnes recently, as you have such an interest in art.' Mrs Jameson sipped her drink. 'Monsieur Rousseau? We saw him at the opening of the exhibition at the Galerie Anglaise. I should like to speak to him again.'

Sophie Leclerc's bright smile stayed in place, but her eyes widened. She shook her pretty head. 'I don't know him,' she said. 'I don't remember seeing him at the exhibition. It was very crowded with people.'

'Never mind. I'm sure we will find him. Haut de Cagnes is not a big village.' Mrs Jameson picked up the framed pencil sketch from the table. 'This is very nice, Madame. It looks like a portrait of you. Who is the artist, if I may ask?'

The woman glanced quickly at the sketch and reached out a hand as if she wanted to take it back.

'That's my mother,' she said. 'I'm not sure who drew it.' But she looked uncertain. Colour had mounted into her cheeks. I looked again at the drawing. The woman stared coquettishly back, head half-turned over a bare shoulder, a heavy coil of hair pinned up on her head. It did look very much like Sophie Leclerc.

'*Mais non!*' declared Claudette, leaning over Mrs Jameson's chair. '*C'est Maman! Oncle Antoine l'a fait.*'

Mrs Jameson gave the child her most benign smile. 'Who is Oncle Antoine, my dear?'

Claudette laughed. '*Le peinteur. Il est très gentil.*' She rushed from the room. Her mother looked aghast for a moment, then tried to stage a recovery.

'Oh!' Her bright laugh rang as false as a broken bell. 'Of course. You must mean Antoine Rousseau, who sometimes visits the village school with my husband to teach the children art. Claudette must have met him at the school. I'd forgotten. And Marcel brought the sketch home one day, after I'd called in to see them at lunchtime. I remember, now.'

Claudette charged back into the room, brandishing a roughly carved wooden doll with features painted onto the face with oils. It too looked remarkably like Sophie Leclerc.

'*Oncle Antoine m'a fait une poupée,*' she announced. '*Je l'aime beaucoup.*' She bestowed a smacking kiss on the doll's face.

Madame Leclerc was looking rather desperate, as well she might. 'I will ask my husband if he knows where M. Rousseau is staying, when he gets home,' she said. 'Now, Madame Jameson, can I get you anything else? Only I have many things to do today.'

Mrs Jameson rose, a glint in her eye which showed she was well-pleased with the results of her visit.

'You are too kind, Madame. Please remember me to M. Leclerc,' she said. 'And M. Rousseau, if you should happen to see him.' She swept out, with me in her wake.

'Whoever heard of a village school employing an artist to teach the children to draw?' she said, when the door had been firmly shut behind us. She let out a hoot of laughter. 'The silly woman. I wonder what her husband knows about her liaison with M. Rousseau.'

We walked along the road to where I had left the car and I manoeuvred it carefully back down the narrow streets. I breathed a sigh of relief as we got safely out of the village and onto the main road through Cagnes-sur-Mer, the lower village, and into open countryside.

A cyclist was making his way along the road ahead of us, labouring on his bicycle with a large portfolio strapped awkwardly onto his back. As I slowed down to overtake, I got a glimpse of his face beneath his blue peaked workman's cap. It was Antoine Rousseau.

Chapter 28

I pulled over and jumped out in front of him before he could pedal away.

'Antoine,' I called. 'It's Marjorie, Hugh's friend. Don't you remember? I wanted to talk to you.'

Caught between me and the car, he had no choice but to stop. He rubbed his hand across his mouth. The noon sun cast a strong glare so that his eyes were barely visible in the shadow of his cap.

'Ah, Monsieur Rousseau.' Mrs Jameson was right behind me. She addressed him in French. 'We have been looking for you at the house of your friend Madame Leclerc. She showed us the portrait you had made of her.'

He looked from one to the other of us, his mouth working uncertainly.

'*Oui?*'

'It is very good. Of course, she is a very pretty woman. Have you made many portraits of her? Were you at the house this morning, perhaps?' asked Mrs Jameson.

He took off his cap and pushed back his hair. '*Non, Madame.*' He looked longingly into the distance towards the sea beyond the fields.

'So where have you been, and where are you off to in such a

hurry? Are you taking your new work to Mr Montgomery? I understand he sent you some money yesterday. Perhaps he will add your work to his exhibition.'

The painter shook his head. He adjusted the portfolio on his back, looked around as if hoping for some distraction.

'Monsieur? Where are you going?' If he thought Mrs Jameson was going to give up and let him get away, he was very wrong.

Antoine shook his head again and put his cap back on. 'Nowhere.'

The hot sun beat down on the dusty road. I was glad of my shady hat. Mrs Jameson put up her parasol and stood foursquare in the road in front of the painter.

'Well, I don't think any of us will be going anywhere unless you are polite enough to answer my questions.' She leaned forward and tapped his portfolio. 'What do you have in there, M. Rousseau? Will you show me, or shall I summon Inspecteur Grignot of the Nice *prefectoire* to take a look?'

To my surprise, Antoine groaned. 'Please. Do not say anything. *C'est très dangereux.*' He looked up and his eyes were hollow with fear. 'You should stop asking questions, Madame. You should be very careful. You should leave Nice, before anything happens to you.'

Mrs Jameson's eyebrows shot up. 'What sort of thing?'

He wiped sweat from his top lip. 'The sort of thing that happened to Mademoiselle Trent,' he mumbled.

And suddenly I had it. The hand across his mouth; the shadow over his troubled eyes. I'd seen him before – and not just in Nice or Villefranche.

'It was you, on the train,' I said. 'Wasn't it?' Add a blonde moustache and a pair of spectacles, swap the workman's cap for the uniformed cap of a carriage attendant on the Blue Train. 'You pretended to be the attendant. But it was you in Miss Trent's compartment, when she woke in the night.' No wonder the man had been avoiding my company. He must have been terrified I'd recognise him, despite his disguise.

'Oh, well done, Marjorie,' said Mrs Jameson. 'Now we are getting somewhere, Monsieur Rousseau, are we not? Give me one reason why I should not summon the police at once.'

He didn't even bother to deny it.

'I wasn't going to hurt her,' he said. 'It was to make her scared, was all. In case she was going to do anything stupid.'

'I see.' Mrs Jameson leaned towards him, eyes glinting. Her voice was silky, but I recognised the deep anger that it covered. 'And at whose behest did you enter Mademoiselle Trent's carriage in the middle of the night, disguised as a carriage attendant, in order to scare a woman travelling alone? And what did you have to do with that woman's death?'

I heard a rumble and looked around as a cart approached along the road behind us, bound for Nice. The driver raised his hat as he manoeuvred the cart carefully past the parked car, showering us with straw heaped high from the harvest.

Before I had time to react, Antoine took his chance. He mounted his bicycle and pedalled off, squeezing past the slow-moving cart which almost blocked the narrowing road ahead. We saw him disappear into the distance, the cart throwing up dust and scattering chaff in its wake.

'Bother,' I said. 'We won't be able to catch him now.'

Mrs Jameson shook her head. 'No matter,' she said. 'We have more than enough to go to Inspector Grignot and ask for his arrest. We'll go straight to the police station.'

'Do you think Antoine killed Miss Trent?' I asked. 'I mean,

we only have Hugh's word that he put him in a taxi back to Villefranche-sur-Mer after the opening.' I was still bitter about my discovery that Hugh's word was not to be relied on.

Mrs Jameson put down her parasol and stepped back into the car. 'No. No, I don't think so. Antoine is a part of this business, but not, I think, the driving force. He is frightened, Marjorie. Very frightened. Fear can drive people to murder, it is true. But if he had murdered Miss Trent out of fear, he would not be so afraid now.'

I started the engine, and we began the drive back towards Nice. After twenty minutes or so, the hay wagon turned off the main road and we were able to pick up speed. There was no sign of Antoine Rousseau or his bicycle. Back in the familiar streets of the city, I navigated along the Promenade des Anglais, then up into the leafy avenues where the police station was located.

As I approached, a policeman in white gloves and a smart uniform waved me to a stop, blowing his whistle. Obediently, I pulled into the kerb and leaned out with a smile.

'Can I leave the car here?' I asked. 'I'm on my way to the police station.'

'Mademoiselle, have you driven this car from Cagnes-sur-Mer?' he asked, looking suspiciously at the scraped paint along the left-hand side.

'Yes, just now,' I said. 'Don't worry – I know it looks bad but it's only a scrape. The drive shaft wasn't damaged.'

He looked at me askance. 'Please remove yourself from the vehicle, Mademoiselle. And you too, Madame.'

Puzzled, I did as the man said. Mrs Jameson got out of her side and put up her parasol.

'*Vos papiers, s'il vous plait.*'

I dug into my basket and found my passport, the first I'd ever possessed. I passed it to the unsmiling policeman. He wrote the details into his notebook, along with the registration number of the car.

He gestured curtly towards the police station. 'Come with me, Mademoiselle Swallow.'

I walked ahead of him, wondering what on earth was going on. Inside the building, the policeman conferred with the man on the desk, and I was ushered into an office. Mrs Jameson, despite her protests, was told to wait outside.

A third policeman arrived and gestured to the upright wooden chair on one side of a plain deal table. I sat down, and he sat opposite me with a sheet of paper and pen.

'*Votre nom, Mademoiselle?*'

'Marjorie Swallow.'

'*Vous êtes Anglaise?*'

'I'm English, yes.'

He watched me a moment longer. '*Parlez-vous Français?*'

'A bit.' I wasn't sure my French was up to a police interrogation, if that was what this was. Perhaps I should suggest they talk to Mr Rubin, so he could explain that he'd loaned me the car.

He rose and called the first policeman in. They conferred in low voices, then the first man, who clearly spoke some English, began.

'You have been driving your car all morning?' he asked.

'Yes, I drove to Cagnes this morning, and then back to Nice,' I said. 'Although it's not my car. It belongs to Mr Rubin, where I'm staying. He said I could drive it. If you telephone the Villa Beau Rivage, he'll tell you.'

He ignored my suggestion. 'And nobody else has driven it

today?'

I shook my head. 'Not unless it was early this morning. We left at about half past nine.'

'Did you see a man on a bicycle when you drove from Cagnes-sur-Mer towards Nice?'

I nodded eagerly. 'I did. Monsieur Antoine Rousseau. Actually, that is why we were coming here. We have some information for Inspector Grignot about him. Is the inspector here?'

The man did not return my smile. 'And why did you not stop when you hit M. Rousseau?'

'What?' I stared at the man.

He sighed. 'Why did you not stop your car when you knocked M. Rousseau off his bicycle?'

'But I didn't!' I exclaimed. Had the artist made some sort of complaint against me, perhaps to stop us from reporting him?

The policeman held out his hands, palms up. 'And yet a car like the one you have been driving hit M. Rousseau. He told the farmer who found him that he'd been hit by a red sports car. And we have a report of a three-wheeled red car driving very fast on the left-hand side of the road, just outside Cagnes.'

I pressed my hands to my forehead. 'But that's ridiculous. I wasn't driving fast, and I know to drive on the right. Ask Antoine. He'll tell you. He cycled off ahead of us after we talked. Someone else must have hit him.'

The man leaned across the table and fixed me with solemn eyes. 'I cannot do that, Mademoiselle Swallow. M. Rousseau died before reaching hospital.'

Chapter 29

'Dead?' I stared at the man, horrified. 'But we talked to him barely half an hour ago.'

'Then, Mademoiselle, you were the last person to have done so with the exception of the farmer who found him,' said my interlocutor. 'I ask you again, why did you not stop? You hit a man – an accident, *bien sûr*, I make no accusations about that. But why did you not stop to help him, to see how badly he was injured?'

I shook my head, trying to shake some sense into it. 'There is a mistake,' I said. 'I didn't hit him. I didn't hit anybody.'

The policeman pushed back his paper. 'And yet the car itself shows that you hit something,' he said. 'There is a scrape all along the left side. From the bicycle, perhaps?'

'No!' This felt like some horrible nightmare. I tried to think clearly. 'That was yesterday. I had to swerve to avoid a branch in the road, on the corniche. And someone came towards me, forced me off the road…' I trailed off. Someone in a red two-seater car.

'*Eh bien?* And you made a report of this to the police department?' asked the man.

'No, I… we were going to do that this morning,' I said. If only I'd done as Mrs Jameson had suggested, instead of playing down the danger. But was it the same red car that had hit poor Antoine?

'But instead, you drove to Cagnes-sur-Mer, with a damaged car? What did you do in Cagnes, Mademoiselle?'

'We went to the village on the hill to see… to see a woman about a painting,' I said, reluctantly. I knew I sounded evasive, but Mrs Jameson would want to put all the facts to Inspector Grignot together.

He was making notes. 'So, you drove straight to the village of Haut de Cagnes?' he asked.

'Yes. No. Wait a minute. We went to Les Collettes first, to see Claude Renoir.'

The man raised his eyebrows. 'You visited M. Renoir?'

'He wasn't at home,' I said, wretchedly. The whole story sounded flimsy, even to me. 'So, we went to the village and spoke to Madame Leclerc. The schoolteacher's wife.' That at least could be confirmed.

'And then?'

'And then we started to drive back to Nice. We saw Antoine Rousseau on his bicycle, on the road. We stopped to talk to him.'

The policeman leaned back in his chair. 'You knew him how?' he asked.

'I met him in Nice, with a friend. And he was at the Galerie Anglaise on the opening night of the exhibition,' I said. No need at this stage to mention that I'd seen him being thrown out of the gallery, or indeed breaking into Sibyl Trent's compartment on the Blue Train.

'And what time did you see Mr Rousseau, on his bicycle?' I could see he was sceptical. I thought back. It had been hot, the sun directly overhead.

'About noon,' I said. I wished I had a wristwatch to tell what time it was now. I looked around the room, but there was no clock.

The man made another note. 'And you stopped to talk?'

'For a few minutes. My employer Mrs Jameson wanted to ask him about the paintings he was carrying.'

The policeman looked up quickly. 'Paintings? On a bicycle?'

'Yes, he had a big cardboard portfolio over his shoulder. It looked rather awkward to carry.' I frowned, seeing the man's puzzlement. 'Did he not have it with him when… when he was found?'

The policeman did not answer, but wrote busily in his notebook, a frown bisecting his forehead.

'And then what happened?' he asked.

'There was a cart,' I exclaimed in sudden relief. 'Antoine rode off ahead of it. We got stuck behind it for a few miles. It turned off by one of the villages.' I racked my brain to remember the name on the signpost. 'You need to find the man who drove the cart. He'd remember, I bet. Antoine squeezed past him on the road.'

For the first time, the policeman's eyes admitted the possibility of doubt. He made a note. 'I will see if we can find this cart driver,' he said. 'What then?'

I hoped that was the light at the end of the tunnel. 'Then I drove straight to Nice. Here, to the police station. Surely you can see I would not have done that if I was trying to escape the consequences of a car crash? Mrs Jameson wanted to talk to Inspector Grignot.'

The policeman checked his pocket watch. 'He will be taking luncheon,' he said. 'I will inform him of the events of this morning when he returns.'

Gloomily I imagined the inspector sitting down to a hearty lunch of beefsteak, fried potatoes, salad and a glass of red wine at the nice cool brasserie around the corner. I wondered how long it would take. With pudding – maybe a bowl of strawberry ice-cream, or one of those vanilla custards with the burnt-sugar topping. My mouth watered. It had been ages since breakfast.

The policeman was on his feet. I got up too.

'Can I go now?' I asked. If we were quick, perhaps Mrs Jameson and I could join the inspector over his dinner. Antoine dying, so soon after warning us about what happened to Sibyl Trent, suggested the killer was becoming even more dangerous.

'Please be seated, Mademoiselle Swallow,' he said. 'You are under arrest for causing the death of a man by dangerous driving. You may not go anywhere until a senior officer decides to let you go.'

'What? But I just told you what happened,' I cried, pushing my chair over in my hurry to follow him to the door. 'There's been a mistake. Please, get Inspector Grignot. Talk to Mrs Jameson – she was with me the whole time.'

He gestured me back. 'Mademoiselle Swallow, I do not wish to have to use restraints, but if you try to leave this room, I will have no choice,' he said. 'The sergeant will take you to a cell shortly. You will be brought some water, and some food. Now, please do not make this more difficult than it needs to be.'

Chapter 30

The rest of that day was nightmarish. After the policeman left, locking the door behind him, I crumpled into my chair and let fall a few tears of frustration. Why did he not believe me?

And yet I knew from my previous investigations with Mrs Jameson that wrongful arrests were sometimes made in the early stages, that the police had to follow the evidence, that suspects often lied and alibis had to be checked.

Had we been in London, I felt sure a quick telephone call from Mrs Jameson to Scotland Yard would have resulted in my speedy release. But this was France, and I didn't know how things were done here. I still had faith that justice would prevail, but when? My only comfort was that I could hear Mrs Jameson raising hell outside. Yet none of her threats or cajoling seemed to do the trick.

Shortly after the policeman had left, the desk sergeant arrived with a big bunch of keys. To my dismay, he handcuffed me to his wrist to lead me through the public entrance hall.

'Oh, for heaven's sake,' cried my employer, who was clearly making a tremendous nuisance of herself. 'Marjorie isn't about to make a run for it. Are you, Marjorie?'

'Silence,' bellowed the sergeant at my side as I tried to turn and speak to her.

'Don't worry, dear,' she called. 'We'll have you out of here in no time.'

We disappeared down a dingy corridor, the grandeur of the public-facing parts of the police station abruptly replaced by olive-green tiled walls and linoleum of indistinct colour. There was a strong smell of carbolic soap. At the end, we went through a set of double doors. My nose twitched. The odour in this section of the police station suggested further use of carbolic soap would be advisable.

A line of black-painted metal doors stretched ahead of us. There was a din of clanging and shouting, as if we were in a munitions factory. The voices, gruff and angry, were all male. One voice wailed over and over, shouting out pleas to the Virgin Mary. Another seemed to be singing, although he could only remember one line of whichever song it was. Others were yelling at him to be quiet.

I looked at the sergeant in horror. Surely he would not put me in one of these cells, with these terrifying-sounding men?

To my relief, we kept walking, then went up a set of metal stairs, painted the same drab olive-green as the tiles. Another shorter corridor of metal doors with hatches and grills. The smell was… not quite as bad. More carbolic, less body fluids. The noise was almost as loud, although the voices were higher in pitch. The sergeant banged on the door of the first cell we passed, where a woman was singing lustily.

'Silence,' he shouted. The woman cackled. Other voices in the cell took up the song. I recognised the tune; I remembered some of the men singing it in the Maudsley Hospital where I had nursed during the War. I wondered if the lyrics in French were as rude as those the soldiers had sung in English.

Halfway down the row, the sergeant stopped, opened a

hatch in the door and peered through. Seemingly satisfied, he grunted and unlocked it, then pushed me in before him.

Two women and a girl of about twelve looked up at me from wooden benches set along the walls. The girl bounced up and tugged at my sleeve as the policeman removed my handcuffs. She asked me something that I couldn't understand, her voice expressing urgency. She pointed to her mouth, and I realised she was hungry.

'Sorry,' I said. I held out my empty hands. I had nothing to offer her. She pulled her coarse grey smock around her and sat back down.

The officer withdrew and the cell door clanged shut. I knew from Hugh and some of my friends from the Harlequin nightclub what it was like to be locked up overnight. But I'd never been on that side of the door when it shut, the metal reverberating with horrible finality. I bit my lip and tried not to whimper.

The two women stared at me. Or, more likely, at my linen frock, which was already dusty from the drive, and I suspected would not be white all that much longer. They both wore cheap black dresses, low-cut at the neck with tight corsets pushing up their breasts. Their shoes were crude and down-at-heel, and they had knitted shawls around their shoulders. I'd seen enough of the street life of Soho to realise what they had probably been arrested for. I only hoped they would be friendly.

I looked around the bare cell. Benches on two sides, a covered bucket, already reeking of urine, in the corner. How long would I be here? I hated the thought of using it. The light came from a narrow barred window high in the cell, too high to see out of. A strip of blue, taunting me with the promise of sunshine and freedom.

'*Bonjour, Mesdames*,' I said. I smiled, hoping to see some response from their hostile faces. One nodded, the other looked away without a flicker of acknowledgement.

The girl burst into incomprehensible chatter again. Was she with the women, or had she been brought in separately? I'm sorry, I told her in my basic French. Can you speak more slowly?

She stared at me, then laughed and took herself off to the corner of the cell, where she curled up in a ball and chattered away to herself, sending sly glances my way every now and again. The two women resumed their desultory conversation. Hesitantly, I perched on the bench between the women and the girl.

A clatter at the hatch, and something was thrust through the bars. The women were on their feet instantly, grabbing tin mugs of water and plates with hunks of bread and cheese. I hovered, waiting to take my rations. But when they returned to the bench, sharing the food and water between them, the hatch slammed shut.

The girl snatched a piece of bread. They shouted at her, but she'd crammed it into her mouth before they could grab it back. I hoped that was not all she'd have to eat today.

I stood before the women, my legs trembling a little. I supposed I could do without bread and cheese. I was more than well-fed as a rule. But my mouth was dry, and I longed for some water. They had four mugs between them.

I pointed at one of the mugs. '*Un peu d'eau, s'il vous plaît?*'

The elder of the two women picked up a mug, locked eyes with me and drank it down, every drop. Then she dropped the tin mug on the floor, where it rolled noisily around. Her friend laughed. She picked up a second mug and took a sip. Then she seemed to have a better idea. She held it out to me, then drew it away as I reached for it. She held it out again. I reached, and she took it back. Finally, after taking a long swallow of the water, she spat in it and held the mug out again.

I licked my dry lips. She was grinning, discoloured teeth made more unpleasant by two missing at the front. I wondered if someone had knocked them out for her. I felt rather inclined to knock out a few more. The woman set the mug down on the bench, and the girl darted in and swallowed the contents thirstily, spit and all.

Defeated, I sat down on the bench, closed my eyes and tried to ignore my thirst. I wouldn't let the women see my discomfort. They obviously found it amusing, so I would deny them the satisfaction.

I remembered how I'd set aside my water at the Leclerc house, disdaining it for the smears on the glass. I'd been an idiot. Why hadn't I just drunk it?

I knew what my mother would say. I'd become too used to the high life. Fancy cocktails, fine food, staff to attend to my every need. I hadn't even bothered to learn the names of the housekeeper at Villa Beau Rivage, the maid who'd pressed my dresses and made my bed, the gardener who raked up leaves and watered the flowers each morning. Even the cook, whose delicious meals I'd been eating for a week, was a stranger to me.

I felt ashamed. Mrs Jameson always took the trouble to learn the names of servants. So did I, as a rule. My mother couldn't buy a newspaper without stopping for a chat with the news boy. The poor state of my French was no excuse.

Well, I'd been taken down a peg or two, that was for sure. A day after sipping cocktails on the terrace of the most luxurious villa in Nice, I was begging for water from two ladies of the night in a fetid police cell. I thought for a moment of what my mother would say if she could see me, and shuddered. Her worst nightmare had come true.

'Too good for us, are you?' I opened my eyes. The older woman was leaning forward, the final mug of water in her hands.

'You speak English?'

'I am English,' she said, thrusting the mug in my direction. 'Peckham. Don't ask. It's a long story.' Her voice was sharp-edged.

'Catford,' I said, naming my own south London suburb. 'Likewise. I'm Marjorie.' I took the mug and drank, grateful for the lukewarm liquid.

'I'm Eliza,' she said. 'And this here's Antoinette. Like the queen they chopped the head off of. But with less sense.'

I glanced warily at her companion, who was grinning her gap-toothed smile. 'Don't mind her. She likes a bit of fun,' said Eliza. 'Doesn't get much.'

'What about the child?' I asked. 'Is she with you?'

Eliza glanced towards the corner, where the girl sat gnawing a piece of cheese. 'Jeanne? She's from the orphanage. She was stealing food from the market in the old town. She's a bit touched. Not right in here.' She tapped her forehead.

'How did you...' I began.

'Told you. Long story.'

I glanced up at the blue strip of sky. Was it darkening, or was that my imagination? 'Well,' I said, 'I don't have any other plans this afternoon.'

Chapter 31

It was a very long night. Eliza and Antoinette stretched out on the benches after using the bucket in the corner, seemingly without embarrassment. I'd eventually had to do the same; the women had done me the courtesy of closing their eyes, whether they were asleep or not.

The child Jeanne curled up on the floor. I'd tucked my cardigan jacket around her, seeing how little warmth there was in her threadbare uniform smock. Finally, I lay down on the bench myself. Clasping my hands behind my head, I stared at the dark ceiling. I didn't expect to sleep.

There was much to think about. I'd had no contact with the outside world, no visit from Inspector Grignot or word from Mrs Jameson. I had no idea whether the French police were following up the leads I'd given them – the other red two-seater, the cart that had overtaken me. I kept replaying in my mind Antoine Rousseau's words to us: 'You should be very careful. You should leave Nice, before anything happens to you.' Had he known or feared something was about to happen to him? From our visit to Cagnes, it had been clear that he had a relationship with Sophie Leclerc. Was her husband, the creepy schoolmaster Marcel Leclerc, behind Antoine's death?

Antoine had not answered Mrs Jameson's questions about

why he had broken into Sibyl Trent's compartment on the train, or who he was acting for. His only link to Sibyl seemed to be through the Leclercs and Ashton Montgomery, and that was a tenuous one. Why would Antoine want to frighten the woman entrusted with bringing the Leclercs' Renoir painting back to the gallery? I could make no sense of the situation.

I sighed and thought instead of Eliza's story. As she had warned, it had been a long one. She'd run away from home aged twelve, she told me, when a circus arrived on Peckham Rye one summer. She stowed away in a wagon with the show horses.

'I was a pretty little thing, believe it or not,' she said. 'And fearless with horses. They put me in a fairy costume, and I danced on the saddle when the big white horse came into the ring.'

The circus crossed the channel at Dover, then meandered through France and Spain. Mucking out the animals and fending off the attentions of the circus clowns got boring after a while, she said.

'I left them in Spain, joined a group of gypsies. But they didn't want me – I couldn't sing, couldn't play guitar, and couldn't even sell flowers without getting picked up by the police.'

When she was about sixteen she'd met a couple of artists in Spain, who were keen to paint the picturesque gypsy troupe. She'd posed for them, then travelled with them to Paris. They lived together in a half-derelict studio in Montparnasse.

'I couldn't choose between them. Beautiful, they were. Lovely-looking lads. But neither of them lasted,' she said. 'I modelled for a bit, then I got into my current situation. I moved south. It's warmer and cheaper than Paris, but it's getting harder to make a living since the Sammies went home.'

'Sammies?'

'Uncle Sams. The American soldiers what they sent here for R and R during the War.'

'How old are you?' I asked, curious. She looked ancient, her face lined and worn down, her shoulders set in a defeated slump.

'Thirty-five.' She gave a rueful laugh at my shocked expression. Just ten years older than me. 'I'm not going to be picked for an advertisement for face cream, am I?'

When I was a small child, my parents had taken me and my brother to the circus. I'd watched entranced the glamorous performers in their sparkling costumes, doing handstands on the backs of beautiful white horses and beaming with happiness. It had seemed to me like the best job in the world. James and I had whispered late into the night, making plans. He wanted to be a strongman, lifting huge weights, but my heart was captured by the bareback riders. Our running-away plans, as was usual, had come to nothing. But what if we had put them into practice? Would that be me, stretched out derelict on the bench of a custody cell?

I reminded myself that I was, actually, stretched out on the bench of a custody cell, even if I wasn't quite derelict yet. I wondered again what was happening outside. Had Mrs Jameson got hold of Inspector Grignot? Had they found the driver of the hay cart? And did she know about the mysterious red two-seater that had hit poor Antoine Rousseau? The more I thought about it, the more I was convinced that this must have been the same car that forced me off the road on my way back from Villefranche-sur-Mer on Thursday.

I thought warily of Hugh, like pressing a bad tooth with my

tongue to see how much it hurt. He'd said he'd been trying to protect me. Was that true? I felt a needle of guilt, and wondered if he knew yet that his friend was dead.

I'd enjoyed his company so much in Nice, promenading by his side and seeing the admiring looks of the passers-by. But how had they seen us? Another artist and his model, I supposed. Like Eliza and her two artists in Montparnasse.

Montparnasse. Infested with inferior painters, Inspector Grignot had said, like Sibyl Trent's husband. Sibyl, who had studied at the Académie in Montparnasse with Ashton Montgomery, before she married. Sibyl, too, had been in her mid-thirties.

'Eliza?' I whispered, not wanting to awaken the whole cell.

No answer, but a long sigh. I tried again.

'What? I'm trying to sleep.' I heard her roll over on the bench, turning her face to the wall.

'When you were in Montparnasse, did you know a painter called…' Bother. What was his name?

'I knew a lot of painters,' she said. 'Cheap bastards, the lot of them.'

'I can't remember his name. But he married an English-woman. Sibyl Trent.'

There was silence for a moment. Then she propped herself up on her elbow. 'Henri. Henri Lejaby. What about him?'

Briefly, I filled her in on Sibyl's death, and how I had met her on the Blue Train.

'Apparently Sibyl met Lejaby on the rebound from an American student, Ashton Montgomery,' I said. 'She tried to blackmail Ashton about their affair. I was wondering…'

'Well, that's wrong,' said Eliza. 'Sibyl never had an affair with Ashton. I know that for certain.' She blew her nose loudly.

'Who's been telling you this rubbish, eh?'

'There was a letter, in her handbag,' I said. 'But hang on a minute. You knew Ashton Montgomery? Back in Montparnasse?'

She laughed. 'Longer than that. I met Ashton and Henri in Spain. They were the ones I lived with in Montparnasse. Until Henri shacked up with Sibyl Trent, and Ashton decided to stop slumming it and married that stuck-up American gold-digger.'

I stared at her. Was she telling the truth? This street walker, scrabbling for bread in a Nice police cell, was once the companion of the suave Ashton Montgomery?

'Don't believe me, do you? I didn't always look like this. And Ashton Montgomery wasn't always the flashy man about town. He was a kid, once. Like the rest of us. Till that woman got her claws in, anyway.'

'Have you seen him since he moved to Nice? Asked him for help?' Surely he would offer to help her, if he saw the position she was in.

'Not blooming likely. Do you think he'd want to see me like this? Ashton never did a thing for anyone, unless they could do something for him in return. He's tight-fisted, for all that his family is loaded. At least, he thought it was, till his dad died.'

'Go on.' I was rapidly adjusting my image of the sophisticated art dealer. 'I thought he was rich.' He certainly acted as if he had plenty of money.

She yawned. 'He and Lois went back to New York, expecting to inherit a blooming great fortune. All they got was a pile of debts. The family business was about to collapse. His older brother cut his allowance. He got a few hundred dollars, which he used to set up the gallery. I have to say, I laughed like a drain at the thought of Lois's face when she found out. Couldn't have happened to a nicer person.' She chuckled. 'Now, shut up and let me get some sleep, there's a good girl.'

Her snores were soon reverberating through the cell, but I was far from sleep. Why had Ashton told us that he and Sibyl had an affair, if they didn't? And why on earth had he told such a thing to his wife? And if the Montgomeries had no money, what were they living on? The gallery seemed prosperous, but modern art didn't fetch all that much money. No wonder he was so keen to sell the Renoir painting, and to hook Mr Rubin as a client.

I rolled over again, trying to get comfortable on the hard wooden slats. Lois Montgomery had seemed nice enough, but then Ashton had left Eliza to marry her. Eliza could hardly be expected to give her love rival a glowing reference.

And one more thing troubled me. If Ashton never did anything for anyone unless he expected something in return, why had he given money to Antoine Rousseau? And, I remembered with a sinking heart, to Hugh.

Chapter 32

The scraping rattle of the metal hatch woke me from the sleep I'd given up hoping for. The strip of sky at the window was once again cerulean blue. I shifted, my limbs aching, and remembered where I was.

Groaning, I sat up. Someone was staring at me through the hatch.

'Miss Swallow? How are you this morning?'

I got to my feet. 'Is that Inspector Grignot?'

'Yes, yes, it is I.' More clanking and scraping and the door opened. Inspector Grignot stood beside the sergeant, smart in his pristine dark suit, heels together. I tried to smooth down the creases of my grubby linen dress and rake through my hair with my fingers.

'I am sorry that you have been subjected to this,' he said. 'However, there were procedures to follow. I'm sure you will understand.'

My companions were awake now, rubbing the sleep from their eyes.

'Lousy hotel, this,' said Eliza. 'Where's my breakfast? I want *café au lait* and a croissant with strawberry jam. Make it snappy.'

Inspector Grignot raised his eyebrows and stood aside.

'Please come with me, Miss Swallow.'

I hesitated, wondering whether to ask for my cardigan jacket back from Jeanne. But the girl had buttoned it around her bony shoulders, and I supposed her need was greater than mine.

'Give my regards to Ashton and Lois,' said Eliza as I walked out. The door closed on her cackles.

Mrs Jameson was in the entrance hall with Mr Rubin, both looking like concerned parents whose lost child had finally been returned.

'There you are, Marjorie. Are you all right? I'm sorry this took so long,' said Mrs Jameson. 'The French police apparently have their own ways of doing things.' She glared at Inspector Grignot. 'I had to insist the British Consulate involve Scotland Yard.'

Inspector Grignot, ignoring her, gestured for me to sit at the desk, opposite the sergeant. 'You will need to sign here, Miss Swallow, to acknowledge the terms of the bond. You must stay at the Villa Beau Rivage, and you may not leave the bounds of the Département des Alpes-Maritimes.'

I looked up at Mrs Jameson and Mr Rubin. 'I've settled the bail bond,' said Mr Rubin quickly. 'There's nothing to worry about. Just a formality.'

I signed. I hadn't been cleared, then. I was still a suspect, but now I was out on bail.

'Come on,' said Mrs Jameson. 'Let's get you back to the villa, then we can talk. I expect you could do with breakfast, couldn't you?'

I was famished. I walked across the marble floor, my legs feeling rather wobbly. I felt very conscious of the prisoners I'd left behind me. At the door I stopped and turned to Inspector

Grignot.

'Please ensure the girl in my cell is given a proper breakfast,' I said. 'Jeanne. She seems half-starved.'

He looked a little abashed. 'All our prisoners are fed, Mademoiselle.'

I held his eye for a moment. 'Children are not always able to get their fair share. And children who are arrested for stealing food from the market are apt to be hungry.'

I was satisfied to see a slight blush rise to his face. 'I shall attend to it.'

I walked down the steps of the police station into another bright morning. The light was dazzling after so long inside. So dazzling that at first I thought I must have been hallucinating. Then I gave a cry of delight and rushed across the pavement.

Leaning against Mrs Jameson's bottle-green Lagonda, cupping a Woodbine cigarette in her hand, was Mrs Jameson's chauffeur, Frankie O'Grady. Overcome with emotion, I threw my arms around her neck.

'Oi, oi, Marge. What's all this about?' She gave me a playful shove, but her smile showed she was as pleased to be here as I was to see her. 'How come you always get in trouble when I'm not around to look after you, eh?'

'I thought it best to wire for reinforcements, especially as you will not be allowed to drive until this business is concluded, Marjorie,' said Mrs Jameson. 'Frankie drove to Dover yesterday and took the boat across.'

'Then I drove all night from Calais,' she said. 'The Lagonda beat the train, I reckon. It needs more of a rest than I do. This is a bit of all right, isn't it?' She waved her arm, indicating the elegant street, the palm trees, the blue sky and sunshine. 'Now, let's get you back.'

I don't think I've ever been more grateful to sit down to breakfast than I was that morning. The big table on the terrace was set with plates of finely cut ham, cheeses, fruit and rounds of warm crusty baguettes, heaps of croissants and pain au chocolat, jugs of orange juice and cafetières of strong black coffee. Frankie and I dived in without restraint.

'What, no bacon?' she asked me, her voice low, with a wink. We shared a love of a full English breakfast, but I wasn't going to complain. Indeed, I took a moment to tell the housekeeper how much I'd enjoyed it.

'Where is everyone?' I asked, pondering whether I could fit in another pain au chocolat without bursting something. Of the usual house party, only Miss Braithwaite and Benjamin Rubin had joined us at breakfast. Miss Braithwaite looked most disapproving of my scruffy appearance, and even more so at the inclusion at the family breakfast of Frankie. She'd left her green livery at home and was dressed casually in breeches, boots and a waistcoat over her shirt, sleeves rolled up and open at the neck. Benjamin was wide-eyed at her mannish attire and cropped hair.

'Andrew's driven Miss Pemberton and M. Brunot to the studios,' said Mr Rubin. 'They hope to finish filming today. Although I believe M. Brunot said that last week.' He smiled conspiratorially. 'Perhaps I shall have to ask my cook to lower the standards. Nobody ever seems to want to leave.'

So, Dulcie had not carried out her threat to take off for a hotel, in umbrage at being questioned by Mrs Jameson. I remembered her admission of love for Andrew in the tower room the night before last. Mr Rubin's dinners were not the only attraction.

'I'm surprised you let that young woman take advantage of

you, Mr Rubin,' said Nanny Braithwaite, who seemed to thrive on disapproval.

He turned his mild gaze on her. 'I'm not aware that I am being taken advantage of.'

She raked the table with a meaningful gaze. 'You are generous to your guests, I know. But surely, with young Benjamin to consider, you must expect certain standards to be upheld.'

'I don't mind,' said Benjamin, cheerfully. 'I like it when there are lots of visitors.' He pushed back his plate. 'Can I bathe? It's Saturday, so no lessons today.'

'That sounds good,' said Frankie. 'I'll join you.'

Miss Braithwaite gasped. 'Not right on top of your breakfast, Benjamin! I knew a little boy who went swimming with a full tummy, and he got cramp and drowned.'

'I'm not a little boy,' muttered Benjamin.

'Maybe you should have saved him,' said Frankie, with a grin. 'Call yourself a nanny?' She got to her feet and stretched. 'Right, I'm going in. Then I'd like a quick kip, if it's all right with you, Mrs Jameson. I'll be right as rain by lunchtime.'

I didn't dare to ask what she was going to wear to bathe. Somehow I couldn't see Frankie in the flounces and frills of my borrowed costume.

'That's perfectly all right, Frankie,' Mrs Jameson said. 'Now, Marjorie, I suggest you get washed and changed and meet me in the sitting room. We have much to discuss.'

Chapter 33

The elegant walls of Mrs Jameson's sitting room were now covered with sheets of paper written over in her large, distinctive handwriting.

'Crimes,' was the heading on one of the large foolscap sheets. '1: Break-in on Train Bleu. Victim Sibyl Trent; perpetrator Antoine Rousseau. 2: Murder at Villa Beau Rivage. Victim Sibyl Trent; suspects Dulcie Pemberton, Andrew Fraser, Hettie Braithwaite, unknown others. 3: Attempted murder on the Corniche. Victim: Marjorie Swallow; suspects unknown driver of red car. 4: Murder on the road from Cagnes. Victim Antoine Rousseau; suspects unknown driver (likely same as 3).'

'How did you persuade Inspector Grignot to let me out?' I asked.

'I sent a telegram to Peter Chadwick,' said Mrs Jameson. Inspector Chadwick of Scotland Yard was a good friend of ours. 'He got onto the police in Paris, and they put a rocket under the Nice prefecture. The relaxed Inspector Grignot was urged to move a little faster. With the result that the police located the driver of the cart, who confirmed our version of events.

'He told the inspector that a man on a bicycle carrying a

portfolio had overtaken him on a narrow stretch of road. He remembers seeing him in the distance, taking a turning down a road towards a farm. That was where he was found after the crash. The farmer who found him had been driving his horse and trap home from Nice, and was overtaken on the way by a red car driving very fast towards Cagnes. A four-wheeled Bugatti, not a Morgan, despite the unknown caller to the police, who reported a speeding red three-wheeler.

'Anyhow, Inspector Grignot was persuaded that the Bugatti was probably the car that hit M. Rousseau. He is seeking its owner with all urgency.'

'Golly,' I said. 'Thank goodness.'

'Was the car that forced you off the road a Bugatti, Marjorie?'

I tried to remember. It had all been a bit of a blur. 'Sorry. I wasn't thinking about the car's make. It happened too fast,' I said, regretful. 'Maybe if I saw it again, I'd know.'

'Of course.' She mused, looking down at her notes. 'I should very much like to speak to whoever it was who made the erroneous report to the police. I have urged Inspector Grignot to attempt to trace the call.'

I took a closer look at the lists of suspects. 'Wait a minute. You suspect Hettie Braithwaite of murdering Sibyl Trent?'

Mrs Jameson sighed. 'Not really. Although I wouldn't put it past her, would you? The difficulty is, apart from Andrew and Dulcie, Miss Braithwaite is the only person we know of who had the opportunity. Everyone else was watching the speeches.'

'Except for Benjamin,' I said, jokingly.

'True,' said Mrs Jameson, adding his name to the suspect list before I could protest that I didn't mean it. 'And, of course, the staff. I think they come under the heading of unknown others.'

I took a pencil from my bag. 'I found out more about Sibyl Trent last night. And Ashton Montgomery. It changes what he told us in the gallery.' I explained what I'd learned about Ashton's rackety student days, living with Sibyl's future husband and Eliza. 'I don't understand why Ashton told us he'd had an affair with Sibyl, if he didn't,' I said.

'Which confirms that it cannot have been the secret she wrote about in her letter,' added Mrs Jameson. 'And the news about Ashton's precarious financial situation is most interesting. We will look further into that.'

She gazed for a moment at the list of crimes, victims and suspects, tapping her index finger on her chin. I waited.

'Sibyl Trent and Antoine Rousseau,' said Mrs Jameson. 'Do you remember when he was thrown out of the gallery at the opening of the show? What he said?'

It was just after Hugh and I had talked to M. Picasso. Antoine had been shouting in French, but I didn't remember his words.

'He called Ashton Montgomery a *faux-cul*, a fraud. And he said he'd tell everyone,' said Mrs Jameson. 'Unfortunately, we don't know what he would tell everyone. But isn't that interesting, Marjorie? Two people who threatened to tell people something about Ashton Montgomery have wound up dead.'

I shivered. 'But Ashton can't have killed Sibyl Trent,' I reminded her. 'He was on the terrace giving a speech, in front of everyone. You were there yourself.'

'Yes. But it is interesting, all the same. I will suggest that the French police ask Mr Montgomery where he was at the time of the car crash yesterday. And indeed, what car he drives. Now, have you worked out yet what his secret is?'

I looked up, startled. 'No. Have you?'

She gave her maddening cat-smile. 'Oh, I think that's becoming clear. I wonder who else knows about it. Apart from those directly involved, I mean.'

I sighed. 'Are you going to tell me, Mrs Jameson?'

She tapped my arm. 'I'm sure you'll work it out. It would be much better for your training if you put the puzzle together yourself.'

Easy for her to say, after a comfortable night's sleep. Tiredness was slowing my brain down and I kept having to smother enormous yawns.

'Perhaps you should think about why you yourself became a target,' she said, seating herself by the window and looking out at the glorious sweep of the bay. 'What did you know that someone didn't want you repeating, and who else knew?'

I couldn't think what she meant. I'd driven Hugh to Villefranche, supposedly to look for Antoine. During the journey, my mind had been entirely on the aftermath of the party and Hugh's kiss on the beach. Then I'd seen Antoine and he'd run away from me, and Hugh had lied about talking to him.

'I think… I think Antoine recognised me when he saw me in Villefranche,' I said. 'Not just from the time I met him with Hugh in the market. But from the train. Maybe he was scared that I was going to recognise him.'

Mrs Jameson inclined her head. 'It's possible.'

'So… I suppose Antoine could have been the one driving the red car, who pushed me off the road? Maybe he followed me, then saw me drive back to Nice.'

Mrs Jameson rang the bell. 'You need more coffee, Marjorie. If he followed you, how could he have driven towards you in the opposite direction? And if he has a red sports car, why does he ride that bicycle? And…'

'And he can't have run himself over,' I agreed. 'You're right. It can't have been him. Or Hugh.' That was a relief, at least. Suspicious as Hugh's behaviour had been, I didn't want to consider the possibility that he had tried to murder me.

The maid arrived to take our requests for coffee. '*Café au lait*, please, Marie. And lots of sugar,' I said, remembering Eliza's quip about breakfast. I wondered if my cell mates had been released yet – and whether Inspector Grignot had kept his word about ensuring Jeanne was fed.

'Who knew you were going to Villefranche?' asked Mrs Jameson. I tried to drag my mind back.

'We were at the gallery,' I said. 'So, you and Hugh, obviously. Ashton Montgomery, and his wife.' I thought for a moment. 'That's all.'

Ashton Montgomery, again. But why would he want to hurt me? I tried to remember what we'd talked about. Mrs Jameson had quizzed him about Sibyl Trent's letter. He'd admitted to an affair – which, it turned out, was a lie. Then Hugh arrived and they'd talked about Antoine Rousseau. Ashton had agreed to give Antoine some money and gave Hugh a bonus.

'Eliza said that Ashton never gave anyone a thing unless he was getting something from them in return,' I said, slowly. 'But he gave Hugh a bonus, and he gave him money for Antoine. I thought maybe he was embarrassed, because I'd talked about Antoine buying second-hand paintings in the market to paint over.'

A slow smile spread across Mrs Jameson's face. 'So you did. I should have realised at the time how dangerous that observation had been.' Her face became serious again. 'Thank goodness you weren't badly injured. Now, can you see the connexions? What do people have in common who take money from Mr Montgomery?'

'They're artists?' I suggested. 'And they're poor. They need money. They'll do what he says.'

'Until they become too demanding, or too dangerous.' Mrs Jameson raised her grey eyes, suddenly wide with anxiety. 'Have you heard from Hugh since Thursday night?'

'No.' I felt a clutch of fear. 'Not a word.' Not since I'd shouted at him, and he'd slammed his way out of the villa, claiming he was trying to protect me.

Mrs Jameson was half-way across the room before I'd put down my coffee cup. 'Frankie,' she called up the stairs. 'Sorry to wake you, dear. We need you to take us to Villefranche.'

Chapter 34

The Rue Obscure seemed much less creepy with Mrs Jameson beside me, but I was dry-mouthed with apprehension.

'I remember this place.' Mrs Jameson reached a hand to the chiselled stone walls. 'I visited Villefranche before the War and stayed at the Hotel Welcome. M. Cocteau, the artist, was here too. We did have fun.'

She knocked firmly on the ancient timber of the door to Hugh's lodgings. The same woman I'd spoken to before opened it, narrowing her eyes with suspicion at the sight of me.

'*Bonjour, Madame.*' I tried to look confident.

'*Il est mort,*' she said.

'He's… he's dead?' All the life seemed to drain away from me. My legs felt queer and I leaned against the door jamb to support myself.

Mrs Jameson put a hand on my arm. 'I think she means M. Rousseau. *C'est vrai, Madame? M. Rousseau a été tué dans un accident de voiture?*'

The woman straightened at the sight of Mrs Jameson, upright and elegant in her travelling costume.

'*Oui, madame, c'est vrai. Le pauvre Antoine.*'

I breathed again.

The woman bowed her head. Perhaps she thought Mrs Jameson was a rich relative of Antoine. She bobbed a quick curtsey and said something in French that I didn't catch. Mrs Jameson smiled and reached for her purse.

'He owes rent,' she murmured to me. 'Perhaps if I pay his arrears, she'll tell us more.'

We introduced ourselves and the landlady, Madame Durand, ushered us into the apartment building. We passed through a dingy hallway with a narrow staircase, into a parlour with an oilskin-covered table, three upright chairs and an astonishing collection of art hanging on the walls.

We gazed around in wonder. I spotted several rather good Impressionist views of Villefranche harbour, a head of a man that had Hugh's style about it, a Jean Cocteau painting of fishermen hauling nets, something that looked suspiciously like a Picasso drawing of a bullfight… the dozens of paintings in this bare little room must have been worth a fortune.

Mrs Jameson switched into her effortless French. 'You have a most magnificent collection here, Madame.'

Madame Durand beamed. 'Thank you. Many artists stay with me here. They sometimes give me pictures instead of…' She rubbed her thumb and fingers together in the universal gesture for money.

'Is that really a Picasso?' I asked, peering closer at the pen-and-ink depiction of an elegant matador waving his cape before a bull, captured in a few pen-strokes.

She laughed. 'Ah, non. But it is very good, no? A good joke.' Her laughter dropped away, and she shook her head. '*C'est un dessin de Antoine Rousseau, le pauvre. Très gentil, et très ingénieux.*'

Mrs Jameson bent to look. 'Indeed, very clever. How

interesting.' She straightened. 'However, we are looking for another of your guests, Madame Durand. An Englishman, Monsieur Hugh Williams.'

A Welshman, actually, but Mrs Jameson like many Americans did not differentiate between the different countries of Great Britain. I held my breath again.

The woman clasped her hands. '*Ah, je suis désolé. Il est parti.*'

We had come too late.

'He's gone? When did he go, and where?'

Hugh had been at his lodgings on Friday afternoon, when the police arrived with news of Antoine Rousseau's death, reported Madame Durand.

'*Il était vraiment désolé. Très agité.*' He'd been very upset and agitated. He had packed his things at once and paid his rent in full from a wad of francs in his wallet.

'And did he usually pay his rent on time?' asked Mrs Jameson.

Madame Durand laughed. 'He is an artist. They never pay their rent on time,' she said. She gestured at the works hung floor to ceiling around us. 'It is fortunate that I appreciate art.'

To my disappointment, Hugh had not told his landlady where he was going. He'd left the address of the Slade School of Art in Bloomsbury for forwarding any mail.

'I suppose he has gone back to London,' said Mrs Jameson. 'He must have realised that he was in danger when he heard of Antoine's death.' She scribbled down the address and telephone number of the Villa Beau Rivage and handed it to Madame Durand. 'Please do let us know if you hear from him. And thank you for your hospitality.'

We walked back to the waterfront. I tried not to take it personally that Hugh had not told me he was leaving.

Although, I supposed, he would not have been able to do so anyway, as I'd been locked up in a police cell when he left.

By the time we found Frankie, who had parked the car opposite the harbour, she had attracted a considerable amount of attention. She had the bonnet of the Lagonda open, and a gang of street urchins was watching carefully as she gave an impromptu lesson on how an engine worked. Several sailors sat on their heels, smoking and making jokes, quite possibly at Frankie's expense. A couple of smartly dressed women with hair cropped almost as short as her own lingered nearby, clearly puzzled as to whether her trousers and waistcoat were a new fashion they should be adopting.

She straightened up. 'Nosy lot, ain't they? I had a couple of policemen stop by earlier, wanting to know if I was a man or a woman. I said it was none of their blooming business and they pushed off. I think they'd made a bet about it.'

'Oh, goodness,' I said. 'Isn't it illegal for women to wear trousers in France?'

Mrs Jameson laughed. 'That's a common misperception. There was a local decree about *travestissement* in Paris, but I don't believe anyone takes any notice of it. I certainly wore trousers during the War.' She smiled at my look of surprise. 'Much more convenient when one is crawling around the Parisian catacombs or trying to infiltrate enemy lines,' she said. 'Now, I should like to treat you both to lunch at the Hotel Welcome, unless of course you're still full from breakfast.'

We both shook our heads fervently. And whatever the hotel staff made of our unconventional party, they treated us with the utmost courtesy. Mrs Jameson was welcomed back like a prodigal son; a table was set on the terrace and she entered into serious discussion with the maître d'hôtel before he disappeared, beaming.

'Bouillabaisse,' she said, triumphantly. 'You have to have it at least once when you visit the south. It's a Marseilles speciality, but the Hotel Welcome version is impeccable. The monkfish and lobster were swimming in that sea this morning.'

It was quite delicious, fragrant with saffron and richly flavoured, although the garlic in the mayonnaise was strong enough to make my eyes water.

'Not bad,' said Frankie, scooping up the last of hers with a round of bread. 'Could do with some chips, though. And you can't beat a nice bit of batter.'

Chapter 35

Frankie and I both slept all afternoon, the effects of the last couple of days catching up on us. When I eventually emerged in the early evening, she was already on the beach making friends with Benjamin. To my surprise, she had a bathing suit of her own – a stripy, sporty number that suited her athletic frame. She emerged from the waves, slicking back her cropped hair.

'The water's lovely, ain't it? Warm as the Poplar Baths, and a blooming sight cleaner.'

Benjamin was keen to demonstrate the jiu-jitsu moves I'd taught him, but he found it impossible to throw Frankie. She was an expert practitioner of the martial art, much better than me. She only got him to let her alone by promising to teach him some advanced moves the next day. Then she raced him to the rocks, climbed up and dived back in, a perfect swallow dive that left barely a ripple on the surface. I felt dizzy just watching her.

Over dinner, Mrs Jameson outlined a plan to return to Cagnes-sur-Mer the next morning.

'I believe that is where we will find the explanation for the deaths of Sibyl Trent and Antoine Rousseau,' she said. 'I have spoken to Inspector Grignot and learned more about Antoine's death.'

'Did you find out if Ashton drives a red Bugatti sports car?' I asked. The car was still haunting my nightmares, and I'd woken from my afternoon nap with a start, convinced it was heading straight for me.

Mrs Jameson set down her knife and fork. 'No. He has a Citröen, a big one so he can transport artworks around. What's more, at midday yesterday when Antoine Rousseau met his death, Ashton Montgomery was entertaining clients and local dignitaries to lunch at the Nice Casino. Guests included the chief of police. Even allowing for the lax standards of the French constabulary, I think we have to rule him out as a suspect.'

* * *

The next morning I dressed in my green and blue Madras cotton frock, while the laundry maid did what she could with my once-white dress. Although the style was outdated – the wide skirt flaring unfashionably from the waist instead of dropping straight from the hips – it was at least cool and clean.

I spread apricot jam on a croissant and washed it down with *café au lait*, then went to find the others. Frankie was in the garage, lying on her back under the jacked-up Morgan. Andrew Fraser watched the car possessively.

'It's a lovely bit of kit,' she said. 'But I reckon that knock it took threw the shaft out of alignment a touch. Pass me a spanner, would you?'

Mrs Jameson swept into the garage. 'There you are, Frankie. Come along, dear.'

She turned her gaze on Andrew Fraser. Dulcie Pemberton and Maxim Brunot had announced at dinner that they had finally completed their film and were due to depart the villa in a day or two. They were meeting newspaper reporters and photographers this morning to create publicity for *La Femme Honnête*. Andrew was despondent as a puppy whose owner had abandoned it by the side of the road.

'Would you like to come with us, Mr Fraser? After our last trip to Cagnes, it might be as well to have company. And a witness.'

'I'm driving, though,' said Frankie quickly. She didn't often let anyone else drive the Lagonda.

Andrew brightened up. 'Happy to help, Mrs Jameson. I'm glad to hear you're not leaving, too. The house is almost empty.'

I sat with him in the back seat as Frankie took us on the now-familiar route along the seafront. 'I suppose the season will be starting soon,' I said. 'Will you teach tennis again at one of the hotels?'

He sighed. 'I suppose so. But I'm getting a bit sick of it, to be honest. It's not much of a job for a man, is it? Teaching bored young women to hit a ball over a net. And what about when I'm too old for it? I need to find something steady. Something I can do all year round.'

I nodded sympathetically. 'That sounds sensible. Maybe you should talk to Mr Rubin. He might have some ideas.'

'That way,' called Mrs Jameson. Frankie swung the wheel left and took a turning into a side road. 'That's it. Pull over here for a moment.'

I leaned forward, puzzled.

'Where are we?' We were still a few miles from Cagnes village. I'd thought we were going to call on the Leclerc family.

The roadside showed nothing of interest that I could see, apart from some scrubby weeds and a ditch.

'This is the road where the farmer found Antoine Rousseau after the car hit him,' said Mrs Jameson. 'His bicycle was in the ditch, and he had crawled out onto the roadside.'

She stepped out of the car and walked into the road, scanning the dusty surface. I climbed out to join her, bending down to scrutinise the criss-crossed tracks of cars, carts and horses.

'I don't think we'll find anything of use,' said Mrs Jameson. 'There have been police cars and farm carts up and down the road ever since, no doubt obliterating all traces of the crime. But I wanted to see the spot.' She met my eyes and I saw deep anger there. 'It was a despicable crime, and I will find the culprit. However, that's not why we are here. I know where Antoine was heading.'

We got back in the car and resumed our journey. A few minutes later Mrs Jameson directed Frankie down a narrow farm track. We bumped along the rutted path past fields of stubble.

Frankie pulled up in a scruffy yard. Rusting farm implements lay abandoned in front of a half-derelict barn, choked with thistles and brambles. A small cottage alongside was not in much better condition: tiles missing from the roof and paint peeling from the shutters. The sun beat down on the dusty ground. There was no sign of life.

'Park around the back of the barn,' said Mrs Jameson. 'No need to advertise our presence.'

We picked our way across the yard, heading for the barn. Mrs Jameson pulled aside the broken timbers of the door. As my eyes adjusted to the gloom, I made out bales of straw, pungent pigeon droppings on the floor, a broken-down cart.

Something long and low, covered with an oilskin cloth, sat in the middle of the barn.

'What are we looking at?' asked Frankie. Then she saw it. 'That looks interesting.' She crossed the floor and whipped off the cover. Beneath was a bright red Bugatti two-seater, gleaming in the scattered light from the dilapidated roof. 'Blimey. What a beauty.'

'Don't touch it,' said Mrs Jameson. She walked carefully around it. 'No signs of blood. It's been washed clean. But there may be fingerprints, or blood stains on the tyres that we can't see.'

'This is the car that hit Antoine?' I crouched down and looked at it head-on. 'I think it might be the one that forced me off the road. It was so quick that I can't be completely sure. But it looks like it.'

'That's interesting,' said Frankie, peering into the cockpit. 'Do you see those bolts? The seat's been adjusted.'

'What is this place?' asked Andrew. 'It doesn't look like anyone lives in the cottage anymore.' He walked to the door and looked out. 'Wait a minute, though. There's someone coming down the lane. I think… yes. It's that Leclerc fellow. The schoolteacher who came to lunch.'

'Dash it,' said Mrs Jameson. 'I suppose we'll have to hide. This is his place now. It belonged to Sophie Leclerc's parents, until her mother died last year. She grew up here.'

Frankie threw the oilskin back over the car. The barn was dim and cluttered, and it wasn't hard to find places to hide. We crouched behind the mouldering bales of straw and waited.

Chapter 36

Marcel Leclerc pushed aside the broken door and came into the barn, breathing heavily. I peeked around the straw. He was dressed in black trousers and a white shirt with the sleeves rolled up, carrying something awkwardly under his arm. A flat oblong parcel tied up in brown paper. He took it over to a wooden manger on the far side of the barn.

M. Leclerc set down his burden and unwrapped something in the manger. Then he put his parcel inside and wrapped it up again. He stretched, massaging his lower back with his hands. He glanced around and I ducked down quickly. There were footsteps, which soon stopped.

I peeked out again. M. Leclerc stood by the car and lifted the corner of the tarpaulin. He looked at the Bugatti for a moment, longing clear on his face, then dropped the cloth. Was he the driver who had forced me off the road and killed Antoine? It seemed unlikely that a schoolteacher could afford such a vehicle on his salary alone.

Finally, with a last lingering look at the car, he left. We waited a few minutes, then Frankie tiptoed to the barn door, looked out and gave us the thumbs-up.

We rushed over to the manger to see what M. Leclerc had hidden there. Mrs Jameson took out the cotton gloves she always kept in her handbag, unwrapped the oilskin cloth and the brown paper, then stood back with a smile.

'There we are,' she said.

It was a painting, unframed, of a pink-and-white nude with bundles of chestnut hair cascading down her back. The woman stretched her arms above her head, against a background of hazy blue sea. There was a squiggly signature in the bottom right corner.

'Another Renoir!' I exclaimed. This must be Sophie Leclerc's mother.

Mrs Jameson lifted it aside. Beneath it was another painting; this one of a serious-looking girl in a white dress reading a book, light dappling her face. A thick braid of chestnut hair hung over her shoulder. The resemblance to Sophie – and the girl in the Renoir painting that Sibyl Trent had been travelling with – was clear.

And beneath that, further down in the manger, was another painting, and another. All of women and girls, in the garden or on the beach. I counted twelve canvasses and remembered what Mrs Jameson had said about the price of the painting Mr Rubin was considering.

'These must be worth…'

'Absolutely nothing.' Mrs Jameson set the paintings back down. 'In monetary terms, at least.'

'But… but they're by Auguste Renoir,' I protested. 'You said yourself, a painting of his sold for ninety thousand francs last year.'

Mrs Jameson smiled, the superior look on her face almost insufferable. 'Indeed. Which is why he has become such a tempting target for forgeries. Do try to keep up, Marjorie.'

'Blimey,' said Frankie, starting to laugh. 'You mean this lot are all fakes?'

Andrew Fraser stared at the pile of paintings. 'All of them? But they're quite good paintings, these. I wouldn't mind one of those on my wall.' He realised he was staring at the glorious nude, and blushed. 'I mean, I like the colours,' he finished, lamely.

I was trying to adjust the reality in my head. 'Antoine?' I said. I remembered the landlady in Villefranche-sur-Mer, pointing out the 'little joke' of the pastiche Antoine had drawn of a Picasso bullfight. Very ingenious, she'd called it. And Hugh had said Antoine's technique was brilliant, but his own paintings were too old-fashioned to sell. 'Did he paint these?'

If he did, then Marcel Leclerc knew. And Sophie, I realised, must have posed for them; at least for the nudes. The two of them must have been in on it. And what about Hugh? Did he know about the forgeries? Cold knowledge seeped into my heart. He did. Of course he did. That's why he'd lied to me about seeing Antoine when we went to Villefranche. He'd wanted to stop me from seeing him, talking to him in his studio. And that day when we'd seen Antoine buying old paintings in the market. Was he using them so that the canvas would not be obviously brand new? If so, Hugh must have realised what was going on.

'They are the work of Antoine Rousseau,' Mrs Jameson agreed. She worked her way to the bottom of the pile in the manger. 'Look. This is his portfolio.'

I stared at the scuffed black cardboard, tied with a frayed black ribbon that had gone green with age. 'He had it with him when he died,' I said. 'The car driver must have taken it after he hit him.' I shuddered. Who would steal from a dying man, and leave him lying in the road?

I shook my head, trying to get things straight. 'So, did Marcel Leclerc kill him? He forced Antoine to make paintings of his wife and offer them for sale as if they were by Renoir? And then for some reason, he decided to kill him. Because he was having an affair with Sophie, I suppose?'

Mrs Jameson gave her maddening smile again. 'The Leclercs said they'd discovered a pile of paintings in the attic of Madame Leclerc's mother's house, remember? Maxim Brunot gave me a telephone number for Jean Renoir in Paris, and I spoke to both him and Claude while you were cooling your heels in Nice police station, Marjorie.

'Claude does recall Sophie Honfleur and her mother visiting Les Collettes, when he was a boy of ten. He remembers thinking Sophie was very pretty. But he says they came two or three times, no more than that. He remembers his father presenting Madame Honfleur with an unfinished painting of her daughter. Renoir thought it wasn't working, but Madame Honfleur liked it. Claude is quite sure they were not given any others. His father didn't often give paintings away, even if he was unhappy with them. It was unusual, which is why he remembers.'

'So, the painting that Mr Rubin was going to buy – the one that Sibyl Trent had on the train…?'

'Fake,' said Mrs Jameson, firmly.

I thought again. Sibyl Trent was an expert. She said she'd authenticated the painting. She must have known that it was not a genuine Renoir. And yet she'd been prepared to take money to say that it was.

'Sibyl knew,' I said, slowly. 'And Antoine knew. And now they're both dead.' Hugh had known as well, which was why he'd fled to London. Maybe that was as well. I shivered. Was that why someone had tried to kill me, and then to frame me for Antoine's death?

'I only wish I had seen it sooner,' said Mrs Jameson, sorrowfully. 'Perhaps those deaths could have been avoided. But, we all see what we want to see in this life. It's very easy to fool someone if you show them what they want to see.'

'Shouldn't the police be here?' asked Andrew. 'I mean, isn't it illegal to make fake paintings?'

'Actually, no. It's not illegal to make copies of paintings, or art in another artist's style.' Mrs Jameson turned her cat-like smile on him. 'But it is illegal to offer them for sale as the real thing. And that's the baited hook we shall use to catch the killer.'

Chapter 37

After Sunday lunch back at the Villa Beau Rivage, Mrs Jameson dismissed Frankie and me for the afternoon.

'I will talk to Mr Rubin, then make a telephone call to Inspector Grignot. I have some suggestions for him, if he can rouse himself from his post-luncheon torpor. Why don't you two relax for a while? I'll need you sharp as needles again tomorrow.'

'Let's go down to the beach,' said Frankie. 'Mrs Smithson sent you a present. We can eat it there.'

I changed quickly into my borrowed bathing costume, picked up a beach towel and my big straw hat. Frankie topped off her swimming suit with a boater. We slumped into deckchairs, took off our shoes and wriggled our toes against the warm stones.

Mrs Smithson, the cook at Bedford Square, had sent a whole Dundee fruitcake, which Frankie had carried ceremoniously down to the beach and carved up with her pen-knife. The rest of the household sent their best wishes, and Jenny the maid had sent me a pile of freshly ironed pocket handkerchiefs. Graham Hargreaves, the butler, had tried to insist on coming with Frankie.

'I had to check the back of the car twice,' reported Frankie, taking an enormous bite of cake. 'I thought he was going to stow away, he was that worried about you when Mrs Jameson wired to say you were in clink.'

'I wish he had come,' I said. 'I've missed you all. How's Sooty?'

Frankie pushed the cake tin towards me. 'Sooty's fine. Although Mrs Smithson says she's been consorting with the ginger tom from next door, and she wouldn't be surprised if there were kittens on the way.'

The familiar taste brought a sharp pang of homesickness for the big house in Bloomsbury, the cosy kitchen downstairs and my own little room up in the attic. Even the London rain was a comforting thought.

'You all right, Marge?' Frankie tipped back her hat to look at me. 'I mean, apart from the night in the cells and the murders and everything.'

Should I confide in her about Hugh? Although I loved her like a sister, we'd never indulged in girl chat. Frankie was five years younger than me, and she wasn't interested in men. But she did know Hugh, who frequented the Caravanserai club in Soho where I had first met Frankie.

'I made a bit of a fool of myself,' I admitted. 'The night of the party, when Sibyl Trent died.'

She nodded encouragement, her mouth full.

'I was with Hugh. Down here, on the beach. He… he kissed me.' I stared at the water lapping the bay. 'And I let him. But now I feel badly about it.'

Frankie burst out laughing, spraying cake crumbs. 'Is that all? If I felt bad about every girl I kissed… never mind. Is that why you're upset he's gone back to London? What did he say about it?'

'He said he wasn't sure what he wanted.' I didn't mention that I'd said the same. 'And then, later, he lied to me. He said he was trying to keep me safe, but I think he's involved in this business with Antoine Rousseau. I feel such a fool.' I also felt guilty about betraying Freddie, who I suspected would not take kisses as lightly as Frankie did.

'Was it nice?'

I swivelled to look at her merry face, rather shocked at the question.

'Go on, Marge. Did you enjoy it?'

I blushed to my hair roots. 'Well, yes. It was very nice. But that's not the point.'

'Good. Don't worry about it, then.' Frankie jumped up. 'Let's swim. Honestly, Marge. You're not the first person to make a fool of themselves over Hugh Williams, I can tell you. Male or female.'

That didn't exactly make me feel better. She splashed me. 'Hugh isn't a bad sort, but he's not reliable. He picks whichever team looks like winning and does whatever is most likely to work to his advantage. I'm sure he didn't mean to hurt your feelings. His sort never does. He just always puts himself first.'

I followed her into the sea, wondering not for the first time how Frankie had managed to acquire so much knowledge of the world in her twenty years, despite barely leaving the East End of London.

Mindful of Miss Braithwaite's dire warnings about swimming on a full stomach, I floated on my back, enjoying the gentle motion of the water and the warmth of the sun, while Frankie swam out to the rocks, clambered out and dived back in.

'Oi, Ben! Are you coming to join us?' she shouted, on

resurfacing.

I looked towards the beach. Benjamin climbed down the spiral staircase in his bathing suit, but seemed dispirited and threw himself down on the pebbles. We came out and sat down next to him.

'What's wrong?' I asked. 'You look a bit glum.'

He kicked moodily at the pebbles. 'I'll need those advanced techniques soon,' he said. 'Nanny Braithwaite says she's going to tell Father that I should go to boarding school in England.'

'Really?' I was surprised, remembering how she had reacted with horror when I'd suggested the boy should be in school.

'She says the boys won't like me. She says they might pretend to, when the masters are around, but they'll get their own back after dark.' He shivered, even though the sun was at its warmest. I flushed with anger.

'She has no right to say any such thing. What on earth does she mean, get their own back?'

Frankie looked uneasy. 'The mean old cat.' She reached for the tin and offered Benjamin the remains of the cake.

He carefully cut a thick slice, then turned his big brown eyes on me. 'Because of what I am. Because of my father. He came from Russia, when he was younger than me, you know. Him and his parents, and his brothers. They were forced out.'

I gazed at his solemn face. 'The Russian pogroms?' I asked. I'd heard the stories: Jewish families massacred, their houses burned to the ground. Thousands of Jews had fled west in the 1890s.

'Nanny Braithwaite says we're lucky that England took us in. But she says nobody likes us because we killed Jesus. She says that Christian boys won't accept me, no matter how rich my father.'

I pulled my towel around me. 'Benjamin, what she says is wicked. We must tell your father. I'm sure he'll be horrified.'

He shook his head. 'She says that she might be able to keep me here a bit longer to protect me, if I'm good. If I keep quiet. Anyway, she's right about the Jew thing. Isn't she? People don't like us.'

Frankie and I exchanged glances. Miss Braithwaite was clearly a monster, to try to scare her charge in such a way. But unfortunately, there were plenty who shared her nasty views.

'Listen, Ben.' Frankie started to build a tower of stones. 'Where I live, in the East End of London, there's all sorts. Lots of Jews, lots of Chinese, Russians and Lascars and blokes from Africa and Malaya and all over. People like me, too. My grandparents came to Limehouse from Ireland. Most of the time, we all get along just fine.'

She took a deep breath. 'When we don't, it's because some rotten politician comes and stirs up trouble. Tries to make out that being poor is all the fault of the Jews, or that there aren't enough jobs because the Chinese have taken them. But we know better. We tell them to push off. That's what you've got to do to Braithwaite. And if you do go to school, I'll make sure you know how to fight, you bet. Like we fight in the East End, when the troublemakers come.' She shoved over the pile of stones.

'Will you really?'

'Hang on, Benjamin.' I was replaying his words in my head, while Frankie made her stirring speech. 'What did you mean about Miss Braithwaite saying you had to keep quiet?'

His face fell again. 'She says I sneak around too much. Hear things I shouldn't hear. See stuff.'

I smiled at him. 'That's pretty much my job, Benjamin. It's

good to be inquisitive, and to notice things. What have you seen that Miss Braithwaite doesn't want you to know about?'

He looked dubious. 'She doesn't know that I saw her. I'm scared that if I tell anyone, she'll have to leave, and I'll be sent away.'

Frankie shook her head. 'Ben, you'll be better off if she goes. Have you talked to your dad about it? He might not even want to send you away to school. But if you've seen something that worries you, you can tell me and Marge.'

I held my breath as the boy looked from one to the other of us, indecision on his face. Then he nodded.

'All right. It was the night of the party. Just before she screamed.'

'You mustn't tell her I told you.'

If it was important, I'd need to tell Mrs Jameson and possibly Inspector Grignot. But I was pretty sure I could promise not to tell Nanny Braithwaite.

'Cross my heart.'

He looked down. 'She came and found me at the party. I was having a nice time, talking to people about interesting things. M. Brunot said he'd show me how to work a kinema camera. And I was telling Mrs Montgomery about learning to play chess. But then Nanny barged in and said it was very late and I had to go to bed.' He grimaced. 'It was embarrassing.'

I smothered a smile. 'What time, Benjamin?' I vaguely remembered seeing him being escorted away while I got lemonade from the refreshment table with Hugh.

'Ten o'clock. Which isn't all that late really. Sometimes the parties here go on until well after midnight,' he said.

'What happened after the Braithwaite woman took you away?' asked Frankie, her voice betraying impatience. I shot her a warning glance. Mrs Jameson had told me never to rush a witness.

'She fussed around in the room for ages, making me brush my teeth and wash my face before I got into my pyjamas.

And then she made me say prayers, which she doesn't usually bother with.'

'Christian prayers?' I asked.

'Yes. She says I should learn them, so I can be converted when I'm older. But I just say the words. I don't think them, if you know what I mean. I don't think my father would like that.'

I wondered if Mr Rubin knew that the nanny had been trying to convert his son to Christianity.

'What next?' asked Frankie.

'She made me get into bed, looked at her watch and turned the light out. Then she went outside.' He looked solemnly between us. 'I was a bit fed up with being treated like a child. I tiptoed to the door and opened it a crack, to see if she'd gone away. I thought I could at least put the lamp back on and read for a while.'

'And had she gone?' I asked.

He shook his head. 'That was the strange thing. She wasn't going downstairs to her room. She was going up the spiral staircase to the tower.'

I thought back to our questioning of Miss Braithwaite. She'd told us she heard something – a gasp or cry – when she left Benjamin's room, then she'd run up to the tower.

'Did you hear anything?'

He shook his head.

'Just her sighing as she went up the stairs. She always says they'll be the death of her. She never goes up if she doesn't have to, which is why it was strange.'

'So, she wasn't running up?'

He chuckled. 'No. She never runs. She had her handbag with her. Halfway up, she stopped and got something out, and then looked at her watch again. She went right up, past where I could see. And a moment later, she screamed like mad.'

'There you are, young man,' said a sharp Yorkshire voice.

Benjamin flinched and looked up guiltily. Miss Braithwaite was crossing the beach, her tread heavy. 'I hope you're not bothering Miss Swallow and…' she gave Frankie a withering look, 'her friend.'

Frankie leaned back in her chair and tipped the brim of the boater so she could see the woman better.

'Ben's not bothering anyone,' she said. 'We're having a nice chat. And we don't want your company.'

The woman stopped dead. Her colour rose until she was puce in the face.

'There's no need for rudeness,' she said. 'I'm in charge of this boy, and I answer to Mr Rubin. I've come to bring him in for his bath.'

'I don't need a bath,' said Ben, rebelliously. Frankie's influence seemed to have rubbed off on him quite fast. 'I'm going to swim. I'll have one later.'

'Now, then. What's got into you, Benjamin?' Nanny Braithwaite wiped sweat from her face, and I saw she was nervous. 'Come with me at once, and don't be a silly boy.'

'He said he'll have one later,' said Frankie. 'Why don't you push off, Nanny? You're not wanted.'

She gasped as if she'd been slapped. 'I won't stand for this. I'll complain to Mr Rubin. Your American employer might let you get away with that sort of insolence, but it's not how we do things in England.'

'But you're not in England.' Frankie smiled up at her lazily. 'And I bet Mr Rubin would like to hear about you trying to convert his son to Christianity and scaring him half to death with your nasty stories. Go on. Shove off back to the house and keep your mouth shut, if you don't want to be out on your lardy arse.'

Miss Braithwaite gaped like a beached haddock for a moment, threw me a reproachful look and stalked back to the stairs. Oh, dear.

Benjamin was staring in fearful delight at Frankie. 'Aren't you scared she'll get you in trouble?' he asked. 'I wouldn't dare talk to her like that.'

'Not me.' Frankie laughed. 'She's a bully, Ben. You won't have any trouble dealing with bullies at school if you learn how to manage Braithwaite. You have to stand up to them, that's all. The minute you do, they lose all their power.'

If only that was true. But I was more interested in what Benjamin had been saying before Miss Braithwaite arrived.

'You said she got something out of her handbag, when she was climbing the stairs,' I said. 'What was it, Ben? Can you remember?'

He frowned. 'Well, that's the strange thing. It was a long white scarf. And then, later, she said she'd found it on the railing in the tower room after Miss Trent fell down. But she took it up there herself.'

I leaned forward. 'Benjamin, that's really important. I promise I won't tell Miss Braithwaite you told us. But I do need to tell Mrs Jameson. Is that all right? You know she's trustworthy, don't you?'

He looked reluctant. 'But she might tell my father.'

'She might.'

'And he might tell Nanny Braithwaite.'

I took a deep breath. 'Ben, this means that everything we thought about Miss Trent's death could be wrong. If Miss

Braithwaite hasn't been telling the truth about it, the whole investigation changes.'

Frankie got to her feet and solemnly placed her boater on Ben's head. 'Come on. Let's tell Mrs Jameson together. Time to face up to the bully, Ben. Don't worry. We'll be with you. Promise.'

Chapter 39

Mrs Jameson paced the sitting room, pausing every few paces to scribble on the sheets of paper pinned to the wall.

'This changes everything,' she said. 'The timeline, for a start. Nobody saw Sibyl Trent fall, remember? I always thought that was odd. No-one on the terrace, no-one on the beach.'

She stopped and crossed out the time of death. 'It wasn't necessarily half past ten. Or at least, we have no proof it was.' She stared at the paper for a moment longer. 'I saw Miss Trent on her own at about ten o'clock, in the lower garden. I assumed she must have gone up to the tower room afterwards without my seeing her.'

I was wondering about the scarf that Ben had seen Miss Braithwaite take from her handbag. How had she got hold of it?

'Miss Trent's scarf came undone when Dulcie Pemberton broke her pearl necklace. She said she was going to the cloakroom to fix herself up. Was she wearing it when you saw her in the garden, Mrs Jameson?'

My employer turned and gazed out of the window, her eyes unfocused as she ran through her memory. 'I'm not sure.' She threw me a sour glance. 'What a pity you were absorbed with your partner, Marjorie. You're usually so good at noticing costume details like that.'

Frankie was sitting on the edge of the table next to Benjamin, both of them swinging their legs. 'If Braithwaite had it, she must have got it before she took Ben to bed,' she observed.

'Which means before Miss Trent went down to the garden,' I added, relieved. 'There you are, Mrs Jameson. She can't have been wearing it.'

'Hmm. Yes, that's true,' Mrs Jameson accepted. 'Perhaps she left it in the cloakroom. Miss Braithwaite might have picked it up there.' She frowned, dissatisfied. 'The question then, of course, is why she did it.'

She turned to the next sheet of paper, which listed our suspects.

Benjamin looked over her shoulder. 'I say! That's my name. Did you think I did it, Mrs Jameson?'

Mrs Jameson laughed. 'Everyone's a suspect, Ben. But no, I didn't think that. You weren't on the terrace when Miss Braithwaite screamed, that's all. I'm afraid that this list gets considerably longer now that the time of death cannot be pinpointed with precision. Many people at the party might have had a chance to slip away at some point between ten and ten-thirty, before we gathered for the speeches.'

I stood at the balcony and looked up at the tower room. 'But they would have had to get up to the tower, past Dulcie's room and Benjamin's nursery. As would Sibyl.'

'It's not a nursery.' Ben's voice was indignant. 'It's my bedroom and study.' He seemed to have grown up about ten years in half an hour.

'I apologise, Benjamin. While you were in your bedroom with Miss Braithwaite, did you hear anyone going up the stairs?' asked Mrs Jameson.

He shook his head decisively. 'No. Although there was quite a lot of noise from the band.'

Mrs Jameson stopped again, this time before the report from the doctor. 'Wait. Marjorie, look at this.' I joined her. 'Cause of death: broken neck. Other injuries: superficial cuts and bruises consistent with a fall.'

She stalked to the window and pointed to the tower. 'How far would you say it is from the tower room to the rocks, Marjorie?'

I gave my best guess. 'About thirty feet?'

'Exactly. Because she was found on the rocks, and because Miss Braithwaite's evidence suggested she'd fallen from the tower, we assumed that was what had happened. But we should have asked more questions.'

She pressed her lips together and shook her head in annoyance. 'It was really very sloppy of me, not to mention of Inspector Grignot. How could a body fall thirty feet from that tower to the rocks and suffer only superficial injuries?'

'But she broke her neck,' I pointed out.

'And there is more than one way for that to happen,' said Mrs Jameson. 'As the murderer will discover, when they are convicted of this rather horrible crime.'

'Blimey,' said Frankie. 'You mean she might not have fallen – or been pushed – from the tower at all? So how come she ended up on the rocks? Whoever did her in couldn't have dragged her body all through the party, could they?'

'Unless she was killed on the beach,' I said, feeling rather sick. Had Sibyl Trent's neck been snapped while Hugh and I were kissing in the shadows?

Mrs Jameson shook her head. 'I saw her in the lower garden after you and Hugh had left the dancefloor,' she said. 'You would have seen Sibyl and anyone with her coming down the iron steps to the beach.' She fixed me with a gimlet eye. 'At least, I assume you would have noticed.'

I flushed. 'I would,' I said quietly.

'What about the tunnels?' asked Benjamin.

We all turned to look at the boy.

'What tunnels?' asked Frankie.

'The smugglers' tunnels,' he said, looking surprised. 'Don't you know about them? They're brilliant. But I'm not supposed to go into them on my own.'

'Of course,' said Mrs Jameson. 'The murderer might have used a tunnel to get the body down to the rocks. Benjamin, you're a genius.'

The boy beamed.

'Have you explored them? Do you know where they go?' she asked.

Andrew Fraser had offered to show us the tunnels, I remembered, when we first arrived at the villa. I'd been feeling too lazy to take him up on his offer. And Eleanor, the girl on the bicycle who had rescued me after the crash, had also said she'd seen the tunnels before the villa was owned by Mr Rubin.

Benjamin jumped up with excitement. 'Some of them. There's one from the lower garden that goes down to the beach. But it's partly blocked at the top, so we don't use it. And one that goes from the terrace down to the lower garden. Do you want me to show you?'

'You bet,' said Frankie. 'Let's go.'

She'd changed into loose khaki trousers and a checked shirt with the sleeves rolled up and looked ready for anything. I looked dubiously down at my blue and green Madras cotton, which was my only remaining decent summer day dress. I didn't really want to get it grubby by scrambling around dusty old tunnels.

'I'll change into my travelling clothes,' I said. The thought of putting on woollen tweed in this weather was unpleasant, but I had nothing else.

'Don't do that. You'll broil yourself. Why don't I lend you a pair of overalls?' suggested Frankie. 'Save you messing up your nice clothes.'

'Good idea,' said Mrs Jameson. 'I think I'll leave you to it. I'm not built for squeezing through narrow tunnels any more. And I must speak to Inspector Grignot again. He needs to know about Hettie Braithwaite's duplicity.'

Narrow tunnels. I swallowed. I'd forgotten my dislike of being in enclosed spaces. Heights, I could manage. Spiders didn't bother me. But narrow tunnels made my mouth dry and my heart speed up. Oh, well. I was going with Frankie. She wouldn't let me get stuck.

Chapter 40

'Are you all right, Marge?'

I closed my eyes in the darkness and tried not to panic. 'I think I'm stuck.'

We had begun on the beach, to investigate the tunnel that led up to the lower garden. Tucked next to the jagged rocky outcrop where Hugh and I had found Sibyl's body was a narrow metal grate, not quite as tall as a man. It was across the entrance to a set of worn steps cut into the rock, a padlock holding it in place.

Before Frankie could unlock it with a set of picks she pulled from her canvas roll of tools, I examined the padlock. It was rusty, stiff and gave no signs of being used recently. I stood back and let her do her work. We'd once spent an entertaining afternoon in the Bedford Mews garage while she taught me to pick locks. I had got the hang of it, but she was quicker. I didn't like to ask where she'd acquired the skill.

The stairs were slimy with weed and worn shallow in the middle from footsteps. They twisted around in a spiral, the wall side oozing moisture, so narrow that I had to turn my shoulders at an angle to pass. Before we set off, I'd checked for footprints or scrapes on the wall, anything to indicate that someone had used the staircase recently. There was nothing of note.

Benjamin scampered up first, gleeful to be taking a lead role in the investigation. Frankie followed him, equally enthusiastic about the adventure. I brought up the rear. Until we got to the top of the steps, where the passage took a sharp turn to the left.

'You're almost there,' called Frankie. 'Can't you see the light?'

I couldn't see anything, although I could hear her voice clearly enough. I'd ducked my head down to avoid the low ceiling, stumbling over a pile of broken rocks and bricks making the passage even tighter. My left shoulder was pressed against the damp rock, my right shoulder twisted behind me. Benjamin and Frankie, unencumbered by bosoms, had slipped through the tight spot easily. Unfortunately, my unfashionably curvy bust had me wedged in place. I tried to calm my breathing. Every time I inhaled, it felt as if the walls were pressing closer in on me.

'I think I'm going to have to go back,' I said, trying to keep the panic out of my voice. I braced my feet on the rubble and tried to back myself into the corner where the passage turned. I whimpered, feeling the baggy overalls snag on the rocks.

'Take it slowly,' said Frankie. 'You got in. That means you can get out again.'

My sweaty fingers smoothed down the creases in the overalls. I could do this. I pressed my shoulder to the wall and eased my hips backwards. An inch or two of space opened up. Thank goodness. I gasped as I almost lost my footing on the rough ground and slammed my hand into the wall to steady myself. Then I was in the corner at the top of the steps.

My relief was tempered by the realisation that I now had to go down the treacherous spiral staircase. Without room to turn around I'd need to do it backwards. The stairs were slippery. I licked my dry lips and began, one step at a time.

I had never been so pleased to see daylight as when I emerged from the bottom of the stairs on the beach. Frankie and Benjamin were waiting for me. I felt idiotic, having failed to make it through when they had both managed with ease.

'Well done,' said Benjamin, kindly. 'That blocked passage at the end is quite difficult for adults.'

'Lucky you wore those overalls,' said Frankie. I looked down. I was smeared from top to toe with gunge from the slimy tunnel walls. I rubbed my cheek and saw green slime on my fingers.

'Ugh. Sorry to have made such a mess of them.'

We went back up the wrought iron steps from the beach to the lower garden, where we examined the narrow passage into the rocks that I'd failed to get through. It was half-hidden behind a gazebo covered in white roses, which explained why I had not noticed it before. I had been very close to getting out, but the pile of rocks in the entrance had made it impassable to all but the very skinny.

'I don't think you could get down there carrying a body,' I said. Miss Trent had been taller than me and would probably have had difficulty in making the passage under her own steam. Even if her assailant had been small and wiry, I could not see how they would have managed to drag her down there with them.

I thought of our suspects. Andrew Fraser would have had trouble, with his broad shoulders. Ashton, too. Marcel Leclerc was skinny, but was he strong enough to carry a body? Nanny Braithwaite was too heavily built. Dulcie Pemberton was tall, but perhaps slim enough to have slipped through.

'Have you been down here with Andrew?' I asked Ben.

'Not for ages. We went over the tunnels when he first came to stay. He said it was a tight fit, but I don't think the rocks had fallen down then.'

'Where does this go?' asked Frankie. She was standing to the right of the gazebo at the end of the garden, holding aside a curtain of jasmine that cascaded down the wall from the terrace above. Behind it, a green-painted wooden door hung askew on its hinges. My heart sank. I wasn't sure I was ready to explore another tunnel.

'It's my den,' said Benjamin solemnly, pushing the door open. 'I think it used to be a storeroom for the smugglers. It's sort of my secret place, when I want to be on my own. And there's a ladder through a tunnel up to the terrace. You can come inside if you like.'

We followed him in.

'This is fantastic,' said Frankie. The storeroom was an uneven circle, like a room in a lighthouse. Someone had laid wooden planks across the rock floor and around the walls, so it was dry and snug.

Benjamin lit an oil lamp hanging from a hook in the middle of the low ceiling, illuminating a rather good rug and an old rocking horse, packing crates made into a table and stools, and an old sea chest.

'This was here when we moved in,' he said, throwing the lid open. 'I thought it might be full of smugglers' treasure, but it just had a load of empty bottles in it.' It was now full of other treasure: much-read copies of *The Champion* and *Boy's Own* comics; a glass jar of aniseed balls; several veteran conkers, pierced and threaded with boot laces; and a wooden chess set.

'What's that?' I knelt down. Something shiny glinted in

the light of the oil lamp, wedged between two floorboards. I took a pencil from the breast pocket of Frankie's overalls and wiggled it free.

'A pearl,' said Benjamin, excited. 'So there really is treasure here.'

I stared at the round bead lying in the palm of my hand.

'Not that sort of treasure,' I said. I straightened up. 'I think that's one of the pearls that Sibyl Trent was wearing on the night of the party. Her necklace broke.'

If the pearl had found its way into the storeroom, then so had Sibyl Trent. Or her body.

'Let's go up the ladder,' Frankie suggested. 'See where it comes out on the terrace.'

Thankfully the wooden stepladder in the corner of the room was in decent repair. It looked as if it had been replaced relatively recently. Frankie climbed up first and pushed open the trap-door at the top.

'What can you see?' I asked.

'Nothing. It's dark.'

'It comes out in the tool shed,' said Benjamin. 'You have to open the door.'

I heard clattering and crashing, and Frankie swore.

'Sorry,' she called back down. 'Ben, you're not to use that word, d'you hear? Unless you really need to.'

Light showed through the trap door, and we followed her up.

'Are you all right?'

She showed me a bloodied thumb. 'Caught it in the hinge of the door. Blooming thing.'

'Ouch. You should wash it and get it dressed,' I said. 'I'm sure Nanny Braithwaite will be happy to help with a spot of iodine.'

'I bet she would,' said Frankie. She put the thumb in her mouth and sucked it. 'Maybe I'll go to the kitchen and see if they've got something to bandage it up with. Won't be a tick.'

She headed for the house. I looked around. The shed contained the usual garden tools: trowels, secateurs, piles of terracotta plant pots and balls of twine. Benjamin and I stepped outside. A bougainvillea-smothered trellis shielded the shed from the rest of the terrace, a bright pink curtain.

I reconstructed the night of the party in my mind's eye. The refreshment table had been on the far side of the terrace, by the stairs to the lower garden. The band had set up between the trellis and the house. There were tables and chairs around the terrace, and the dancefloor was in the centre. If you had wished to slip into the tool shed unnoticed, it would not have been difficult. And the band would have masked any noise, I supposed.

'Do you really think Nanny Braithwaite murdered Miss Trent?' asked Benjamin.

'What? No. No, sorry, Ben. I didn't explain properly. I think that she lied about what she saw, though. To cover up for someone.'

'Why?'

That was a very good question. Mrs Jameson thought she'd been paid to lie, and intended to ask the police to investigate her finances. Perhaps she had not even known, at first, what her lie was intended to cover up.

'I don't know yet. Why do people do things they shouldn't?'

He took the question seriously, looking out over the sea. 'Sometimes people steal things, because they're poor or hungry,' he said. 'Or they say horrible things because they haven't been brought up properly and don't know not to. And Father says sometimes people are just jealous, or ignorant.'

'True.' I leaned on the terrace next to him. 'Sometimes people are rude about me, because my father's a shop-keeper and I used to work in the shop. And sometimes they think I'm stupid, because I'm a girl.'

He laughed. 'You're not like a normal girl, though. Nor is Frankie.'

'Ah, but maybe this is what some girls are like,' I said. 'Mrs Jameson isn't stupid. Nor was Sibyl Trent.'

He turned to look at me. 'They're grown-ups, though,' he said. 'Do you really think my father will marry Dulcie Pemberton?'

The change of subject took me by surprise. 'I don't know. Do you?'

He sighed. 'I hope not. I don't think she likes me much. She's pretty, but she isn't very nice. I think she should marry Andrew Fraser, don't you? I like Andrew.'

I smiled. 'Maybe she will.' I took out the pearl from my pocket. 'I'd like to look at your little room again, Ben. But maybe I should show this to Mrs Jameson. Keep it somewhere safe.'

'All right. I'll meet you down there. I'm going to look for more pearls.'

Chapter 41

I crossed the terrace, clutching the pearl in my hand. Mrs Jameson had seen Sibyl Trent alone in the lower garden on the night of the party, at about ten o'clock. What if she'd gone to Benjamin's little room, or met someone there? A struggle, the pearls spilling from her pocket onto the ground, one lodging in the crack between the boards.

But then we were back to the same difficulty – how did her body get from there to the rocks above the beach?

As I reached the hall, I heard heavy footsteps descending the staircase from the first floor, past Mrs Jameson's sitting room. Miss Braithwaite, in her unflattering beige uniform, clumped down and stood foursquare in the middle of the hall, staring with venom towards the kitchen, where I could hear Frankie's voice among peals of laughter from the kitchen staff. I shivered. Frankie had been incredibly rude, but Miss Braithwaite had undoubtedly deserved it. She looked up, saw me and continued unsmiling towards the terrace.

I ran quickly up to the sitting room and burst through the door.

'We found this, in a crack in the floor,' I said, holding out the pearl.

'Bonjour, Mademoiselle Swallow.' Inspector Grignot rose

politely from his chair.

'Oh! Hello, Inspector. I didn't know you were here.'

I remembered that I was still wearing Frankie's overalls and covered in grime. Oh dear. The last time I'd seen the inspector, I was grubby from a night in the cells. I wasn't doing much to improve his impression of Englishwomen's dress sense.

'There you are, Marjorie,' said Mrs Jameson. 'Goodness, you look like you've been down a coalmine. Inspector Grignot has been good enough to interrupt his day of rest and visit us. I telephoned to tell him about our discovery of the cache of paintings in Cagnes-sur-Mer, and I've been bringing him up to date about young Benjamin's revelations.'

'I will ask Miss Braithwaite to accompany me to the police station,' said Inspector Grignot. 'It is most serious, what she has done. The whole investigation is now changed. We shall have to begin again.'

Mr Rubin, who had been standing by the balcony, turned with a sad smile. 'I must thank you, Miss Swallow. You have done me a great favour by learning what my son was suffering. I was very shocked to learn of Miss Braithwaite's behaviour.'

Behind him, I saw the nanny cross the terrace and head for the steps down to the lower garden. I frowned. Where was she going? Benjamin was still in his den, and Frankie was in the kitchen. I felt uneasy. Had Miss Braithwaite overheard the conversation between Mrs Jameson and the inspector?

'I'm just glad he trusted me,' I said. I saw Mr Rubin flinch slightly and wished I'd been more tactful. 'I mean, he obviously trusted you, but he was afraid to say what was happening because of Miss Braithwaite's threats.'

He'd trusted Frankie and me when we'd told him we would support him and face the bully together. And now we'd left him on his own.

'Perhaps I should be getting back,' I began.

'Tell us what you've found,' commanded Mrs Jameson. Quickly I gave her the pearl and explained where we had found it.

'So I thought perhaps Miss Trent was in the storeroom after you saw her in the garden,' I said. 'She might even have been killed there.'

She took it and balanced it meditatively on her palm. 'Yes. Yes, you could be right. I'd like to see this room. Shall we go down?'

We walked down the stairs and crossed the terrace. As we reached the top of the steps, I heard Miss Braithwaite's sharp tones from the lower garden.

'No-one will believe you,' she said. 'Remember what I told you about school. I won't be able to protect you there.'

'I'm not afraid of school. And I'm not afraid of you any more.' Benjamin's voice was high-pitched but clear. 'I'm going to tell the police.' Oh, goodness. He'd decided to confront her himself.

'You don't know what you saw. You were tired and half-asleep.' Miss Braithwaite sounded scornful, but not as confident as usual.

I started forward, but Mrs Jameson grabbed my arm and put her finger to her lips. We stood silently above, watching. Miss Braithwaite had her hands on her hips, confronting Benjamin like a wrestler.

'It was very naughty of you to creep around spying on me, but let's say no more about it,' she said. 'You didn't understand what you saw. You'll only muddle the police if you tell them some silly story now. They might put you in prison, like they did that Miss Swallow. How would you like that, hmm?'

He shook his head. 'They won't,' he said. 'But I reckon they'll put you in prison for telling fibs.'

'You are a very naughty boy,' said Miss Braithwaite, grabbing him by both arms. 'I've a mind to give you what's coming to you.'

Ben took a step back, put his foot outside her ankle and pulled the nanny off-balance. She crashed to the ground, her weight taking her down in a textbook illustration of a jiu-jitsu ankle block. She shrieked.

'Oh, well done,' I cried. Frankie, who'd arrived on the terrace just in time to witness it, whooped.

Inspector Grignot, moving faster than he had given any indication of being capable of so far, shot down the steps and hauled the woman to her feet. 'I am arresting you for obstructing a police investigation,' he informed her. 'And for threatening a witness.' He made a small bow. 'Thank you for your assistance, Master Rubin. I will be back to take your statement shortly.'

Benjamin was grinning from ear to ear. His father took him by the shoulders.

'I am very proud of you,' said Mr Rubin, tears in his eyes. 'And I will never let you get into the hands of a woman like that again.'

Chapter 42

Inspector Grignot returned after dinner. Mrs Jameson, Mr Rubin, and I were already gathered in Mrs Jameson's sitting room, watching the sun descend in a glory of pink and gold over the Bay of Nice. The inspector accepted a large brandy and sank into a chintz armchair, closing his eyes.

'*Ouf*! That Mademoiselle Braithwaite, she is not *sympathique*,' he complained. 'I have had to put her in a cell by herself. I would have a riot on my hands if I imposed her on the ladies commonly accommodated in the custody wing.'

'Her arrest must be kept very quiet,' urged Mrs Jameson, anxious. 'We cannot let news of it reach the murderer.'

The inspector opened his eyes and spread his hands. 'I am not an imbecile, Mrs Jameson. I have interviewed her myself. She maintains her innocence, and says her charge is known for lying.' He saw Mr Rubin start forward and raised a placatory palm. 'Which I am sure is not correct. The gendarmes at the police station have been told she is being held for cruelty to a child. Having met her, they do not find that difficult to believe.'

Mrs Jameson laughed. 'You will give English nannies a bad name, Inspector. Now, we have more news for you. The maid found this, under Miss Braithwaite's mattress.' She handed over a brown paper parcel, wrapped around with string.

The inspector raised an eyebrow and untied it. Inside, a large pile of French bank notes. He began to count, and whistled. 'Perhaps that explains Miss Braithwaite's motive,' he said. 'I will ask her to explain how she amassed such a pile of French money. I am sure you are a generous employer, Mr Rubin, but I would be surprised if she had been able to make such savings in the three years you have lived in France.'

Mrs Jameson took a sip of brandy. 'The question is, how do we proceed with the new evidence? I have sent a telegram to Inspector Chadwick of the Metropolitan Police. He will track down Mr Williams, an important witness to the forgeries, who we believe to be in London.'

Feeling rather mortified, I had helped Mrs Jameson give details of anything that might help find Hugh in London. If, indeed, that was where he was. I only hoped he would co-operate with the police if they found him.

'And in the morning,' continued Mrs Jameson, 'I suggest Marjorie and I pay a quiet visit to Haut de Cagnes. We need to know what role the Leclerc family has played in this affair.'

'Is it safe?' asked Mr Rubin. 'I don't want you putting yourselves in danger, Iris.'

'I will send a police constable to drive you,' said the inspector. 'Don't worry. We can be discreet, I assure you. And there is less danger of your car being recognised.'

He swirled the remains of his brandy around, then put down his glass. 'And on a related matter, Miss Swallow, I am pleased to inform you that all charges against you have been dropped. We have traced the anonymous telephone call that reported the Morgan on the day M. Rousseau was killed. It was not, shall we say, a reliable source.'

That was a relief. But I was still nervous about the trip to

Cagnes. What if M. Leclerc had learned about our previous visit to his wife?

'What else?' said Mrs Jameson. 'We have the letter that Sibyl Trent wrote asking for money.'

'And my colleagues in Paris have been most patient with Henri Lejaby,' added Inspector Grignot. 'He has confirmed, as far as he can remember, the version of events that Mademoiselle Swallow learned about in…'

'In your police cell,' I finished, with asperity. 'Thank you for reminding me.'

Mrs Jameson tapped her chin meditatively. 'Then I believe we have all that we need to proceed. Inspector, will you indulge me in arranging a little theatre tomorrow afternoon? I believe it will tell us what we need to know.'

Chapter 43

Inspector Grignot arrived early on Monday to direct operations from Villa Beau Rivage. Policemen were sent quietly to the farmhouse outside Cagnes to make an inventory of the paintings. Mrs Jameson and I made our discreet visit to Haut de Cagnes, where Sophie Leclerc was inconsolable over M. Rousseau's death, and considerably more forthcoming than she had been on our previous visit. To my relief, her husband was again absent. The pieces were falling into place for Mrs Jameson's plan.

On our return to the villa, Inspector Grignot greeted us with a grin, waving a piece of paper. 'A communication from the Metropolitan Police,' he said. 'I believe this is the last piece of the puzzle.'

At lunchtime, Mr Rubin made a telephone call to the Galerie Anglaise. He was planning to return to London tomorrow for some months, he said. Would Mr Montgomery be good enough to bring the Renoir to the villa this afternoon, so he could make a final decision and arrange the purchase before he left the country? And, if Mr Montgomery wished, perhaps he could bring any other Renoir paintings that he might have for sale.

He replaced the receiver. 'All's well. He will be here at three.

Now, where do you want us, Iris?'

At ten to three, I was in the lower garden, trying to remember how to play chess. Ben had refused point-blank to go to his room. He had become quite assertive in the last couple of days. I wondered if I should apologise to Mr Rubin for Frankie's influence.

I heard a car, and Andrew went through to open the garage.

'Park in here,' I heard him call. 'It's safer than leaving it outside on the street.'

Lois Montgomery sauntered through the green door in a white tennis dress and green cardigan, white Oxfords laced on her feet. 'Good afternoon.' She held out her hand to Mr Rubin and smiled warmly at Mrs Jameson. 'Please excuse the casual outfit. I'm on my way to the tennis club. Ashton will drop me off after you've concluded your business.'

She came down to sit with us in the garden. 'Hello, Benjamin. How's the chess going?'

Ben looked up with a smile. 'I think I'm winning,' he said.

'He certainly is,' I said. 'I haven't played for years. You should take over, Lois.' I felt rather sorry for her. There would be no tennis club that afternoon, or possibly ever again. If her husband was arrested, she would become a social pariah. She took my place and I sat back to watch.

Ashton Montgomery had followed his wife from the garage. He and Andrew carried three packages wrapped in brown paper.

'Where shall we put them?' he asked. 'I brought you all I have. I wouldn't usually offer more than one at a time, but I know you plan to be out of the country for a while, Mr Rubin.'

Mr Rubin bustled forward. 'Yes, indeed. Most kind. Please, put them on the table here, in the shade of the pergola. Now, can I offer you some refreshment?'

Mr Rubin looked remarkably cool. I supposed he would need good nerves, to make such a success in the diamond business.

The preliminaries over, they began to unwrap the paintings.

'This is the one that Sibyl Trent brought back from Paris?' Mrs Jameson leaned over the table.

'That's right. The one I showed you in the gallery, Mr Rubin.'

'Very nice. Very nice indeed,' he said, his voice steady. 'And this is the painting Renoir made of Madame Leclerc as a child, yes?'

'That's right. And I thought you would like to see this, of Madame Leclerc's mother, Madame Honfleur,' said Ashton. 'It really is superb. Part of Renoir's neo-classical period, as you can see.'

'When would you say this was painted?' asked Mrs Jameson.

'It's not dated. From Madame Leclerc's memories, it would be 1910 or 1911, which fits with the style,' said Ashton.

'She really does take after her mother, doesn't she?' said Mrs Jameson, impishly. 'You would almost think it was a portrait of Sophie Leclerc herself.'

They all laughed, Ashton's voice the loudest.

Lois glanced up from the chess board with a smile. 'You've got me there, Ben. You're good at this, aren't you?'

Ben took her bishop with glee.

'One more,' said Ashton. 'Here we are. Another painting of Sophie, as a girl of twelve, reading a book. Children reading was a common theme of Renoir in his later years. There's a lovely painting of his son Claude reading, done at about the same time.'

'Dear me, yes. Very nice.' Mr Rubin extracted a small

instrument from his pocket, put it to his eye and bent to examine the painting more closely.

'And, to be completely clear,' said Mrs Jameson, raising her voice so we could hear every syllable, 'all three of these paintings are being sold as genuine paintings by Auguste Renoir? And they will be authenticated as such?'

'Yes, of course,' said Mr Montgomery. 'As you know, Miss Trent has already prepared the certificate of authentication for the first.' He paused. 'I will arrange for the others to be certified too. But I wanted Mr Rubin to have a chance to buy them, before I showed other collectors.'

'Very kind,' said Mr Rubin.

'I can offer the three of them together, at a very reasonable price of one hundred thousand francs,' said Ashton. 'Bear in mind what his paintings are selling for now, Mr Rubin. I promise, you won't have such an opportunity again.'

I craned my neck to watch what happened next.

'I certainly hope not,' said Mrs Jameson sharply. 'Mr Montgomery, these paintings are not by Auguste Renoir. I spoke to his son Claude, and he is sure of it. His father gave only one painting to Madame Honfleur, of her daughter. You sold that last year.'

Lois Montgomery froze, a chess piece in her hand, and looked up at her husband in alarm.

'Nonsense!' said Ashton. 'Claude was just a child at the time. He wouldn't remember. Sophie Leclerc will tell you...'

Mrs Jameson's voice was like ice. 'I visited Sophie Leclerc this morning. She is distraught about the death of Antoine Rousseau, who painted these pictures and who had become her lover,' she said.

Her words dropped into a sudden cold silence. Lois

Montgomery replaced the chess piece she was holding, and got to her feet, her cheeks flushed.

'But that's terrible!' she cried. 'If these paintings are not by Renoir, then my husband has been defrauded by the Leclerc family. Haven't you, darling?'

'Madame Leclerc told us many things,' continued Mrs Jameson, as if Lois had not spoken. 'That her husband approached you, Mr Montgomery, for help in selling their one genuine Renoir, last year. And that the money you made from that was not enough for you. So you dispatched M. Rousseau to make more paintings of Madame Leclerc, much to her delight. She agreed to go along with the fable. She is young, romantic and bored with her life as a provincial schoolteacher's wife. She fell in love with the artist.'

Ashton pulled at his collar. 'You have it all wrong,' he said. 'The paintings are genuine. And I think you forget that this painting was authenticated by an expert from the Hôtel Drouot.'

'Ah, yes. Your old acquaintance, Miss Trent. She authenticated the first, genuine, painting,' said Mrs Jameson, crisply. 'And then, because she was in dire need of money, she agreed to do the same for the others, despite it being clear to her that they were not genuine. However, she was not prepared to go on with this arrangement unless you increased her share of the proceeds of this crime, Mr Montgomery. And the secret she threatened to reveal, as is now clear, was that the paintings are faked.'

'Nonsense. I was doing her a favour, because she once meant something to me.'

'She meant nothing to you,' said Mrs Jameson. 'Indeed, we now know that your story about an affair with her was untrue.

She was useful to you, until she began to make threats. And that's when you tried to scare her off, Mr Montgomery. A low trick, to send a man to frighten a woman travelling alone on the Blue Train.'

I watched Lois Montgomery's freckled face, as she gazed in dismay from Mrs Jameson to her husband. 'Oh, Ashton…' she murmured.

'Finally, the Metropolitan Police have located the letter that you gave to Mr Williams for Antoine Rousseau.' Mrs Jameson was relentless. 'The scribbled note, which offers him an additional three hundred francs for each so-called Renoir painting, to guarantee his silence. I think that should stand up in a court of law, don't you?'

'It's not true,' he shouted. 'Tell them, Lois!'

Lois Montgomery was staring at her husband in horror. 'Tell them what? I don't know what to believe. You promised me… you said we'd be properly established, once you'd made these sales. You said you'd re-make our fortune. If I'd known you were doing it by fakery… how could you?' She shuddered and turned away, pressing a very clean handkerchief to her eyes.

Ashton stared at her for a moment, then turned and ran for the garage. Inspector Grignot emerged promptly from the garden shed. He had objected strongly to such an undignified hiding place but had to admit it provided the perfect cover. He was at the garage door almost before his prey had reached it, and seized him by the arm.

'Mr Montgomery, I have listened to you offering for sale three paintings which you claim to be by Auguste Renoir, despite knowing they are forgeries,' he said in his precise English. 'Therefore, I am arresting you for attempted fraud.

Please, do not make any further attempts to leave the premises.'

Chapter 44

'Miss Swallow,' muttered Lois, swaying. 'Could I trouble you for a glass of water?'

She looked as if she was about to faint, her face white as a sheet beneath her freckles. I helped her into a deckchair and ran up the steps to the terrace. Halfway to the kitchen I met the maid, Marie, and asked her to bring a jug of water and glass.

On the terrace, Ashton was handcuffed to the inspector. But Mrs Jameson had not finished with him yet.

'Miss Trent got the message, that night on the Blue Train,' she said. 'She realised you were threatening her. But it didn't have the effect you had hoped, and you could not risk her growing discomfort – not when fake paintings had already been sold to other collectors and you had so much invested in the scheme.

'When she threatened to tell Mr Rubin, you killed her. And when Antoine Rousseau, increasingly desperate and unstable, looked as if he might give the game away, you murdered him, too.'

Ashton gazed around wildly like a cornered fighter. 'Absolute nonsense,' he said. 'How dare you? Mr Rubin, is this some kind of joke? You were here with me when poor Sibyl died.

We were standing right here on the terrace when she fell from the tower.'

Mrs Jameson rose. 'Except, of course, she did not fall from the tower. Mr Montgomery, when you came for luncheon last week, you said you were familiar with the house, having visited its previous owner. Presumably he showed you the tunnels. Including the one from this terrace, which leads down to the hidden storeroom that opens onto the garden below.'

Ashton's gaze flicked quickly to the garden shed, which housed the tunnel. He knew it, all right.

'At ten o'clock, you descended by that tunnel, unseen, having suggested Miss Trent join you in the lower garden for a tête-à-tête. You took her into the hidden room, where you broke her neck. There must have been a struggle, since we have found one of the beads from her necklace in the room. You then somehow pushed her body over the garden wall onto the rocks, before heading back up the ladder to the terrace and joining Mr Rubin for the speeches.'

'That's not true,' he said. 'Miss Braithwaite saw her fall. She found her scarf.'

'Yes, that was your plan,' said Mrs Jameson. 'Fortunately, Miss Braithwaite's testimony has been challenged by a most astute witness. Mr Rubin's son saw her take the scarf up to the tower room herself. Miss Braithwaite lied, Mr Montgomery. How much did you pay her for that falsehood?'

At this, Ashton seemed to slump. He opened his mouth, then shut it again.

'No,' he said, but his voice lacked conviction. 'It can't be.'

'Come with me, Mr Montgomery,' said Inspector Grignot. 'We shall continue this interview at the police station.'

'Where do you want the water, Miss Swallow?' Marie

emerged from the kitchen with a jug and glasses on a tray.

'Please take it to the lower garden. Mrs Montgomery is feeling unwell.'

I realised I'd left Benjamin alone. I went to the edge of the terrace, but couldn't see him, or Lois. Her deckchair was empty, the chess board abandoned. There was no-one on the beach. Where had they gone? I had a sudden rush of panic.

There was only one place they could be – Benjamin's little room.

I opened the door to the tool shed, quietly lifted the trap door and listened.

'How exciting,' said Lois, her voice inviting. 'You're very clever to have found it.'

I looked down, but I couldn't see anyone in the wood-lined room. Odd. I could hear the voices, although they sounded a bit distant.

'You're the first person I've shown,' said Ben. 'I was worried people would stop me from coming here. Are you feeling better now you're out of the sun?'

'Oh, much better. Isn't it a long way down to the rocks?'

I was down the ladder in a moment, fear mounting in my chest. I looked around the empty room, then checked outside. Marie was carefully placing the tray on a table beside the fountain. Back in the room, I saw that some of the planks lining the walls were outlined with light. Indeed, they were not planks, but a door.

I pulled it open and passed through the gap into another hidden tunnel. I fought down panic that I'd get stuck again. This tunnel was short. I could see light, afternoon sunshine and a glimpse of vivid blue sea. I quickly emerged onto a rocky ledge cut into the surface of the cliff. The light dazzled me for a second. And then I saw.

Lois Montgomery had hold of Benjamin's arm and was forcing him closer to the edge. Directly below us was the sea, and the black rocks on which Sibyl Trent's body had been found.

Ben half-turned, trying to get away from her, and saw me. I saw his face light up in relief and he darted forward. Too late. Lois's strong arms shoved him hard, and he fell, screaming, his limbs flailing at thin air.

Chapter 45

I rushed to the edge of the cliff. Lois turned and saw me, her eyes widening in dismay.

'He fell,' she said. 'I'll get help.' She pushed past me into the passage and I let her go.

Benjamin hit the blue water and disappeared. Not the rocks. That was something. But he hadn't resurfaced.

I took a deep breath. It was a long drop, and I'd have to avoid landing on the jagged black rocks. My swimming lessons had not progressed to diving. But there was no question in my mind as to what I was going to do. I kicked off my shoes and stared at the azure sea, as close as I could to the point where Benjamin had landed.

My stomach stayed behind on the ledge as I plummeted through the air, trying to mimic the way that Frankie had dived from the rocks. The shock of the cold water hit me hard, thumping into my arms which I'd instinctively wrapped around my head. Then I was deep underwater, going down through the waves, down and down. Finally my descent slowed and my hand touched something solid. Rock. I pushed against it, wriggled up and kicked hard.

I felt as if I was miles underwater. I mustn't panic, I told myself. I mustn't breathe in. I must hold on. But I wasn't sure I could hold my breath much longer. My head started to hurt, and I battled not to open my mouth to scream. At last, I broke the surface, gasping and spluttering against the flurry of waves.

I'd survived. But where was Benjamin? I tried to scan the surface of the water, surprised how difficult it was to see more than a yard or two as the waves broke around me. I took a breath and put my head back under the surface, forcing my eyes open, although the salt stung. Maybe I could see further under the water.

Something… something was drifting in the water, not far away. I kicked towards it, using the rudimentary breaststroke Mrs Jameson had taught me. I stretched out my arms and felt something solid, an arm or leg. I flipped onto my back, gasping for air again, and pushed the water out of my eyes.

Benjamin lay face down in the water. His arms and legs were floating, but he wasn't moving. I seized his shoulders and heaved until he turned onto his back in the water.

'Ben! Can you hear me?'

He was limp. I moved behind him, so I was holding his head and shoulders out of the water. 'Come on, Ben.' I squeezed him around the belly, and water poured from his mouth in a frightening way. I wondered how long I could keep the two of us afloat, feeling the weight of him pulling me down. I squeezed again, trying to shock his lungs back into use.

This time he coughed. 'Oh, thank God,' I gasped in relief. 'Thank you.' A wave broke over his shoulder and hit me in the face. I spluttered, swallowed salt water and began to choke. My arms slipped and Benjamin drifted away from me. I tried to hold onto him, keep him with me, but my strength was almost finished. He coughed again.

Two sleek forms sliced through the water. One seized Benjamin's shoulders and began to swim him back to the shore. The other put her hands under my arms and held me up.

'All right, Marjorie. Well done, dear. You're safe now.'

Mrs Jameson's grey eyes locked onto mine as I retched salt water and regained my breath. 'That was the bravest thing I've seen anyone do,' she said. 'And I've seen a lot. Hold onto me until you're ready, and we can swim back to the beach together.'

By the time we reached the shore, Benjamin was sitting wrapped in a towel, shivering like a whippet. Mr Rubin sat next to him, his arms tight around his son, tears coursing down his cheeks. Frankie crouched next to them, her clothes soaked through. A couple of maids were hovering, their hands full of towels. Marie had brought down the jug of water and glasses.

Frankie gave me a rather wobbly smile.

'Blimey, Marge. I'd have taught you to dive properly if I knew you were going to go straight for the top board. We saw you from the terrace. I thought you were a goner.'

I collapsed on the beach, heedless of my soggy frock. One of the maids draped a towel around my shoulders.

'Is Ben going to be all right?' I asked.

'Yes,' Benjamin croaked.

Relief overwhelmed me and I started to sob.

Mr Rubin looked up, wiping away his own tears. 'I have telephoned for a doctor to be sure. I am in your debt more than ever, Marjorie. Thank you, from the bottom of my heart. Thank goodness you saw him fall.'

I stared at him. 'But he didn't fall, Mr Rubin. Lois Montgomery pushed him. Didn't she, Ben? I saw her. Where is she now?'

Mrs Jameson, who had wrapped herself in a towel and was twisting a second into a turban on top of her head, looked up.

'What? Good grief. We must stop her. Where's the inspector?'

She charged up the spiral stairs to the garden, with Frankie and me close behind. My head still hurt, and my arms and legs felt heavy as lead. But I wasn't going to let Lois get away.

Chapter 46

On the terrace, all was confusion. Inspector Grignot and his sergeant had taken Ashton Montgomery away in the small black Renault. Lois Montgomery was nowhere to be seen – and nor was Ashton's car.

'She said she had to follow them to the police station,' reported the housekeeper. 'She drove off rather quickly, towards Nice.'

We scrambled for the Lagonda. The Montgomeries had arrived in a black Citröen Torpedo, which despite its name was not a particularly fast car.

'We'll catch her,' Frankie vowed.

'Where's she going?' I asked Mrs Jameson. 'Not to the gallery?'

She shook her head. 'The Leclercs' smallholding at Cagnes. Frankie, take us there now. Andrew, call the police and tell them. Then you can follow us.'

We were at Cagnes-sur-Mer in less than half an hour, but with no sign of Lois Montgomery or the Citröen on the way. Frankie drove past the turning, then pulled over, turned the car around and tucked it in at the side of the road, shielded by a scrubby bush.

'Now what, Mrs J?' asked Frankie. 'Should we go down

there, or wait for the police?'

We had our answer a moment later. The bright red Bugatti roared up the driveway, turned right and disappeared in a cloud of dust and gravel. Lois Montgomery was at the wheel, wearing a leather helmet and flying coat.

Frankie pulled out behind her. I pressed a handkerchief to my mouth and nose to keep out the grit being thrown up by the speeding Bugatti. I saw the yellow and black of Mr Rubin's Hispano Suiza come towards us, then brake hard as we passed. Glancing over my shoulder, I saw Andrew execute a U-turn.

'There's an airfield out on that flat grassy land on the other side of the river,' called Frankie over the noise of the engine. 'I noticed it last time we drove to Cagnes. Bet you anything that's where she's headed.'

I held on tightly as we shot across the wide, flat bridge over the Var and took a skidding right turn down towards the sea. A couple of green-painted metal sheds on a wide grassy field were the only sign of the aerodrome. But we could see the Bugatti, a scarlet insect, beetling across the grass towards the second shed, where a pair of overalled men were opening the doors.

'No, you don't,' said Frankie, flattening the pedal to the floor. I squealed as we bumped over the grass, threatening to take off ourselves. As we drew closer, Lois scrambled out of the Bugatti and climbed up a ladder propped against the side of a small aeroplane with corrugated square wings, a satchel swinging over her shoulder. She climbed into the cockpit as one of the men began to swing the big propeller on its nose.

'Caudron 27,' muttered Frankie. 'They demonstrated it at the Paris air show last year. I saw it in the newspaper. I'd love to have a go of one, wouldn't you?'

I wasn't sure I would, but we had more immediate concerns. Frankie put on a final burst of speed as the men prepared to pull the chocks from under the wheels. Recklessly, she skidded to a halt right in front of the plane, despite the men's yells for her to get out of the way.

'You take the little one,' she said, leaping out of the car. Frankie soon had the bigger of the two men on his back, and sat triumphant on his chest. The second, a skinny bespectacled chap, looked at me in dismay and held his hands up.

'*Mademoiselle! Ne me frappez pas, je vous en prie!*'

What a relief. 'I'm not going to hit you,' I said. 'But that lady mustn't take off. She's wanted by the police.'

He shouted to his friend, who yelled at Frankie to let him get up. The four of us stood, watching each other warily, as Lois Montgomery cursed the two men in surprisingly coarse French. A relic, I supposed, of her days in Montparnasse. Fortunately, the men seemed disinclined to follow her instructions as to what to do with us.

I heard another car and turned. The yellow and black bumble bee of the Hispano Suiza, driven by Andrew Fraser, trundled over the airfield. And it was followed by a black police car. Inspector Grignot was out of the door almost before it had stopped.

'Ah, there you are, Inspector,' said Mrs Jameson. 'Would you do the honours? I believe Mrs Montgomery will be joining her husband at the police station.'

Lois Montgomery descended from the aeroplane, throwing a look of icy dislike at me and Frankie.

'You should keep out of my business,' she said. 'Why do you care where I go?'

'You tried to kill Benjamin,' I protested. 'And you killed

poor Antoine Rousseau, and tried to run me off the road at Villefranche.'

She shook her head and gave a sorrowful smile. 'I don't know what you're talking about. The boy fell, and I can hardly be responsible for your careless driving. I would be careful with the accusations you make, Miss Swallow. Your own reputation is hardly unsullied, after a night in the cells with a pair of common prostitutes.'

I flushed. 'That reminds me,' I said. 'Eliza Rudgwick sends her regards to your husband. She remembers you well. She said you were…' I pretended to search my memory, 'that's it. "A stuck-up American gold-digger." I do hope your gold was worth it.'

Chapter 47

I leaned back in the armchair, gazing over the black velvet bay framed by the open French doors. Lights twinkled and a full moon rose into the sky. The drawing room piano played a gentle, hypnotic melody.

'I do love Debussy,' said Mrs Jameson. 'You must admit, Marjorie, it's more relaxing than listening to jazz.'

The pianist was Maxim Brunot. Dulcie was draped over the piano, presumably trying to butter him up for a role in his next film. Andrew Fraser had turned his back on them and was playing chess with Benjamin, who had declared he was going to stay up all night now he didn't have a nanny any more. I'd noticed his yawns were getting bigger and his eyelids had drooped. Mr Rubin didn't have the heart to send him to bed.

'It's very lovely,' I admitted. 'What's it called?'

'*La Mer*. It sounds even better with the full orchestration, flute and harp giving an impression of the waves and the moon. I will ask Freddie to help me find a good recording of this for our gramophone. It helps me to think.'

I wasn't sure Mrs Jameson needed much help in thinking. She explained she had already realised that if Ashton had not been the driver who hit Antoine Rousseau, it might have been his wife. And when she learned that Mrs Montgomery had married Ashton in the expectation of great wealth, which had been disappointed, she'd realised she was also likely to be involved with the forgery plot.

'I suspected Lois Montgomery from that point onwards, but I had little proof. Fortunately, she was foolish enough to try to throw suspicion on you, Marjorie, by making an anonymous telephone call to the police, from the booth at the Hotel Negresco, immediately opposite the Galerie Anglaise. The clerk remembered her placing the call, because he recognised her and wondered why she was not using the gallery telephone.

'Then, when we discovered the hidden car at Cagnes, Frankie pointed out that the driving seat had been adjusted to suit a woman. That's when I knew it was Lois Montgomery's car. The police found blood on the tyres. They also found her passport and an envelope of dollars in a satchel hanging behind the barn door. That's why I knew she would head there when she fled.

'After we'd amassed the evidence pointing to Ashton, the case against her husband was clear, but Lois had left few traces. If I gave her a little bit of rope, I hoped she would run. And she did. Except – and I will find it hard to forgive myself for this, Sol – she tried to eliminate Benjamin, a key witness to the cover-up of Miss Trent's murder, first.'

He closed his hand over hers. 'You were not to know she would be so callous. And all is well,' he said. 'Thankfully.'

I shivered at the mention of rope. 'I suppose they'll hang,' I said. I had once been a firm believer in the death penalty, and I still felt it was appropriate for cold-blooded murderers. But the more criminals I met, the more uncomfortable it made me.

Mrs Jameson shot a quick look at me. 'If they are convicted

of murder, they will be executed by guillotine,' she said calmly. 'As is usual in France.'

I gasped. 'That's horrible! I didn't realise. It's…'

'Quick and efficient,' said Mrs Jameson. 'If one is going to execute criminals, one should adopt a method that does the job without unnecessary suffering. No sense in being squeamish.'

Mr Rubin sipped at his whisky, his expression sombre. 'So much bloodshed,' he said. 'And so little point to it all.'

Frankie laughed. 'Says the multi-millionaire diamond trader. It's easy to forget how much people will do for money, when you've got plenty of it.'

'Frankie!' I was shocked, but Mrs Jameson was chuckling. After a minute, Mr Rubin joined in.

'You know, I used to think that making money was all that mattered,' he mused. 'After my family escaped from Russia, I thought that if I could just amass enough money, we would be safe. So I worked alongside my father, learning as fast as I could. And I worked so hard! Barely took a day off. I found I was good at business. I had an eye; I could see immediately if a diamond was real or fake, even before it was cut and polished.'

He rose and took a silver trinket box from a locked drawer. He offered it to me and Frankie. 'Go on. Pick one.'

The box was full of little shiny pebbles, like crystals of quartz or rock salt. We both picked one out. Mine had a yellowish sheen, while Frankie's had a blue cast. They shone in the soft gaslight. Mr Rubin inspected our choices.

'One of you has chosen a real diamond, and one a piece of quartz. Do you want to know how to tell them apart?'

We watched, fascinated, as he took a brass instrument from his inside jacket pocket and fitted it to his eye, like a tiny telescope. 'There. The best way is to use a jeweller's magnification loupe, like this.'

He handed it to me. 'Diamond crystals are formed in octahedrons. Eight sides,' he said. 'So you can see four sides on each end. Quartz is hexagonal. And the true diamond has a sheen about it, as if coated in oil.'

I fixed the loupe in my eye socket and squinted. At first I couldn't see what he meant. Both pebbles were shiny, both glinted. Then I realised the blue-ish stone looked like two four-sided pyramids stuck together at the base. An octahedron. And compared to the other, it looked almost wet.

'This one,' I said, holding up the blue stone.

He beamed. 'Very good.'

'That was mine,' said Frankie, with a grin. 'Do I get to keep it?'

He laughed, then his expression sobered. 'The other thing I learned, Miss O'Grady, was that no amount of money can keep you safe from those who wish to do you harm. Indeed, the more money you have, the more people wish to deceive you and part you from it.'

He glanced at his son, half asleep over the chess board.

'The most useful skill is to recognise what is truly precious to you. And to be able to distinguish true friends from false ones. Those who would protect you with their lives from those who would risk your life to gain their own advantage.'

Frankie gave him a sideways glance. 'Even so,' she said. 'A bit of bunce don't half grease the wheels of friendship.'

He smiled, balancing the diamond in his hand. 'This stone is worth about six hundred pounds, Miss O'Grady and Miss Swallow. And today you saved the life of my son, the most precious thing I have. I should very much like to give this to you both, if you promise to let me sell it and share the proceeds equally between you. Young women need money of their own, I know that. More even than young men, who have a better chance of earning it. Perhaps Mrs Jameson will help you decide how best to invest it?'

We were both speechless for a moment. Then Frankie surprised everyone by bursting into tears. She scrambled over and hugged Mr Rubin tight.

'You have no idea what that means,' she sobbed. 'I was joking, you know? But thank you. Thank you, Mr Rubin, so, so much.'

I echoed her fervent thanks, my mind spinning with possibilities. Three hundred pounds. That was more than I earned in a year. I could stay in Nice. I could travel. I could save it and put it towards renting a flat of my own – or even buying a house one day.

'What's happening?' asked Dulcie, wafting over from the piano. 'Did I miss something?'

Mr Rubin smiled at her, rather sadly. 'I think you might have done, Miss Pemberton. Now, if you will excuse me, it's time I put my son to bed.'

Chapter 48

'Good afternoon, ladies.' The comfortable East End tones of Graham Hargreaves announced the arrival of a laden tea trolley, dissipating the gloom of the blustery October afternoon with the promise of scones, jam and fruitcake.

'Marvellous. Thank you, Graham.' Mrs Jameson set aside the police report and telegram from Nice that she'd been translating into English for our files.

'Marjorie, the magistrate has accepted the charges against Ashton and Lois Montgomery for the murder of Sibyl Trent and Antoine Rousseau, respectively. They will go to trial. I'm afraid they are dropping the case against Lois Montgomery for trying to run you off the road, for insufficient evidence. But they are proceeding with the fraud case relating to the paintings, and the charge of attempted murder of Benjamin.'

Sooty the cat had inveigled her way in with the tea. She jumped into my lap, curled up, sneezed and went to sleep. She was heavier than usual; her litter of kittens was expected in a couple of weeks. I'd been instructed to find homes for them, Mrs Jameson having made it clear that she had no intention of supporting them all in Bedford Square.

'That's good.' I didn't mind about the dropped case. There was more than enough to convict them.

I took just one scone. My stomach was still settling after the previous day's crossing from Calais, during which gale-force winds had tossed the steamer mercilessly in the wild waves. Frankie and I had joined the other passengers leaning over the rail in misery; only Mrs Jameson seemed unaffected by sea-sickness. The white cliffs of Dover, looming up through the storm clouds and driving rain, had never seemed so welcome.

'Glad to be home, ladies?' asked Graham.

'Oh, yes,' I said.

Mrs Jameson glanced out of the window. The wind was whipping the leaves off the tall plane trees and heavy pewter clouds scudded across the London sky. We had left Nice two days ago in perfect blue skies, the sun beating down on the olive trees as Frankie drove the Lagonda north across Provence.

'It's always good to be home,' she said, with barely a trace of irony.

Our last two weeks at the Villa Beau Rivage had been blissfully quiet. We'd swum, driven up to picturesque mountain villages and even visited the Casino at Monte Carlo, although I hadn't dared put any money down on the spinning roulette table. My share of Mr Rubin's diamond had been safely invested towards future needs, once I'd replaced the clothes I'd lost or ruined on our adventures. Mrs Jameson, however, had won a surprising amount at roulette, cashed in her chips and left immediately. That, she'd explained, was the only way to gamble.

'Miss Marjorie,' said Graham, 'you have a visitor.'

I tucked Sooty under my arm and followed Graham down the back stairs.

'Who is it?' I knew from Graham's rather disapproving tone

that it wasn't Freddie, who was still away on tour. Everyone in the house liked Freddie.

'Mr Williams.'

I paused, my mouth suddenly dry, and smoothed down my hair, which badly needed a trim. 'Oh, goodness. Do I look all right, Graham?'

He didn't turn around. His voice was kind, but stern. 'You look more than good enough for Hugh Williams, Marjorie.'

Hugh stood by the door to the servants' dining room, as if unsure of his welcome. His suntan had faded, and his eyes no longer sparkled like the sea. But when he smiled, my heart still gave an answering thump.

'Hullo. Frankie said you were back.'

Frankie herself sat by the fire with a mug of tea, ostentatiously flipping through a catalogue of car parts, boots up on the fender.

'Hullo.' I wasn't going to make it easy for him.

'Could we… is there somewhere we can talk privately?'

I looked around. In the pantry, Mrs Smithson was doing something complicated to the chicken we were to have for dinner; Graham sat heavily down at the scrubbed deal table and began adding up the household accounts; Jenny the maid carried in a basket of clean laundry for folding.

'This will do just fine,' I said.

He looked down at his hands. 'I wanted to apologise. Again. I should have told you I was going, before I left Villefranche. And I should have explained about Antoine. I'm back at the Slade School now. The new term's just started.'

I waited.

'The thing is… I was scared, when I heard about Antoine's death. He told me about the forgeries on the night of the exhibition. I suppose you've worked that out. He was drunk, threatening to tell everyone. He shouldn't have threatened Ashton.'

I raised my eyebrows. 'You lied in Villefranche about seeing Antoine, because you didn't want him to tell me about the forgeries. You wanted to keep in Ashton's good books, because he was selling your paintings.'

He swallowed. 'That's true. But then I heard about Antoine's death. I thought that if Ashton had killed Antoine because he knew, and I knew too, then I was in danger. So I left.'

I looked at him steadily. 'I expect you were. And so was I.'

He looked down, a bit shamefaced. 'Yes. That's true.'

'But it wasn't Ashton Montgomery who killed Antoine,' I told him.

He looked up in surprise. 'Really? Then who?'

'His wife,' called Frankie, from the hearth. 'Marjorie and I managed to stop her from killing again.' She winked at me. 'The female of the species is more deadly than the male, Hugh.'

He gave a rueful grin. 'I never doubted that. Well, that's all I wanted to say. If,' he glanced at Graham, who was watching over the top of his spectacles, 'if you fancy going to see an exhibition or something, that would be nice. I'd be happy to take you. I meant what I said, Marjorie, about wanting to be friends.'

'I'll keep it in mind,' I said. I certainly wasn't going to commit myself, even if a tiny bubble of glee was rising inside me.

He nodded, raised a hand to Frankie, and backed out of the door. I bent and released Sooty onto the floor, and she went to curl up by the fire.

Frankie burst out laughing. 'Poor Hugh,' she said. 'You sounded as stern as that awful Nanny Braithwaite.'

I sat down, a little shaken.

Graham looked up from his accounts. 'I know it's not my business, but he's not a patch on that nice Mr Gillespie,' he said. 'Which reminds me. These came for you in second post. I thought you'd like to have them privately.'

He handed me two letters. The first, postmarked from Paris the day we left, was from Dulcie Pemberton.

'Good heavens,' I said. I read it twice, wanting to be sure I'd deciphered the loopy handwriting correctly. 'She's going to marry Maxim Brunot. I suppose he will keep her in line. And in couture frocks.'

I felt a pang on Andrew's behalf. I'd retained some hope that Dulcie might finally marry him, after he was offered the post of games master at a boys' day school in Nice. He and Benjamin would start on the same day, new boys together. I was glad Benjamin had someone to look out for him. Andrew had been surprisingly enthusiastic about the idea, which Mr Rubin had suggested. It was steady, worthwhile work, and Andrew said he'd always liked teaching children sports. But clearly it was not lucrative enough for Dulcie.

My second letter was from Whitley Bay, a seaside resort in the far north east of England.

'Hello, Marjorie. I hope you had a wonderful time in France. I bet it was warmer than here. I've honestly never been so cold as last night, playing the Spanish City ballroom on the seafront. But the Geordies are a hardy lot and like to enjoy themselves. You never saw so much goose-pimpled flesh!

'We've got one more night in these digs, then we'll be on the Flying Scotsman heading south. We're booked for the Cafe Royal in Piccadilly until Christmas, so I'll be back in London for a good while. I'll call for you next Wednesday afternoon, if that's all right with you. Maybe we can go to a tea dance?

'Yours ever, Freddie.' There was a PS. 'Never go to Redcar.'

I folded it up and put it in my skirt pocket.

'All right, Marge?' asked Frankie.

I nodded. 'Freddie's coming home. He's going to take me dancing.' We'd never danced together, I realised. He'd always been playing piano. How would he be on the dancefloor? I firmly shoved Hugh out of my mind.

I poured myself a second, blisteringly strong, cup from the big brown teapot on the table. A holiday romance was all very well in the sunshine, but best left behind when one came home, I supposed.

'There we are,' said Mrs Smithson, carrying the chicken through to the kitchen range. 'Goodness, the nights are drawing in, aren't they? Soon be Christmas, Mr Hargreaves. We've been here a whole year, now.'

So we had. A year of adventures in Bedford Square. I wondered what the next year would bring.

* * *

Enjoyed The Riviera Mystery? Get the prequel novella free.

So how did a nice girl like Marjorie Swallow end up working for a lady detective? And what happened during her interview for the job, in the Palm Court at the Ritz Hotel?

Subscribers to my Readers Club can download a free novella, *Murder At The Ritz*, which answers these questions and more! Readers Club members get a monthly newsletter with news about my books, events, exclusive short stories, recommendations and special offers. Sign up at my website, https://annasayburnlane.com/.

I loved writing *The Riviera Mystery*. If you enjoyed reading it, I would be so grateful if you left a quick review to let me know. I read all my reviews, and they make a huge difference in helping other readers find new books to enjoy.

Historical Note

I couldn't resist the idea of setting a Marjorie Swallow mystery in Nice, which is one of my favourite places. Last year I travelled there by sleeper train from Paris, clutching my copy of Agatha Christie's *Mystery of the Blue Train* and hoping not to be murdered on the way. The experience inspired the opening chapter of *The Riviera Mystery*, with Marjorie travelling south on the famed Blue Train when… well, when something happened. That was as far as I'd got.

Back home, I delved into the British Newspaper Archive for insight into the 1920s on the French Riviera. There was a wealth of society articles, including enthusiastic reports by *Vogue* and *The Bystander* of the new Blue Train sleeper service direct from London. The 'season' ran from October to March, when the English upper classes escaped there for the winter, but by the mid-20s American visitors had begun to spend summer on the Riviera, too.

On YouTube, I discovered *French Riviera: a history in pictures*, a documentary which gave an entertaining overview of the artistic history of the area, from Renoir and Monet to Picasso, Dufy and Cocteau, not forgetting the burgeoning film industry and the Nice film studios. I investigated further, and details about Renoir's time in Cagnes come from Jean Renoir's memoir, *Renoir My Father,* and Barbara Ehrlich's *Renoir: an intimate biography.*

The general history of the Riviera was well-covered in Jim Ring's *Riviera – the rise and rise of the Cote d'Azur*, which had interesting nuggets about the 'Sammies' visiting the coast during the First World War. This may have sparked American interest in the area. Ted Jones's *The French Riviera: A Literary Guide for Travellers* was good on the literary and artistic set around Gerald and Sara Murphy, who feature briefly in *The Riviera Mystery* along with their friend Pablo Picasso.

Different sources give slightly different dates for when the Murphys and Picasso first summered on the Riviera, so I don't feel bad about placing them there in 1923 in time to meet Marjorie!

Villa Beau Rivage owes something to the exquisite Villa Beau Site, apparently owned in the mid-20s by 'a diamond merchant about whom little is known' – who promptly became Solomon Rubin in my book.

My friend Emma gave me a copy of her cousin Claudia Parsons's fascinating memoir, *Century Story*, from where I picked up details about art students at the Grande Chaumière studio in Montparnasse, horses in Nice wearing straw hats and police measuring swimwear for decency. Claudia also drove 'an oil-cooled Morgan two-seater, in which one lay almost prone, not a yard from ground level', which sounded very much like Marjorie's sort of car.

Acknowledgments

Thanks to Vivienne and Roger Bishton for a memorable lunch in St Juan Les Pins, and to Viv for correcting my French (any remaining errors are my own). Thanks to Emma Parsons for *Century Story* and inspiring conversations. Thanks to my editor Alison Jack and cover designer Donna Rogers, both of whom continue to be the kipper's knickers.

Thanks to my ace beta reader team: Christina, Rosalie, Radhika, Madeleine, Jean, Emma, Michelle, Cynthia, Candice, Victoria, Deborah and Dana.

Thanks to my husband Phil for pointing out that a Morgan three-wheeler doesn't have a reverse gear. And for everything else.

About the Author

Anna Sayburn Lane is a novelist and journalist. She writes historical cozy mysteries and contemporary thrillers.

Anna studied English and History at university, then began her career as a reporter on a London newspaper, later moving into medical journalism.

She published her first novel, *Unlawful Things*, in 2018, followed by *The Peacock Room*, *The Crimson Thread* and *Folly Ditch*. *Unlawful Things* was shortlisted for the Virago New Crime Writer award and picked as a Crime in the Spotlight choice by the Bloody Scotland crime writing festival.

In 2023 she began writing the 1920s murder mystery series of classic detective stories. *Blackmail In Bloomsbury* is the first in the series, featuring apprentice detective Marjorie Swallow. *The Soho Jazz Murders, Death At Chelsea* and *The Riviera Mystery* continue the series. There will be more!

Anna lives between London and the Kent coast.

You can connect with me on:

- https://annasayburnlane.com
- https://www.facebook.com/annasayburnlane
- https://annasayburnlane.substack.com

Also by Anna Sayburn Lane

Step back into the roaring twenties with classic detective novels set in the jazz age. *The Riviera Mystery* is the fourth in the series featuring plucky apprentice detective Marjorie Swallow.

Blackmail In Bloomsbury

Everyone at the party had a secret. Someone killed to keep theirs…

When a bohemian party ends in murder, there's no shortage of suspects. Half of Bloomsbury wanted Mrs Norris dead – but who wielded the knife?

Was it the handsome but troubled artist? The vivacious young actress? Or the aristocratic lady novelist? Marjorie and Mrs Jameson must find the true killer to save an innocent man from the noose. From the garden squares of Bloomsbury to the seedy backstreets of Soho, they navigate the glamour and peril of Jazz Age London in a thrilling story of secrets and lies.

The first in the 1920s Murder Mystery series, *Blackmail in Bloomsbury* will delight fans of Agatha Christie and classic crime.

The Soho Jazz Murders

It's January 1923 and London feels dreary after the festivities of Christmas. So Marjorie is excited about meeting the American Ambassador's niece, a genuine 1920s flapper with a love of jazz, dancing and fun.

But their night out at Soho's infamous Harlequin Club comes to a tragic end. Soon Marjorie is working undercover as a dance hostess in the club to unmask the drugs gangs that threaten the West End. It's a perilous occupation - and there are more deaths to come.

The Soho Jazz Murders is the second in the 1920s Murder Mystery series, featuring the irresistible apprentice detective Marjorie Swallow.

Death At Chelsea

The prettiest flowers can be deadly...

Mrs Jameson and Marjorie are called to investigate when a renowned garden designer suspects that someone is sabotaging her priceless Himalayan Sapphire Lilies, ahead of the 1923 Chelsea Flower Show.

But soon it's not just the flowers that are dying. Rival gardeners, intrepid plant hunters and even King George V himself are caught up in a poisonous bouquet with its roots deep in the mountains of Tibet.

www.ingramcontent.com/pod-product-compliance
Lightning Source LLC
Chambersburg PA
CBHW051142190726
48290CB00006B/1956